"Would yo
asked. "Y

As much as she wanted to assure him she'd be fine on her own, the idea of walking the two blocks to her house made her skin crawl. "I'd appreciate that. I just need to get my things and lock up."

Not saying a word, he walked beside her as she went through the motions of gathering what she needed and making sure the bar was secure.

Secure. She mentally rolled her eyes at the thought. No matter how many locks were in place, she wasn't sure if she'd ever feel safe again. At least not once she was left alone with the memories of what happened.

But for now she was protected. Reid stood guard, even if only for two more blocks, then she'd be forced to face the impending nightmares all on her own.

Dear Reader,

One thing to know about me is that I take my friendships very seriously. My mother has always teased me, saying I like to collect friends. But it's true! Once you're in my life, you're stuck like glue! I like my tribe big. I still have annual sleepovers with my third-grade bestie, leave multiple voice memos a day to my current bestie and make as much time as possible for the friends I've collected all around the country who've added so much to life. And I won't even tell you how frequently I talk to my mom and sister because you might find it alarming. I treat my relationships with care, always striving to make sure the people who mean so much to me always know I value them.

I think this is one of the reasons I like to write a series. I love returning to a town and seeing all the people I've met and love. Coming back to Cloud Valley to learn more about Eve and Reid was like sitting down and visiting with old friends. I loved discovering more about Eve's past and how she ended up the owner of the bar and grill, and uncovering what brought Reid to Wyoming filled in so many gaps about what made him the strong, protective hero I admire so much.

I hope you enjoy jumping back into the action in Cloud Valley with the boys from Sunrise Security as much as I did. I'm honored you've found the time to come back for a visit, and now that you're here, you're officially part of my tribe—forever and always.

With all my love,

Danielle M. Haas

PERSONAL BODYGUARD

DANIELLE M. HAAS

ROMANTIC SUSPENSE

MIX
Paper | Supporting responsible forestry
FSC® C021394

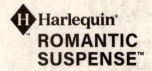

Harlequin®
ROMANTIC SUSPENSE™

ISBN-13: 978-1-335-47180-2

Personal Bodyguard

Copyright © 2026 by Danielle M. Haas

For questions and comments about the quality of this book, please contact us at CustomerService@Harlequin.com.

TM and ® are trademarks of Harlequin Enterprises ULC.

Harlequin Enterprises ULC
22 Adelaide St. West, 41st Floor
Toronto, Ontario M5H 4E3, Canada
www.Harlequin.com

HarperCollins Publishers
Macken House, 39/40 Mayor Street Upper,
Dublin 1, D01 C9W8, Ireland
www.HarperCollins.com

Printed in Lithuania

Danielle M. Haas resides in Ohio with her husband and two children. She earned a BA in political science many moons ago from Bowling Green State University but thought staying home with her two children and writing romance novels would be more fun than pursuing a career in politics. She spends her days chasing her kids around, loving up her dog and trying to find a spare minute to write about her favorite thing: love.

Books by Danielle M. Haas

Harlequin Romantic Suspense

Sunrise Security

Wyoming Bodyguard
Personal Bodyguard

Matched with Murder
Booked to Kill
Driven to Kill

Visit the Author Profile page at Harlequin.com.

To my husband, Scott. You are my best friend, my number one supporter and the model for all my heroes. Thanks for being you, babe.

Chapter 1

Eve Tilly struggled to keep her smile in place as she waved at a group of young women who giggled their way out of Tilly's Bar and Grill. "Thanks for stopping by."

A brunette with large blue eyes and too-tight jeans threw a smile over her shoulder before they disappeared out the door.

As she hurried to the now-empty table, the corners of Eve's mouth dropped a little. She couldn't let her guard down completely. Not with the last patron of the night hunched over his nearly empty plate and half-filled beer at the bar. She should have flipped the closed sign ten minutes ago, but she couldn't shut things down until her bar was completely empty.

God, she was tired.

When she'd taken over her family's bar in Cloud Valley, Wyoming, right before her twenty-eighth birthday, she'd poured her blood, sweat and tears into keeping the traditions alive. She loved her job. Loved her customers. Loved the community she served.

But tonight, after working nonstop for the past two days with the annual rodeo in town, she'd give anything to kick out her last diner and bury her head under her covers for the next week.

Becca, her best friend and manager, joined her at the dirty table. "I told Rick he could leave, so the kitchen's officially closed. As soon as that guy's done, we can clean up and head home." She nodded toward the haggard cowboy with the overgrown beard and weathered hat pulled low over his eyes.

She waited for Becca to clear the table and pocket the tip before wiping her dishcloth over the crumbs. "Why don't you take off, too? No reason for both of us to stand around and wait. I'll finish the rest while he eats."

Becca's frown dipped her dark eyebrows into a deep V in the middle of her smooth forehead. She flicked her gaze above Eve's head, an easy feat since she was a good four inches taller, and scrunched her nose. "Are you sure?"

Eve fisted a hand on her hip. The rag dangled down her leg, dampening her jeans. She cringed and tossed the towel on the table. "I'm fine. Besides, you're opening tomorrow. Might as well get some of that beauty sleep while you can. You'll be lost without it."

Becca rolled her big blue eyes. "Sleep I want, but it never comes easy with a teething toddler. Which, by the way, Suzy's asking to see Auntie Eve. You need to stop by soon."

Just the sound of her goddaughter's name was enough to turn Eve's insides to mush. She didn't begrudge her parents' decision to retire and see the world, but taking over the business at such a young age had cost more than she'd anticipated. Her baby was the bar, plain and simple. And as much as her heart yearned for a family of her own, there simply weren't enough hours in the day to devote to anything beyond profit margins and inventory.

Besides, she'd tried that once, and it hadn't ended well.

She'd been left with a broken heart and her dreams further away than ever.

But at least she had her adoptive family to dote on whenever she could find the time.

"Once the rodeo moves out of town, I'll grab my favorite little girl for a slumber party. I'll get some quality girl time. You and Bobby can get some sleep...or whatever else it is you need." Laughing, she wiggled her eyebrows.

"That sounds amazing. I'll hold you to it." Becca pointed her index finger at Eve then hauled away the dirty dishes, disappearing through the swinging door that led to the kitchen.

Eve made a mental list of everything that still needed done before leaving for the night and headed to the cash register. Screw it, she didn't want to wait for this guy to pay before counting the till. She'd comp his meal so she could take off as soon as he was done.

"All righty," Becca said in a singsong voice as she returned from the kitchen. "You sure you're okay?"

Eve nodded, this time flashing a genuine smile. "I'm sure. Go. I'll see you tomorrow."

With her friend gone, she counted the money in the register then cleared her throat loud enough to gain the diner's attention. "Don't mean to interrupt. Just wanted to let you know I took care of your bill. Thanks for your business and have a great night."

He gave a brief nod then drained the rest of the amber liquid in his tall glass.

She noted his mostly eaten food. Shouldn't be too long before he finished. Not wanting to pressure him, but fine with giving subtle hints, she crossed over the scuffed wooden floors to the neon lights that dotted the dark-paneled walls. She tugged on the cords of the lights, shutting down the colorful advertisements and slogans she'd known since she was a child.

When she'd taken over ownership, a tiny part of her had considered giving the place a facelift. Adding brighter colors and replacing all things old with new and more modern. But when the time came to make the changes, she couldn't erase what her parents had created. The attachment to the things she'd loved since childhood was deeper than she'd realized.

So she kept everything exactly the way it'd always been, down to the giant buck head mounted above the stone hearth—the hat between its antlers changing along with the seasons. Tonight, he wore a tan cowboy hat, and someone had added a giant pair of sunglasses that made her smile.

Okay. Signs turned off. Tables cleared. Money counted. All she had left was to clean the floors and bus the last plate. A quick glance told her the man was still in his seat. She hurried to the small hallway closet where she kept the broom. She wouldn't start sweeping until he left, but maybe he'd notice her waiting and leave a little bit quicker.

Stepping back into the dining area, she let out a big sigh. He was gone. Good. Now she could finish her list and get the hell out of there. Tomorrow would come soon enough, filled with another busy day of tourists.

Hurrying to clean the bar, she grabbed his plate and glass. Something slid from the bar and hit the floor near her feet. Curious, she returned the dishes to the bar and crouched to find a small piece of wood that resembled a flower of some kind.

Huh?

She turned it in her hand, trailing her fingers over the tiny crevices carved into the wood. Hopefully someone hadn't left it behind accidentally, but she didn't have the energy to care too much at the moment. Standing, she tossed the whittled flower onto the dirty napkin she'd placed on the plate.

Suddenly she was hyperaware of a presence behind her.

"Appreciate the meal, ma'am." A brush of warm breath skimmed the back of her neck and raised the hairs on her arms.

The low, gravelly voice turned her stomach. It was close. Too close.

She swallowed past the sudden lump in her throat and attempted to step to the side and take back her personal space, but a hard grip on her bicep pinned her in place.

"No reason to be scared, miss. Just wanted to give you a proper thanks. It was awfully nice of you to give me such a great meal for free."

"No thanks necessary." She yanked her arm, but he refused to release her.

He spun her around, letting go of her arm just long enough for her to face him. He reclaimed her bicep with his clammy hand, bracing his other on the bar at her back. He leaned close, the smell of cigarettes and sweat mixing with the beer on his breath.

Fear tightened her chest, but she refused to let him see it. She lifted her chin, staring him straight in the eyes. "You need to let me go. Now."

His soft chuckle grated her nerves. He lowered his mouth to speak softly into her ear. "I'm just trying to be friendly. Give a man a chance, darlin'."

"I said, let me go." She couldn't stop the quiver that shook her words.

He moved his lips to her jawline. His wiry beard scratched her skin.

She hiked up her knee as hard as she could until it connected with the sensitive spot between his legs. His grip loosened and she lunged away.

He fisted the neck of her shirt and hauled her to him, molding his big, lean body to hers. A sneer twisted his lips. "You shouldn't have done that."

Eve opened her mouth and screamed.

Disconnecting the call from his sister, a little bit of the tension wrapped around Reid Sommers's neck loosened. As much as he loved his baby sister, their conversations got harder and harder. She might stay in their hometown in Indiana to help their dysfunctional father, but Reid had run as far away from that mess as he could the moment he'd turned eighteen.

The Marines had made him into a man. And twelve years later, the town of Cloud Valley, Wyoming, gave him a home.

A home he'd spent the last year protecting as best he could as a security specialist at Sunrise Security.

Madden McKay, his boss and best friend, leaned against the door frame and crossed his arms over his chest. "Hey, man. You done with the case at the Wilson ranch?" The lines around Madden's eyes told him his friend had suffered just as long of a day.

Reid propped his elbows on the desk. "Yeah. Finished late this afternoon. Was making my notes when Tara called."

Madden's dark brows rose. "Everything okay?"

"As okay as they can be." Reid dropped his arms and shoved away from his desk. Needing to move, he paced between the lone window in his office and the cream-colored wall on the other side of the room. "Dad talked his way out of rehab then stole money from Tara. She's upset, and I feel for her. I really do. But damn it, Dad will never change, and she'll never accept that. I can't keep getting sucked into this mess."

Madden frowned. "I'm sorry, man. Wish there was something I could do."

Stopping in front of the window, he stared at the mountains in the distance. The jagged peaks and explosion of colors that came with late summer calmed his jangled nerves. He pulled in a large breath. "I learned a long time ago there's nothing anyone can do."

Enough. Don't waste another second on trouble hundreds of miles away. Not my problem anymore.

Except when Tara called and dragged him back into the middle of the mess he tried to avoid at all cost.

"Anyway," he said, facing Madden. "We should talk about hiring more help. Things have finally picked up. I've finished the Wilson case and have three more waiting for my attention. Have you considered hiring Dax?"

Madden scowled but gave a tiny nod. "We've talked. I've also spoken with Ben recently. He's searching for his place after leaving the Marines. This could be a good fit."

"Agreed."

After struggling to win over the citizens of Cloud Valley and the surrounding area, Sunrise Security had grown beyond anything Reid could have imagined. Business was booming, which left him and Madden with full hands and even fuller schedules. He trusted Dax, Madden's younger brother, and Ben Besler, whom they'd served with in the Marines.

A quick glance at the clock ticking on the wall reminded him of the time. "Can we discuss more tomorrow? I need to get my head on straight after that call, and I've been here all day. I need to find some dinner and head to bed."

"Sure. I'll see you in the morning."

He waited for Madden to slip into his own office across the hall before shutting down his computer and gathering his things. He flipped off the light and hurried through the empty lobby—the receptionist desk long abandoned for the day and sitting area nice and neat—then headed out the front door.

Main Street was quiet this time of night. Bright bistro lights zigzagged above the street and competed with the starry sky for attention. Lit lampposts chased the shadows from the empty sidewalks. Shops and restaurants had closed, sending citizens off to their homes. Even the horde of tourists in town for the rodeo had found somewhere else to pass the rest of their night.

Hope beat inside him with every step that at least one business remained open. Tilly's Bar and Grill was the only place in town to grab an ice-cold beer and a good meal past nine.

And the only place to find Eve Tilly, the beautiful owner who could make him laugh no matter how sour his mood.

Although he enjoyed the breeze, he quickened his pace. Odds were that Eve had closed for the night, but if he caught her before she left, he might persuade her to let him in for a drink. If he was being honest with himself, he could get a cold drink at home. What he really needed was a few minutes with Eve to loosen the rest of the tension coiled in his gut.

As the golden letters etched into the glass of the front window of Tilly's came into view, a shrill scream sent his pulse into a gallop. He sprinted toward the front door, yanked it open and red-hot anger pounded against his temples.

A tall man wearing a faded jean jacket and worn brown cowboy hat towered above Eve. He used his body to pin her against the bar. His long, scraggly beard hid his facial features, but there was no disguising his intent as he gripped her wrist in one hand while the other clamped over her mouth. He struggled to press his lips to her neck.

Eve clawed at the man's face with her free hand.

"Get the hell away from her." Reid stormed across the room and yanked the man away from Eve.

Eve's hazel eyes flew wide. She lunged to the side, but the man kept a firm grip on her wrist. He spun around, holding Eve to his chest, and grabbed the dirty knife off the plate from the bar. "Don't make me hurt her."

Reid stopped and balled his hands at his side. Every instinct screamed to slam his fist in the asshole's face, but he couldn't risk injuring Eve. "Let her go."

The man clicked his tongue. "You think I'll give up that easily?"

Aiming for a calmness he didn't feel, Reid shrugged. He focused on the man. If he stared too long at the fear in Eve's face, he'd crumble. "Don't see how you have many options."

The man grinned, showing off crooked teeth. "I'm

going to walk with the lady to the door, and you aren't going to do anything stupid."

Reid swallowed his rage and watched the man maneuver toward the exit, Eve trapped against him. Reid took small steps, keeping the two of them within reach. His heart beat a frantic rhythm in his chest as his brain went into overdrive to think of a way to get Eve away.

With his back to the door, the man's grin grew. "So long."

Eve firmed her mouth and jabbed her elbow into the man's gut.

Grunting, her captor bent at the waist, and his hand slipped from hers.

Reid sprinted forward, the need to spill the other man's blood like fuel in his veins.

The man reached for Eve's hair, his long fingers snaking through the auburn strands. He jerked her head back before shoving her in Reid's path.

Reid caught her seconds before she fell on the floor and the man ran out of the bar.

Chapter 2

Eve's body trembled, and she held tight to Reid. His strong arms wrapped around her, securing her. Saving her. Protecting her.

"You're all right. I've got you." Reid spoke softly, as if raising his voice above a whisper would be too frightening.

But nothing could be more frightening than being attacked. She didn't even want to imagine what would have happened if Reid hadn't appeared. How far things would have gone.

Wanting to escape from the ugliness clawing at her psyche, she buried her head in the crook of Reid's neck and closed her eyes. The scent of his cologne—a mixture of pine and leather—surrounded her, comforted her. She should tell him to go after her attacker, but she couldn't stand the thought of being left alone.

She gave herself a few more seconds to fall apart before pulling herself back together. "We need to call the police."

Reid grabbed his phone and scooted out a chair from the nearby table. "Take a seat. I'll make the call. Do you want any water or anything?"

"Maybe a shot of whiskey," she said on a short, humorless laugh.

Reid's eyebrow shot up. "Seriously? I can get that."

"I'm joking." She held up a palm to stop him. "Just sit with me."

Nodding, he took a seat beside her and pressed his phone to his ear. "Hi, Mary. This is Reid Sommers. I need an officer at Tilly's Bar and Grill right away. Eve was attacked."

The matter-of-fact statement made her brain buzz and replay the horrible scene all over again.

Disconnecting, Reid placed his phone on the table and shifted to face her. He widened his legs to sandwich hers and gathered her hands in his own. "Are you okay? Did he hurt you? Touch you?"

His concern warmed the cold pit in her stomach. He'd been a good friend over the last year, one who crossed her mind more often than he should. Their flirty banter and easy conversations fulfilled her in ways nothing else could. She hated showing him her vulnerabilities, but the bearded cowboy who'd tried to force himself on her had stolen her choice to keep up her guard.

At least for the night.

"My head hurts from where he pulled my hair, but other than that, I'm fine. Just shaken. I can't believe something like that happened. I can't believe——" Tears closed off her windpipe, stealing the rest of her thoughts. She shook her head as if the motion could wipe away the stain that now marred her second home. A place filled with memories of laughter and friends and family.

"Hey, now. You're safe. I promise."

As if to punctuate that point, the door swung open,

and two sheriff's deputies entered the restaurant. They wore matching frowns and uniforms, but everything else about them was opposite of one another.

Deputy Hill, a twentysomething man with deep dimples and dark hair, dipped his chin. "Evening. Deputy Silver and I heard you folks have had some trouble."

Eve wanted to laugh at the word *trouble* but held it in. "You could say that. A man was in the bar and waited until we were alone to attack me. Reid showed up and scared him off."

"No, I showed up and put him on edge enough for Eve to get herself away from the asshole." Reid shoved his hand through his shaggy brown hair, his ever-present tan cowboy hat forgotten on the table. "He tossed her to the ground then took off."

Deputy Silver pulled out the chair across from Eve and sat. Kindness filled her big brown eyes, and her blond hair was pulled back in a long ponytail. "I'm sorry this happened. Can you describe the man who attacked you?"

"He was a little older than me, I think. Long, brown beard that covered a big portion of his face. He wore a dirty cowboy hat low over his eyes, sat hunched over his plate the whole time he ate." Describing him brought back his scent, the hard edge in his eyes, and she swallowed past the lump in her throat to steady herself. "He smelled like cigarettes. His eyes were green."

The deputy wrote in a tiny notebook then refocused on Eve. "Did you recognize him?"

Holding back tears, she shook her head.

"I didn't, either," Reid said. "I'm not from around here, but I've lived in Cloud Valley long enough to recognize most people who venture into town. This guy didn't ring a bell." He pressed his mouth into a firm line as fury rolled off him in large, hot waves.

"Deputy Hill, why don't you head out and see if there are any witnesses? Try to track this guy down before he hurts anyone else." Deputy Silver's tone made it clear her question wasn't a suggestion.

"I'm on it." Deputy Hill tipped the brim of his wide hat then hurried out the door.

"Ms. Tilly, are you injured? Do you need me to call a paramedic?" Deputy Silver flicked a quick glance at Reid. "We can always speak in private if that would make you more comfortable."

The idea of being separated from Reid sent another spike of panic through her system. She reached for his hand, not caring if she came off as needy. "No. I'm fine. Reid got here before things went too far. If he hadn't come… Honestly, I don't want to think about what would have happened."

"You don't have to worry about that," Reid said. "He's gone."

She blew out a long, shuddering breath, wanting to believe Reid was right. That whoever the guy was, he'd stay the hell out of her bar and far away.

"Okay then." Deputy Silver stood, her small stature similar to Eve's. "If there's nothing else, I'll help Deputy Hill try to find this guy. With any luck, we'll have him behind bars before the night is over. I'll be in touch, and don't hesitate to call if you think of anything else."

Eve should stand, should walk the deputy to the door, but her trembling legs probably wouldn't carry her across the room. "Thank you."

When the deputy was gone, she returned her focus to

Reid. He watched her, his expression a mask she couldn't quite read.

"Is your car parked in the lot?" Reid asked.

Wrapping her arms around herself, she shook her head. "I didn't drive today."

"Would you like me to walk you home?" he asked. "You shouldn't be alone right now."

As much as she wanted to assure him she'd be fine on her own, the idea of walking the two blocks to her house made her skin crawl. "I'd appreciate that. I just need to get my things and lock up."

Not saying a word, he walked beside her as she went through the motions of gathering what she needed and making sure the bar was secure.

Secure. She mentally rolled her eyes at the thought. No matter how many locks were in place, she wasn't sure if she'd ever feel safe again. At least not once she was left alone with the memories of what happened.

At least for now, she was protected. Reid stood guard, even if only for two more blocks. Then she'd be forced to face the impending nightmares all on her own.

Indecision slowed Reid's steps as he and Eve approached her bungalow. The porch light highlighted the explosion of flowers in the white boxes on the two front windowsills. Large flowerbeds looped around the perimeter of the house, packed with plants and foliage of all shapes, sizes and colors.

They hadn't spoken during the walk, and he'd kept his hands shoved deep in his jeans pockets to keep from reaching for her.

Back at the bar, he'd needed to comfort her. To touch her. To feel for himself that she was okay.

But now it wasn't acceptable. Not when they stood outside her turquoise door. An awkward silence he'd never experienced with Eve made him uneasy—made him second-guess how to act and what to say.

"Well, thanks for…everything." Eve dug in her purse for her keys, hesitating when she found them. "Do you want to come in?"

"Sure." He waited for her to step inside before following and closing the door behind him. Curiosity had him peeking around her, the open concept allowing him a view of the tidy living room and kitchen beyond.

Eve kicked out of her shoes and made a beeline for the couch. She sank against the light gray cushion. "I should offer you something to drink or eat, but I don't have it in me to play hostess."

He snorted. "Don't worry about it. I could use a drink, though, if you don't mind me poking around your kitchen."

She waved a hand in a go-ahead gesture.

He noted the simple and polished furnishings and the way framed photos added splashes of color to the tan walls. The same simplicity met him in the kitchen: clutter-free marble counters and no streaks on the stainless-steel appliances. The whiskey she'd mentioned at Tilly's sounded appealing, but he opted to search the refrigerator for a couple of cold beers instead.

"Grabbed one for you in case you wanted it," he said, rounding the sofa to sit beside her. He passed her the brown bottle then opened his top and took a sip. The cool liquid slid down his throat and relaxed the tight muscles along his shoulders. He'd had a bitch of a day before he got to Tilly's. Since he'd walked into that god-awful scene, the day had gone straight to hell.

Damn, he was a self-absorbed bastard.

Nothing that had gone wrong in his day could compare to the horror Eve had endured.

"What's that look?" Eve narrowed her eyes, but the exhaustion clinging to her like a burr kept him from spilling his thoughts.

He took another long pull from the bottle. "Nothing. Just worried about you. I hate the thought of you here alone all night."

A light blush stained her cheeks, and she busied herself opening her beer. "I'll be fine. I'll make sure the doors are locked, and a few drinks of this will knock me out cold. Now that the adrenaline has leaked from my system, I can hardly keep my eyes open. It's been a long week."

He cringed. She'd obviously only invited him inside to be polite. He should have seen her safely inside then made his own way home. He'd be lying if he told himself not wanting her to be alone was his only motivation for accepting her invitation. Eve had piqued his curiosity from the first time they'd met. Always matching him word for word with a smart-ass comment and able to hold a conversation about what players the Colts had traded in the off-season.

She was unlike anyone he'd ever met, and he couldn't pass on the opportunity to see a different side of her. To see where she let her guard all the way down at the end of a long day. The place she called home.

"I'm sorry. I'm intruding. I really just wanted to see you here safe and sound, and now that I have, I'll get out of your hair." He set his bottle on the end table beside the sofa and stood, wiping the condensation from his palms onto his thighs.

"I didn't mean you had to go. Honest. I was just saying…well, I don't know what I was saying." She let out a long breath. "Please. Sit. Finish your beer. Tell me something about your day. Anything to take my mind off what happened tonight."

"Are you sure?"

She grabbed his forearm and pulled him back down beside her. "Yes. Positive. Why were you walking by the bar so late? Hope Madden's not working you too hard."

"Work's been steady—crazy, actually—but that's not why I was heading to see you."

"You were coming to see me, huh?"

The tiny smirk that slid up the corner of her mouth urged him to tell her more. "I needed a drink," he said, grabbing his beer and saluting her. "And some good company to take my mind off a phone call with my sister. I'd hoped you'd let me in, even if you'd already closed."

She frowned. "Is everything okay with Tara?"

The fact she remembered the name of his sister, whom she'd never met, spoke volumes of the kind of person Eve was. "She's fine. She's dealing with stuff about my dad that always brings back bad memories. I wanted to unload a bit before heading home." He didn't want to burden her with more details. She didn't need to hear about how his dad had conned Tara into picking him up early from rehab and then stolen money from her before disappearing.

Same old story. A Sommers man who couldn't keep his shit together and hurt the woman in his life who loved him. A stark reminder of why he couldn't get too close to Eve. He couldn't risk turning into his father—hurting her even if he tried his hardest not to.

"And instead, you found yourself in an even bigger mess. Sorry about that."

The sadness in her voice twisted his gut. He ducked his chin to stare her in the eyes, tucking a long strand of hair behind her ear so she had nothing to hide behind. "Listen to me, don't you ever apologize for anything that happened tonight. You aren't responsible for a criminal acting like an asshole or for the bad mood my dad's actions heaped on me."

Tears glimmered in her eyes. "I know you're right, but I can't help but think of things I could have done differently. Should have done differently."

"Nope," he said, catching her chin between his index finger and thumb. Her skin was so soft, so smooth. What he wouldn't give to slide his palm up to cradle her jaw and finally discover how she tasted.

But that was a line better left uncrossed. Especially with Eve.

"I won't let you place blame on yourself," he continued. "And if you keep at it, I'll have to camp out on your couch and talk your ear off about all the fascinating things I've learned in my time in Cloud Valley."

A hint of humor danced across her face. "Like what?"

"Like how many cattle are on the Wilson ranch or what old man Hackney was up to last week when his wife was afraid he was cheating."

She wrinkled her nose. "Do I want to know?"

"Well, his wife hired me to protect her but later revealed she wanted me as arm candy to escort her around town to make her husband jealous. She thought he was with another woman when he was really paying for a hotel room to nap. He didn't want to hurt his wife's feelings by complaining about her snoring."

Eve let loose a full belly laugh. "Wow. You have been busy keeping the fine folks of Cloud Valley safe, haven't you?"

There it was. The pure, genuine laugh he'd give anything to hear. "You have no idea. Luckily, I could help keep one safe who means an awful lot to me."

Her laughter melted away, replaced by wide eyes and her mouth agape.

Shit. He'd gotten lost in the moment and said more than he should. He forced a chuckle and stood. "I mean, I need you around to keep those cold beers flowing. Listen, it's getting late, and I've taken up too much of your time. You sure you're good by yourself?"

"Absolutely. Go on home. I'll see you later."

He hated the flicker of disappointment she tried to hide beneath a tight smile, but he couldn't sit here any longer. Not with all the pent-up feelings he'd buried now simmering at the surface. He had to leave before he said something he couldn't take back.

He may have helped keep Eve safe tonight, but if he was completely honest with them both about where his feelings truly lay, he'd be the one who could hurt her the most.

Chapter 3

With close to an hour before sunrise, Eve gave up on the idea of sleep. She'd tossed and turned throughout the night, stealing a few minutes of slumber here and there. But every time she closed her eyes, the memory of the way her attacker's beard scratched her chin and his foul odor flooded back.

She'd rather prepare for a full day on very little rest than replay one of the scariest moments of her life over and over.

Being alone in her empty house had been much harder than she'd anticipated. She should have asked Reid to spend the night.

Hell, her entire being had screamed at her to stop being so stubborn and admit she wanted him to stay with her. But if she admitted she wanted him in her home, then she would have been forced to admit to herself she wanted a whole lot more from him. And that was something she couldn't do.

Needing to shut off her mind, Eve wrapped herself in her plush robe and shuffled into the kitchen. She scooped flour and sugar, losing herself in the mundane task of mixing and stirring until the mouthwatering scent of homemade banana bread hung in the air.

She glanced at the time flashing on the oven. Becca would be awake with Suzy. She could stop over and tell her what happened while they stuffed their faces with sugar. Decision made, she hurried to dress for the day, gathered her baked goods and headed out the door.

Outside, the cool morning air promised fall would be there soon. She was ready for summer to vanish, taking with it the hot weather and stream of tourists. After the business of the past few weeks, she was ready for things to slow down a little. Ready to take some time off to enjoy the things she loved outside of work.

A shiver raced down her spine, and she hurried to her car. The back of her neck tingled as if she was being watched.

Relax. Just your mind and lack of sleep messing with you.

She opened the passenger door to place the still-warm pan on the front seat before heading to the driver's side. Her foot slid on something lying among the pebbles. Bending for a closer look, her heart dropped to the ground.

A wooden flower like the one from the bar.

She snatched it up and stood. Her breath quickened, and she glanced around as if someone would charge forward any second.

Stop it. You're being paranoid. You must have put it in your pocket, and it fell out.

Yes. That was it. With all the craziness of the night before, she'd forgotten to place it on the plate and took it home by accident. Or at least that's what she told herself as she made the short drive to Becca's cabin at the edge of town.

Lights blazed inside the two-story home, confirming her friend was awake. Eve secured the pan of banana bread and half jogged up the brick sidewalk to the front door. After she rang the bell, she tapped the toe of her tennis shoe on the wooden planks of the porch.

She hated this—hated feeling exposed. Hated how every snapping twig or rustling of the bushes around the house made her nerves jump.

"Well, this is a surprise," Becca said, answering the door. "When you told me you'd make time, I didn't expect it to be first thing in the morning before I head to work."

The sound of her best friend's voice crumbled the last wall of resistance keeping her from falling apart. She sniffed, but it did nothing to keep tears from streaming down her face.

"Oh my goodness, what's wrong? Come in." Becca looped an arm over Eve's shoulders and led her into kitchen. "Set down whatever you brought that smells so dang good and tell me what happened."

Eve slid the bread onto the island that dominated the center of the spacious kitchen and slumped onto the stool. She dropped her head in her hands as all her emotions leaked from her still-shocked system.

"Honey, please. Tell me what's wrong." Becca took the seat beside her and rubbed circles between her shoulder blades with her palm.

Letting her hands fall, Eve drew in a shuddering breath. "Last night, after you left, the man who was at the bar attacked me."

Becca gasped and her hand stilled. "He what? Are you okay? Did he hurt you?"

"I'm fine." Eve winced, remembering her sleepless

night. "At least, I'm mostly fine. Reid came by the bar and walked in on the attack. He scared the guy off before things took an even worse turn. I'm not hurt, but I can't stop replaying everything in my mind. When I close my eyes, I see this guy's face. I smell him. I swear, on my way here, I could feel him near me. Watching me."

"That's horrible. I can't believe that happened." Becca pulled her into a fierce hug. "Did the police catch him?"

"Not that I know of, which is terrifying. If the police can't find him, hopefully he was a tourist in town for the rodeo and he went back to where he came from." The thought that he could hurt someone else if he wasn't detained turned her stomach, but she couldn't handle the idea that he was still in Cloud Valley.

Becca released her then gripped her hands. "I shouldn't have left you there alone. If I had stayed, this wouldn't have happened. I'm so sor—"

Eve shook her head. "Nope. Stop that. I won't let you take an ounce of blame. You did nothing wrong, and neither did I. Some creep attacked me because he's an asshole. Plain and simple." She couldn't help but think back on Reid's words.

"What's that look?" Becca asked, eyes narrowed.

"I did the same thing last night. I placed blame on myself, and Reid put a stop to it right away. He told me almost the exact same thing when he walked me home."

"He's a good friend." Becca bumped her shoulder to Eve's. "Maybe more if you pursued him a little."

"I don't have time for more than a friend. Hell, I hardly have time for you and Suzy. My life revolves around Tilly's. Besides, you should have seen him jump up, wanting to leave as soon as things got a little too personal. Everyone in town knows Reid isn't the type of guy to want anything more than casual and short-lived with a woman. We're the perfect combination of no chance in hell. Best to keep everything platonic." She had to remind herself of that. Seeing him in her home had awakened a desire to have him there more. To see him outside of her job. To know him deeper than their surface-level banter.

But that was nonsense. A silly fantasy she used to entertain herself on long, lonely nights. Reid was a friend, and that's all he'd ever be.

"I'm sure that's not true," Becca said, bringing her back to the conversation. "I've seen the way he looks at you."

Eve opened her mouth to tell Becca how ridiculous she was, when a pint-size toddler with messy blond curls and wearing adorable footie pajamas padded into the room.

"Ebe!" Suzy said, holding up her pudgy arms.

Needing one of the little girl's hugs more than she needed her next breath, Eve rose and scooped Suzy into her arms. "Good morning, Suzy Q."

Suzy planted slobbery kisses on Eve's cheek.

"No one looks at me the way she does, and that's good enough for me." With the child squeezing her tight, most of her worries melted away. She savored the innocent and pure love heaped on her.

Or at least that's the lie she told herself. Because if she didn't have time for romance before, she definitely didn't now. Not when a criminal who'd tried to hurt her was on the loose and she was barely holding herself together.

Not even the punch of black coffee could chase away the lingering bits of fatigue in Reid's brain. He shuffled forward in the line at Cloud 9 Café like a zombie to wait for his pastry and second cup of the day.

"Here ya go, Reid." Tiffany, the owner's granddaughter, handed over a brown bag and a carrier with two to-go cups. "Black for you, and one coffee with cream and sugar for Madden. Have a great day."

Dipping his chin, he took his purchases and headed for the door. Temptation to sit and finish his drink before heading to work slowed his footsteps. Sunrise Security's office was only three doors down, but as tired as he was, it might as well be miles.

Sleep hadn't come easy. He'd even climbed into his car in the middle of the night to drive to Eve's house, idling on the side of the road to make sure everything was all right. Once he was positive she was safe, he'd driven back home just to toss and turn until the sun came up.

It'd taken every ounce of self-control not to call and check on her. He'd wait until he settled into work and talked to Madden before casually swinging by the restaurant. Knowing Eve, she wouldn't take the day off after her ordeal. She'd be back behind the bar, serving her customers with a smile.

The bell chimed above the entrance and gained his attention. Deputy Luke Hill strolled inside, his cowboy hat in his hands. His face was clean-shaven and dark hair a little disheveled.

Reid lifted his hand in greeting. "Hey, Luke. Any news about last night? I'd love to hear that son of a bitch who went after Eve is behind bars this morning."

Luke winced. "I wish I could tell you that, but the guy's vanished."

The news was like a fist in the gut. "Damn it."

A voice crackled from the radio clipped to Luke's shoulder. "Sorry, I've got to see what's up."

Reid waited for the young deputy to leave then followed him outside, peeling off in the opposite direction. The sun was already warm, but a faint breeze stirred the air. People milled about, popping into stores or sitting outside on benches to enjoy the morning.

He waved at a happy couple strolling hand in hand then stepped into Sunrise Security.

Peggy Reynolds sat behind her desk. Her straight, gray hair skimmed the top of her shoulders and her ever-present pink lipstick showcased a mouth that always smiled. "Good morning."

Her singsong voice usually lifted his spirits, but it wasn't enough to shove aside the heavy cloud hanging over him. "Hi, Peg. Madden in?"

She twisted her chair to face the filing cabinet behind her and pulled out some paperwork. "Yep. In his office."

"Grabbed your favorite." He tossed the pastry bag on her desk on the way down the hall.

"Thanks," she called out. "Chocolate. You always know my weakness."

Stopping outside Madden's open door, he tapped on the door frame then stepped inside. "Got your usual."

Madden accepted the coffee and gestured toward the chair across his desk. "You're bringing in all kinds of treats today. I could hear Peggy hollering about chocolate all the way down the hall. Have a seat."

Grunting, Reid sat and took a sip of his drink. The hot, bitter liquid burned his tongue before sliding down his throat. He closed his eyes for a brief second, willing the caffeine to work.

"Get any sleep last night?" Madden asked.

Reid shook his head. After he'd left Eve's place, he'd

called his friend to fill him in on what had happened. Talking it over had helped process everything, as well as made him realize there wasn't anything else he could have done to find the guy who'd hurt Eve.

"That explains the early trip to the café. Appreciate it. You talk to Eve this morning?"

Again, he shook his head. "Figured I'd stop by when I know she's at Tilly's. Don't want to overwhelm her. I'm sure she'd rather just forget the whole thing. No need to drag it all up again as soon as she wakes up."

Madden snorted and leaned back in his seat. "You think she's not running it through her mind over and over? Chances are you got more sleep than she did last night. I'm still shocked you didn't stay at her place. She had to be terrified."

Reid scrubbed a hand over his face. His friend was right. He should have stayed—hell, he'd wanted to stay. But sitting with her in her home, sharing a drink, had held the type of intimacy he hadn't experienced with a woman in a very long time.

Was the type of intimacy he'd avoided at all costs most his life.

"You know Eve. She's tough as nails. Swore she was okay and couldn't keep her eyes open. I didn't want to keep her up any longer, but that doesn't mean I didn't check and make sure she was all right."

Madden's dark brows shot up. "And how did you do that if you haven't spoken with her?"

Well, hell. He hadn't meant to confess his late-night drive-by. "Nothing. Forget about it. I planned to stop by Tilly's this morning. Give her a little time before checking in."

The widening of Madden's green eyes told Reid he'd noticed the defensiveness in his tone. He opened his mouth, but the ringing phone on his desk kept him from saying anything.

Reid hunched low in the leather chair and took another sip of coffee. The temperature had gone from scalding to hot, allowing him to take a longer drink. An internal war waged, blocking out Madden's voice as he talked to whoever was on the other end of the line. The complicated feelings he had for Eve combated with a lifetime of not wanting to become his father and twisted him up inside. Because of that, he'd left a woman alone all night after she'd experienced a traumatic event. What a dick move.

He'd make it up to Eve. As soon as Madden got off the phone, he'd track her down and let her know he was around for anything she needed.

Frowning, Madden ended his call.

Reid rose to his feet. "You're right. I'll get a hold of Eve right away and see if there's anything else I can do."

"Sorry, but that's going to have to wait. That was the sheriff. A woman was found dead down at the rodeo. Sheriff's department has requested our assistance. We need to go now."

Chapter 4

Eve wiped a wet cloth over Suzy's messy cheeks then smoothed back an unruly curl. The blond pigtails made her face impossibly cuter. She tossed the dirty towel in the hamper then washed her hands in the pedestal sink. Spending her morning with her best friend and favorite little girl was the perfect way to start her day. Especially after such a traumatic night.

Fisting her hands on her hips, she faced Suzy with a wide grin. "All clean, baby girl. Nana will love the pink bows we put in your hair. So fancy."

Suzy's bottom lip jutted out, and her blue eyes grew larger. "I want you. No Nana."

Eve's heart melted. She gathered Suzy in her arms and settled on the edge of the tub in the small bathroom. She'd always assumed she'd have a child of her own at this point in her life, but at least she could pour all her love into her goddaughter. Suzy filled the holes in her life, smothering her in unconditional love and slobbery kisses. "I'm sure you'll have a blast with your nana today, honey. She always has the most fun things planned."

Becca popped her head in the room. "Suzy, be happy you got to see Eve at all today. Now be a good girl and grab your shoes."

"No." Suzy burrowed her head against the curve of Eve's neck.

"Didn't you get new purple sneakers?" Eve hurried to find a way to get the child to listen before Becca lost her patience. Giving Suzy an opportunity to show off new shoes would always entice cooperation. "I want to see them. Can you show me?"

"Okay!" Suzy jumped onto the ground and ran from the room.

"I don't know if I should be appreciative or annoyed she listens to you better than me," Becca said as she fastened a golden hoop earring into place.

Eve shrugged, happier than she should be with Suzy's cooperation. Her dream of having a family one day might never come true, but no matter what, she had a bond with Suzy that could never be severed. "I have a gift and, to be honest, some free time this morning. I could hang with her for a few hours before I need to head to work. Give your mom a morning to herself."

Scrunching her nose, Becca studied Eve. "Are you sure? You've had a tough night and not much sleep. You should relax. Take the day off. Nellie and I can handle everything."

The idea of spending the whole day and evening alone sent a shiver down her spine. She trusted her staff to handle the restaurant without her, but right now she needed to be busy. Not sitting idle while her mind played tricks on her.

Made her feel like her attacker was watching her. Waiting for her.

The pitter-patter of little feet snapped Eve out of her spiraling thoughts. Suzy wiggled past her mom and stormed into the room, hoisting her little shoes high in the air. "Look!"

"Oh my! Those are beautiful."

Suzy beamed.

Eve gathered her in her arms and sent a pleading look toward Becca. "I know what would make me feel better today, and it's more of this." She gave Suzy an extra-big squeeze to accentuate her point. "We can have some girl time before I head to work for the dinner shift. We'll be slammed tonight, and there's still a lot to plan before tomorrow night. Fridays are always busy with locals coming in to listen to the band and dance. With the rodeo in town, we should expect at least double the usual crowd. We need all hands on deck."

"We could cancel the band. The fine folks of Cloud Valley can go one week without some line dancing." Becca secured her hair in a low ponytail then fixed concerned eyes on her. "People will understand."

A part of her wanted to agree, wanted to cancel the weekly entertainment. But that one event brought in half the revenue for the week, and on the one night a year when a horde of tourists were in town, that revenue went through the roof.

"I can't do that. Besides, there's no real reason to cancel anything. Yes, I'm a little shaken, but I'm totally fine. I just need a few hours with Suzy and I'll be right as rain."

Becca didn't look convinced. "If you're sure, I'll call my mom. But if you need a break or change your mind, let me know. I'll tell Mom to be on standby. I still think you should take the night off work."

"We can argue about that later. Right now, I have a

fun day to plan with my favorite girl. Maybe some flower picking? What do you think, Suzy?"

"Yay!"

"You spoil her," Becca said, rolling her eyes but grinning. "I'll pack up some stuff for her."

Eve snorted out a laugh then tickled Suzy's sides while figuring out a perfect way to spend her suddenly free day. There was only one place where she felt totally at ease and completely happy. A place she couldn't wait to share with her goddaughter.

Reid hopped out of the passenger side of Madden's truck, and his weathered boots kicked up a cloud of dirt. The sun hadn't climbed all the way into the sky yet, which kept away everyone except those who worked for the rodeo. In a few hours, the parking lot would be jam-packed with vehicles carrying loads of visitors to enjoy the last couple days of festivities.

But for now, he only spotted a handful of people bustling around, attending their duties, as he and Madden wound through the maze of vendors and food carts preparing for the coming crowds.

"You know where we're meeting the sheriff's deputies?" Reid sidestepped a man the size of a world-class steer pushing a wheelbarrow filled with hay toward one of the large barns.

"On the far side of the fairgrounds. There's a spot where a lot of the vendors and riders park their trailers. Kind of like a makeshift campground. Dax and I used to sneak out here as teenagers when the rodeo was in town and drink with some of the cowboys. Dax always wanted to be just like them."

Reid snorted. "I can see that. A hardened bull rider who enjoys drinking as much as flirting. I bet your pops loved that idea."

"Pops never knew." The side of Madden's mouth slid into a smirk. "Son of a bitch probably did know, but never busted us. He had a hard enough time keeping everything moving after my mom died. We didn't make things easier on him, that's for sure."

Reid slapped a hand on his friend's shoulder and gave a little squeeze before letting his arm drop back to his side. "Ain't nothing wrong with two young boys enjoying a cold brew with some new friends. We all should have been so lucky."

Luck wasn't exactly something he'd experienced growing up. Living with an addict, he could have gotten his hands on his fair share of alcohol. Hell, his father had been delighted when Reid had become a teenager and he'd figured he'd have a live-in drinking buddy. At first, Reid had thought sharing a beer or two with his dad had been the best fun, but that hadn't lasted long. Even at a young age, he'd known he wanted a life as far away from his dad as possible.

That included a one-drink maximum and tight control over his actions. He lived with a constant fear he'd slip and make a wrong choice that would send him down the same slippery slope his dad had been trapped on for most his life. Afraid he'd hurt the people he loved the most and destroy their lives.

He followed Madden as he turned down the long, dusty pathway that snaked around the grandstands. The trail circled the arena where most of the rodeo's major events took place, and the sound of galloping hooves echoed off the empty stadium walls. Fifty yards away, a cluster of campers parked under a canopy of trees came into view.

Reid let out a low whistle. "I knew it took a whole lot of people to put on a rodeo, but I never gave much thought to where they all stayed. This is like a little traveling community."

Madden nodded. "Sure is. Folks usually don't give us much trouble. They're professionals who understand they won't be welcomed back if they get too rowdy. But the odd incident occurs. Mostly when people party a little too hard after a long day's work."

The shelter of leaves gave a welcomed reprieve from the sun as they hurried forward. "You think that's what happened? Things got out of a hand last night and someone ended up dead?"

"Not sure," Madden said with a shrug. "Would be odd to call us in for something that straightforward, though."

Scratching his chin, Reid gave that some thought. Sunrise Security might have started out as a company that provided protection for people and their property in the area. But after a high-profile case that had proven their skills in solving crimes as well as protecting against them, business had shifted. Instead of solely providing surveillance equipment for managing ranches, they'd become the go-to agency for personal protection as well as aiding the local authorities when needed.

A woman who ended up dead from a night of partying wouldn't need either of those services.

Reid studied the variety of trailers clogging the area. Some were small and dingy, while others rivaled the size of his apartment. People dressed in worn jeans and cowboy hats loitered on their temporary lawns, concern and curiosity clear on every face. "Looks like word's gotten around."

Madden mumbled his agreement and nodded at a couple of parked deputies' cruisers on the narrow lane. "We found the right place. Time to figure out what the hell happened."

Yellow crime scene tape wrapped around the perimeter separated the lookie-loos from the cluster of deputies speaking close to the small camper. The two deputies who'd assisted Eve the night before stood with their heads together. An older man frowned as he spoke into his phone.

Reid fought the urge to ask if the man who'd attacked Eve had been found. As hard as it was, he needed to focus on what had brought him here. He could get more information regarding Eve once they were finished.

Madden ducked under the tape and cleared his throat. "Hey."

Following close behind, Reid dipped his head in greeting and shoved his hands in the front pockets of his jeans. He'd let Madden take the lead on this one. Better to stay silent and wait for instructions.

The older deputy—Deputy Sanders—disconnected his phone then aimed his frown their way. "Hey, Madden, Reid. Thanks for coming out all this way."

Reid shook Deputy Sanders's hand and offered a tight-lipped smile. As one of the few citizens of Cloud Valley who'd welcomed him into town despite his friendship with Madden, he'd spent his fair share of time with the weathered officer. Now that the town's tension toward Madden had thawed regarding the sale of part of his family's land, the old deputy's willingness to overlook bullshit made him one of Reid's favorite people.

"Surprised to get your call," Madden said. "Can't remember the last time there's been an incident like this around here. I'm a bit confused as to why you called us, though. Not sure how we can help."

"The department's stretched pretty thin right now. Always is this time of year. We could use some help with security while we try to make heads or tails of what happened to that poor girl." He hooked his thumb over his shoulder and shook his head.

"Wait, you want security services?" Reid asked, confused about why he and Madden were needed. "For who?"

Deputy Sanders heaved out a long breath. "The girl in that trailer was strangled, and we need to make sure we keep the rest of the community safe until we find her killer."

Chapter 5

Filling her lungs with fresh air, Eve tilted her head toward the sun and relished the warm rays on her face. This was exactly what she needed. Time in the great outdoors, enjoying the simple pleasures she'd loved since childhood.

And now she could share her favorite spot in Cloud Valley with her favorite girl.

"Ebe! Out!" Suzy wiggled against the straps holding her in her seat.

"Sorry, girlie," she said with a small laugh. "I needed a moment."

Ducking down, she struggled with the multitude of straps and buttons to release Suzy from her car seat. She swept the little girl into her arms then set her on her feet. She reached for Suzy's hand and found something wedged in her tight little fist.

"What do you have?"

Suzy scrunched her nose and hid her arm behind her back.

Eve thought back to buckling Suzy into the car seat. The toddler hadn't carried any toys with her, and Eve had placed the backpack filled with extra clothes, snacks and water bottles in the front seat. "Can I please see?"

Heaving a dramatic sigh, Suzy held out her hand with her palm facing the sky.

A small wooden flower stared back at Eve, and her heart rate shot through the roof. Delicate lines carved into the wood created the illusion of intricate petals. She snatched the figure from Suzy and studied the carving.

A small cry escaped Suzy's pouty lips. "Mine."

"Where did you find this?" Eve struggled to keep her voice calm, but she had no control over the trembling that took over her body.

Suzy's cries morphed into loud wails. "I found it. It's mine." She curled her fingers in a give-me motion.

Eve stared at the piece of wood. It had to be the same one from her driveway—the same one from last night. She must have tossed it in the back seat and Suzy found it. Simple as that. A desperate need to search her car to confirm her theory made her skin itch, but a hard yank on her arm brought her back to the quickly spiraling situation in front of her.

"Please, Ebe. Please." Tears filled Suzy's blue eyes and her face crumpled as if having the flower taken away from her caused her heart to shatter.

Crouching low, she brought herself eye to eye with Suzy. "Honey, you can't have this. Okay?"

"No. I want it." The tears vanished. Suzy crossed her arms over her chest like a tiny dictator, refusing to accept anything other than exactly what she wanted.

"You can't have it, but we can pick flowers. Doesn't that sound fun? This is my favorite trail. We'll probably see lots of birds and maybe even a bunny."

The cries quieted a little but didn't stop.

The sound of tires crunching on gravel shifted Suzy's attention toward the entrance of the parking lot. She frowned, as if irritated by the interruption of her tantrum.

Relieved, Eve stood and shoved the wooden flower into her pocket before Suzy turned back her way. "Look. Lily's here. She wanted to see us."

Although Eve had insisted on spending the morning with Suzy, she wasn't ready to be alone. Or at least alone with only a toddler. She'd called her friend Lily Tremont and asked her to meet them at the state park.

An invitation Lily had quickly accepted.

Lily hopped down from her vehicle and waved an arm high over her head. Her long, blond hair was secured in a high ponytail. Black shorts showed off her lean legs, and her hiking boots were as dirty and worn as her old truck. "Morning!"

Suzy squealed and jumped up and down.

"Morning," Eve said. "Great timing."

Lily arched one perfectly sculpted brow and crossed the deserted lot. "Why's that?"

"I'll tell you later." No need to redirect Suzy back to why she'd been so upset seconds before. "Thanks for coming."

"Of course. I always love a chance to get outside and catch up with good friends. Besides, work's been so busy lately I've hardly had a free second to myself. I still can't believe how many people are interested in using my ranch as a wedding venue." She held up her palms and winced. "Don't get me wrong, I'm happy my business is growing, but it's been a lot."

"Trust me, I understand that sentiment more than you know. But enough shoptalk—let's hit the trails." She grabbed her backpack from the passenger seat and shoved aside all thoughts of creepy wooden carvings and the men who made them.

"Yeah. Hit it!" Suzy beamed up at them then darted past the oversize board at the beginning of the trail that highlighted all the flora and fauna waiting to be explored.

"Slow down there, sister." Eve jogged to reach the little spark plug before placing her hands on the girl's shoulders and bringing her to a slower pace. "You have to stay close. We don't want to lose you."

Suzy giggled. "No lose me."

Eve gave her goddaughter her best don't-test-me look, and Suzy returned to skipping casually along the tree-lined path.

Lily fell into a comfortable step beside her. Silence lingered between them, only the rustle of leaves and morning birdsongs combining with Suzy's giggles to keep them company.

"Do you want to talk about it?" Lily finally asked.

The question tensed all the muscles in Eve's body. "Did Madden tell you?"

Lily winced. "I overhead him on the phone. Reid called to fill him in. Once I realized what they were discussing, I left the room. But not before I understood what had happened. I'm so sorry."

Eve blew out a long, shaky breath. She wasn't upset that Lily had found out about the attack, but it cemented something she'd been dreading: Everyone in town would soon know. It was the nature of life in a small community. And Lily was only offering her support, not much different than what Eve had done for Lily not that long ago.

"I've gone over things a thousand times in my head. I can't stop picturing it—picturing him." A chill slid down her spine. "I don't know how to stop replaying it. That's why I wanted to spend time with Suzy and bring her here. She always makes me forget my problems." She smiled as she watched the little girl study a black-and-orange butterfly resting on a purple flower petal.

"Trust me, I understand. This kind of trauma grabs you by the throat and refuses to let go. Threatens to suffocate you. Everyone has their own way of dealing. You'll figure out what works for you. Just know I'm here."

Gratitude trickled through her like a calming stream. She and Lily had always been casual friends, but their bond had grown deeper in the last few months. Something she'd be forever grateful for.

"What made you want to come here?" Lily asked, picking up the threads of their conversation.

Eve couldn't help but smile. "My dad brought me to this park, to this trail. I loved the evergreens that caged me in like I was walking through a magical tunnel. One that led somewhere special." She nodded toward the opening ahead.

Lily gave her a curious look then lengthened her strides to keep up with a jogging Suzy.

Eve lingered behind, enjoying the gentle breeze on her skin and the moist smell of dirt and trees. Jagged peaks of the mountaintop loomed tall. As much as she loved the tougher trails, those weren't an option with Suzy. Besides, she needed the magic her father had shared with her now more than ever.

Shrill laughter lifted her lips, and she hurried to catch up with Lily and Suzy. An awning of leaves gave way to the giant, blue sky. The wide stream gurgled in the distance, and a field of wildflowers erupted like fireworks as far as the eye could see.

Suzy gasped. "Pretty!"

She took Suzy's hand and led her to a cluster of red flowers that lined the trail. "Do you know what this is?"

Suzy shook her head, and her pigtails bounced with the exaggerated motion.

"This flower is called Indian paintbrush. It's the state flower. And you see the fuzz on the petals?"

Squinting, Suzy pushed her face as close to the flowers as she could. "Uh-huh."

"Do you know what that fuzz is good for?"

"What?" the girl asked, not taking her attention off the flowers.

Eve grabbed the stem and wiggled the petal against Suzy's cheek. "Tickling!"

Suzy giggled. "Again!"

Eve obliged, and pure joy filled her.

"It's beautiful. I can't believe I've never been here," Lily said. "But then, the ranch has enough space and land to explore. There was never much need to venture far. Your dad brought you?"

"Yeah. He spent hours telling me the names of all the flowers. He owned a bar, but the man was born to be a gardener. He passed that passion to me, and whenever I want to feel closer to him and my mom, I come here. This spot is different than most others because the town owns this patch of land within the park. People are continuously planting seeds so we can actually pick the flowers without destroying what makes it so special. It always calms my nerves and reminds me of the magic of nature."

"I love that," Lily said.

"I want magic," Suzy said, eyes wide.

Eve picked a couple flowers and handed them to Suzy. "Every time we'd come, Dad said we needed to take a little magic back for someone special. Usually that meant a bouquet for my mom. But today that means you, my girl."

Suzy grinned then hugged Eve tight.

Lily placed a hand over her heart. "How sweet. I think I might have to take some magic home to Madden."

"Magic for Mommy?" Suzy asked.

"Sure, sweetheart. But not too many."

"What about you, Eve? Suzy already has her flowers. Who else is special enough to deserve such a meaningful gift?"

Reid's shaggy brown hair and kind eyes came to mind, and she struggled not to smile. She should bring him some flowers as a thank-you for saving her life. Something small but meaningful—and the perfect excuse to see him again.

In the hour it'd taken for Reid and Madden to go over what the sheriff's department had pieced together of Dana Fishel's murder, as well was what was needed from them, visitors had flooded the fairgrounds. The scent of fried dough mixed with grilled meat made Reid's stomach growl.

"It's not even lunchtime yet and people are already eating giant turkey legs. God bless this great country." Reid gave a mock salute to the middle-aged couple who walked by while stuffing their faces with fair food.

Madden chuckled. "Anyone who eats much here, a heart attack can't be far away."

"Everything in moderation." Reid studied the PDF file

on his phone one more time before putting his device in the back pocket of his jeans. "So how do you want to handle this job?"

"It's a logistical nightmare." Madden scrubbed a palm over his face. "Too many people, not enough officers to keep them safe. And two of us can't be effective. Not here. We need more guys."

"Dax?"

Madden nodded. "I'll ask him. He's hemmed and hawed about working for his big brother, but he'd be good at it."

Reid nodded but bit back his comments on Madden's younger brother. Families were often complicated, and he didn't need to put his nose in anyone else's business. "And Ben?"

A beat of silence proceeded Madden's sigh. "I'll call him. I know he's looking for work and needs to figure out where his life's heading. But I need to know his head's on straight if he's going to work for Sunrise Security."

"Not sure his head will ever be like it was before the accident, but he seems better."

At least that's what their fellow Marine had told him the last time they'd spoken. After leaving the military, they'd all had a hard time readjusting to civilian life. But the loss Ben had suffered outweighed the burdens he and Madden had brought home.

"You make the calls, and I'll scout the area," Reid suggested. "Deputy Sanders told us where the department has a few deputies stationed, but it'd be good to see locations that need surveillance. You might think back to your wilder years. Try to remember a few places that the presence of a couple bodyguards would have discouraged some bad behavior."

Madden snorted out a laugh. "I have no clue what you're talking about. I never got out of hand as kid. Never even thought about it. But good plan. Make a lap around the place, take some notes, and we'll discuss after I speak with Dax and Ben."

While Madden peeled off to find somewhere quiet, Reid shoved his hands in his pockets and walked back the way they'd first come earlier that morning. The once-deserted path was now filled with hyper kids and smiling couples. Vendors had opened their shops, hollering at passersby to try a sample of homemade soap or look at specialty pieces whittled from wood. He wished he could be like one of the couples, here to enjoy a beautiful day at the rodeo with an even more beautiful woman.

The thought slammed against his chest like an anvil. Eve was the only woman he'd want to laugh with about eating a giant turkey leg or delight in tasting fried candy bars. She'd cheer and holler over a glass of beer while watching bull riders then swoon over baby goats at the petting zoo.

He should check in on her. A quick call to make sure she was doing all right before he got to work. He wouldn't be able to think straight until he heard her voice.

He reached for his phone, but commotion in the stable to his left caught his attention. Shrieks and calls for help had him putting his phone back in his pocket and sprinting toward the large, white barn that housed the bulls and horses.

People clogged the entrance, racing to escape the barn. Reid shoved his way through the crowd, his hand on the butt of his weapon. He didn't want to draw it and create more chaos but needed to be ready in case the killer was inside. Hunting for his next victim.

Making his way into the barn, he collided with a teenager with spiky hair and wild eyes.

"You don't want to go in there, man," the boy said as he bounced off Reid. "Someone let out one of the bulls. That thing is pissed and on a rampage."

Shit. Maybe not a killer, but just as deadly. Reid might have grown up among more cornfields than cattle, but he'd spent his fair share of time around livestock. Any large animal could pose a threat, but an angry bull among a crowd of people was an invitation for disaster.

A piercing cry for help hurried Reid around the corner to the aisle that housed the animals. His blood froze in his veins. A mother shielded her child from a giant bull, her kid against the back wall with the bull blocking her means of escape.

Reid spied the open door to the empty stall. He grabbed a broom resting in the corner then yanked his cowboy hat off the top of his head and waved it high in the air. "Hey there! Over here!"

The bull spun toward him, his nostrils flailing and murder in his eyes. He pawed at the ground. His long ivory horns spiraled out from the top of his lowered head.

Reid braced himself, moving forward until he stood next to the stall door. Replacing his hat on his head, he gripped the broom with both hands and brought it parallel to the ground, chest high. "Get goin' now."

The bull snorted and charged. His muscled frame ate up the concrete, erasing the distance between them in seconds.

Reid jutted the broom forward one end at a time. A quick jab smacked the animal between the eyes. He reared up his head and twisted, the sharp dagger of his horn slicing into Reid's side. Pain tore through his body. He gritted his teeth and hit the bull in rapid succession, forcing him to turn back into his stall. As energy and adrenaline leaked from his body, he fastened the lock then fell to the hard ground.

Warm, sticky blood oozed from where the bull's horn grazed against his skin. Hunching forward, he applied pressure to the gash and hissed out a breath.

The crying mother ran to him and dropped to the floor. "Oh my God. What can I do? How can I help?"

He squeezed his eyes closed against the crushing agony ripping along his side. "Call 911. I need medical attention now."

Chapter 6

After an enjoyable morning and eating a packed lunch under the wide Wyoming sky, Eve returned Suzy to her grandmother and sat paralyzed in her car. The wildflowers she'd picked for Reid rested on the passenger seat beside her. She stared at the front window of Sunrise Security, mentally urging herself to move.

Maybe he'd be weirded out by the flowers. Hell, he hadn't called to check in on her, which hurt more than she wanted to admit.

Shoving aside her insecurities, she grabbed the flowers and hopped out of the car. She had no reason to second-guess a nice gesture toward a friend who'd supported her. She'd drop off the flowers, say a quick thank-you, then head to work. Easy-peasy.

Before she could change her mind, she approached the front door to Sunrise Security, smiled and stepped inside.

Peggy sat behind her desk, her stare fixed on her computer screen and worry lines around her puffy eyes. She lifted her head, and her pink-painted lips drew down in a pronounced frown before she shot to her feet and rushed to greet Eve with a hug. "Oh honey, are you okay? I heard what happened. How scary. And now Reid's at the hospital. What a day."

Eve's body went rigid against Peggy's soft embrace and she crushed the flowers in her tight fist. She pulled back, and her blood turned cold. "What do you mean? Why's Reid at the hospital? Is he hurt?"

Peggy swished her lips to the side. "I'm sorry. I thought you knew. He and Madden were called out to the rodeo, and he was hurt by a bull. Madden filled me in but didn't give me many details. I swear, these men don't understand how much I worry about them. They're like my own sons."

"Wait," Eve said, holding up both hands to stop Peggy's rapid rambling. "So Reid's at the hospital now? Is he seriously injured?"

"Like I said, not many details." Clicking her tongue, Peggy shook her head. "I assume he'd tell me if things were really bad, but who knows. I've thought about calling Madden, but he has his hands full and he doesn't need me interfering."

Eve swallowed her fear and tried to keep her expression steady. The older woman was already worried. There was no reason to add her own anxiety to the mix. "I'm sure you're right. Why don't I swing by the hospital and get some answers for us?"

Relief spread across Peggy's face. "Yes. That's a great idea. Then I don't have to look like the nervous mother hen over here. I try my hardest not to nag, but those boys don't always make it easy."

"I'll call when I have any news, okay?"

Peggy nodded.

With one more quick hug, Eve ignored her racing heart and struggled to not press the gas pedal to the floor as she raced to the county hospital just outside town. All the peace she'd fought to find vanished. The stretches of towering trees and mountain views from her windshield did nothing to calm her nerves. One thought continuously echoed in her mind—Reid had to be all right.

The lot was nearly empty, so she parked in the spot closest to the door and jumped out of her car. Warm air combined with her tangle of nerves and caused heat to slam against her cheeks. The whoosh of automatic doors welcomed her inside, and she made a beeline for the information desk.

A young nurse in dark purple scrubs with a pleasant face glanced up from a pile of paperwork. "Can I help you?"

"Yes, I'm looking for Reid Sommers."

"Are you family?" the nurse asked, her smile in place but not quite genuine.

Eve wrinkled her nose. She'd been so hell-bent on getting there and seeing Reid for herself she hadn't stopped to consider she wasn't authorized to receive any information. The heat from her cheeks engulfed her entire body.

Before she could answer the lingering question, Madden rounded the corner. "Eve? What are you doing here? Are you hurt?"

Fumbling with the purse strap across her chest, she forced herself to face Madden. "I stopped by the office to thank Reid for helping me last night and Peggy told me Reid was injured. She was concerned, so I offered to come by and get more information."

Okay, so that wasn't the entire truth, but it was close enough and didn't make her look like a stalker.

Madden rolled his eyes, but a smile cracked though his gruff expression. "She's a worrywart. I told her he was fine. Just some bruises and stitches. You want to head back to his room? I'm sure he'd enjoy seeing your face a hell of a lot more than mine."

She nodded, not wanting the intensity of her excitement to squeak out of her mouth.

A buzz sounded, and Madden held up a finger before fishing his phone from his pocket and checking the screen. He winced. "I really have to take this. Actually, I need to get going. Any chance you can give Reid a ride back to town? It'd be a big help. He's in room 202."

Madden answered his call and headed for the exit, waving before he disappeared.

The nurse pointed toward the hallway where Madden had emerged seconds before. "Room is that way on the left."

Before she lost her nerve, Eve walked down the wide hall until she found the right room. The door stood open. She stopped in the hallway and the sight of Reid on the bed, eyes closed and hand resting gingerly on his side, misted her eyes.

She took a tentative step inside and cleared her throat.

His eyes shot open, and he jerked to a seated position then cringed.

"Sorry," she said, hurrying to stand in front of him. Instinct had her placing a palm on his shoulder to ease him back on the mattress. "I didn't mean to startle you."

"I'm a little jumpy." He leaned back and sighed. "And wasn't exactly expecting you."

She couldn't tell if her appearance was a good or bad thing, but tried not to dwell on it. "I ran into Madden when I got here. He had to leave and asked if I could take you home. Hope that's okay."

"As long as you don't mind, that'd be great. I just want to get the hell out of here. Hospitals aren't my favorite place."

An unspoken emotion skittered across his face, but she couldn't put a name to it. "I don't think many people enjoy them. The food sucks." She wouldn't mention the lingering scent of strong disinfectant that could never quite the hide the smell of sickness.

He snorted out a laugh, and their eyes locked. "Thanks for that. You always put things into perspective."

"What can I say, I've got a knack. You ready to head out?" She had a hundred questions about what had landed him in the big, ugly bed, but there was no need to do that here.

Nodding, he eased off the bed and hissed out a long breath.

She hurried to his side and looped an arm around his waist to offer support. "I've got you."

He smiled down at her, curling her toes in her tennis shoes. "You think you can keep me on my feet?"

Shrugging, she swallowed a smart-ass response. She could make light of this moment—hell, she probably should. Reid hadn't been in town too long, but it was widely known he liked to flirt with every woman who crossed his path. Their friendship was based on witty banter and easy laughs. Anything more serious than that would complicate things.

But after last night, she didn't want easy and surface level. At least not right now.

Butterflies swarmed in the pit of her stomach. "Reid, I think I'm strong enough to do anything you want."

Reid picked up a bundle of wildflowers from the passenger seat and set them in his lap as he settled into Eve's car. The pain in his side had numbed, but he didn't think it had anything to do with the medication the doctor had given him. His brain was too centered on what Eve had said before leaving his room to register any discomfort.

Eve sent him a long look then stared out the windshield and merged onto the quiet street. "Anything I can do? Anything you need before we get to your place?"

"Nah, I'm fine. I have to get back to the office and talk to Madden. We have too much going on right now to just take off the rest of the day."

She shot him a pinched expression that told him exactly what she thought of him going back to work. "Are you sure that's wise? What exactly happened?"

The flash of the bull's horns and anger in his eyes came rushing back, melting away the numbness in his side. He shifted in the seat. "I was at the fairgrounds. Madden and I went out for a job. There was a ton of commotion by one of the barns, and when I checked it out, a damn bull had gotten out of his stall. I jumped in before he rammed into anyone else and got him back behind a locked door."

Her jaw dropped. "Oh my God! That's terrifying. You were charged by a freaking bull. You're lucky you walked away. How bad are you injured?"

"Got a horn scrapped across my side, right above my hip bone. Just needed a few stitches. Nothing too serious." He wouldn't mention the terror of a two-ton beast charging toward him at full speed. Thank God he'd handled his fair share of livestock before. Quick thinking had turned a deadly situation into one with only a minor injury and bad memory.

"Must be something in the air," Eve said. "The rodeo comes into town every year, and I've never heard of an animal escaping. Especially one as dangerous as a bull. The people who handle the animals are professionals. How could something like that happen?"

"I had the same thought. Madden pulled the security footage to see if someone was goofing around and things got out of control, or if someone had more nefarious intentions."

Eve shot him a quick frown. "What do you mean?"

Suddenly exhausted, he leaned his head against the seat as a stretch of green meadows passed by the window. News about the death of the young woman would be common knowledge soon. Better for Eve to be aware of the situation than left in the dark. With a killer on the loose, she needed to be on high alert.

"A woman was murdered at the fairgrounds last night, and the sheriff's department is hiring us for extra protection at the remaining rodeo events."

Tense silence smothered the inside of the car. He studied Eve's face as she kept her gaze locked forward. Stiff lines hardened her features. "Do the deputies have any idea who killed her?"

"Nothing yet, but they're working hard to find the person responsible."

"Do you think it's connected to what happened to me?" Her voice was barely above a whisper.

He weighed his words. He didn't want to scare her but also wanted to be honest. "I spoke with Deputies Hill and Silver, and neither has mentioned the incidents being connected. They are being investigated as separate cases."

She wiped at the tears leaking down her face and blew out a long breath. "I sound selfish. I'm worried about me when a poor woman is dead."

Reid bunched his hands into fists so he wouldn't touch her—comfort her with more than meaningless words. "You're not selfish. You're human. Anyone would be worried if they were in your position."

Finding a parking spot on the road in front of Sunrise Security, she faced him with eyes as wide as saucers. "Should I be afraid?"

He weighed his words carefully before speaking. "You should be on alert, but not more than you would have been before you received this news."

She nodded and deflated a bit against her seat.

"You also should tell me where you got these flowers," he said, needing to bring a bit of levity into the car. He waved the bundle of wildflowers, and the smell of the blooms wafted up his nose.

She scrunched her face. "I picked them today with Suzy and brought them by earlier to give you as a thank-you."

"No one has ever brought me flowers." No gesture could have meant more to him, and her obvious embarrassment was downright adorable. He stared down at the pinks and reds and purples, and his chest tightened. "I'm sure Suzy loved picking flowers with you. That girl is the cutest. Sounds like a fun way to spend your morning."

A genuine smile spread across her face and chased away the lingering fear. "It was exactly what I needed. I took her to my favorite spot in Cloud Valley—a place my dad used to take me when I was a kid. I loved sharing that with her."

Her face lit in a way that only enhanced her beauty when she spoke about the little girl. He could stay in the car with her all day, listening to her describe every moment in detail then leave still wanting more.

The door to Sunrise Security swung open, and Peggy stepped outside. She stood on her tiptoes and waved her arm high in the air. People clogged the sidewalk, and Peggy bobbed and wove to keep her eyes on Eve's car parked a few feet away.

He chuckled. Peggy was more like a surrogate mother than a receptionist, and he hated that she'd been so worried. "She must have been standing by the door, waiting for me to arrive."

"Crap," Eve said, cringing. "I told her I'd call and let her know any information I found. Apparently, Madden didn't tell her much. I feel bad she was left in the dark all this time."

He whistled, long and low. "I'd tell you to bring her flowers to apologize, but these bad boys are mine."

She grinned, and a light blush flooded her face.

"But you should come in and say hi. She'll be even more upset if you leave without a hug. And when Peggy ain't happy, nobody's happy."

Her grin slid into a smirk. "I thought that phrase was a little different."

He shrugged and shot her a wink. "Well, Lord knows I don't have a wife, and who knows if I ever will."

Her expression tightened, and she shut off the engine. "Then we don't want to upset Peggy. Let's head inside."

He watched her climb out, and a pang of regret echoed through him. Marriage would always be out of the question, but for the first time in his life, he wished it wasn't.

Chapter 7

Fifteen minutes later, Eve found herself back behind the steering wheel of her little car. A myriad of emotions left her exhausted, and she rested her head on the hard, worn leather. Her day had been filled with enough anxiety, terror, relief and disappointment to fill the Grand Canyon.

Maybe she should take the night off work. Soak in a hot bath with a glass of wine before cuddling up with a book. Something with dragons and badass women who fought for what was right. A story to remind her she didn't need a man in her life.

A reminder she didn't need Reid.

At least not in this new, almost overwhelming way she wanted.

A deep ravine of regret split her in two. She'd spent the last year keeping Reid strictly in the friend zone, a place where they both seemed happy. Now that she'd lowered her guard, she wasn't sure she could resurrect those walls.

Strengthening her resolve, she straightened and started the engine. It didn't matter what box she wanted to put Reid in, he was clear as crystal about what he wanted. And a relationship with her—or anyone else—wasn't an option. She was just raw and vulnerable from the attack, and the last thing she needed was to let her emotions get in the way of what really mattered.

And what mattered right now was focusing on her business and making sure everything was in place for tomorrow night's event.

She drove out of her parking spot, and a quick glance at the clock on the dashboard told her she had a little time before she needed to head to work. A shower and a cup of coffee called her name. Once she indulged in both, her head would be back on straight.

With a plan in place, she maneuvered away from the brightly colored awnings shading the mom-and-pop shops lining Main Street. A few people moseyed from store to store, carrying to-go cups and pastry bags, but it wouldn't be long before the dinner crowd swarmed the town.

She turned onto her quiet neighborhood street. Ancient trees bathed the road in shadows. The stamp-size front yards were empty of playing children or men mowing their grass. A perfect picture of a small-town lull she'd experienced a thousand times.

Her car shook as if she was suddenly driving over marbles and veered to the right. A flapping sound penetrated her closed window, and the shaking increased.

Great. How much more crap could her plate handle right now?

Forcing herself to keep calm, she pulled to a stop along the side of the road and flipped on the hazard lights. Chances were high she had a flat tire. Something she could change herself but would cost her time and that relaxing shower.

She pushed the button to pop the trunk then stepped outside, snatching her phone from where she'd placed it in the cup holder before slamming the door. She'd have to let Becca know she'd be late for her shift. If not, her best friend would worry. As she rounded her car, she scrolled through her phone to Becca's number.

"Hey, change your mind and taking the night off?" Becca asked when she answered.

"I wish," she said, crouching next to her now-deflated tire. "I was on my way home to get ready and I got a flat. I have everything I need to change it, but I might be late. I wanted to give you a heads-up."

"You've had the worst luck," Becca said. "Take your time. We're holding down the fort. Dinner crowd won't be in for a few more hours."

"Thanks. I'll keep you posted on when I should get there." She disconnected and sighed. Becca was right. Luck hadn't been on her side the past twenty-four hours. But at least this was something she could fix, so she might as well stop lamenting her misfortune and start changing the flat.

A low whistle skittered down her spine like a pack of angry ants. She glanced up, and a ball of terror lodged in her throat. A man wearing a dirty cowboy hat pulled low over his eyes and an overgrown beard strolled down the empty sidewalk. He shoved his hands in the pockets of his worn jeans and kept his gaze locked on her as he moved.

She lunged for the trunk and yanked out the tire iron. This asshole might have caught her off guard last night, but she wouldn't be a shrinking violet. Wouldn't stand and wait for another attack. With the hard metal in her hand, she used her shaking finger to call for help then ran for the driver's side door. She dived inside, slamming the door shut and engaging the locks.

"Nine-one-one, what's your emergency?"

"This is Eve Tilly. I'm in my car on Cherry Street and the man who attacked me in my bar last night is walking toward me. My car has a flat tire. I can't leave. I need police here now." She started the engine and locked the doors. Fleeing on a flat tire could seriously damage her vehicle, but if the man tried to attack her again, she'd risk the damage to get to safety.

"I'm sending a sheriff's deputy to you right away. Is the man still there?"

She glanced in her rearview mirror.

The man closed in on her, a slow smile growing on his face. He kept his steady pace even and unhurried like a madman from one of those cheesy 1980s horror movies.

She kept a tight grip on the tire iron. Her heart thundered against her chest as anxiety spiraled higher and higher. "Yes. He's walking toward the car."

"Help will be there soon."

Words caught in the dryness of her mouth so she nodded, gaze locked on the mirror as she watched the man approach her car. She shifted the vehicle into Drive, prepared to take off and rip her wheel to shreds if necessary.

The man stopped mere feet from the back of her vehicle, lifted a hand to wave, then turned around and strolled back the way he'd come. Disappearing into the line of trees on the far side of the street.

"He left. Just walked away. I don't know where he went. What do I do?" She searched for another sight of him, the unknown of where he'd gone almost as unsettling as knowing he was right behind her.

"Stay where you are. You're okay."

The welcoming sound of sirens released the ball of

tension pressing down on her lungs seconds before she spotted the deputy's cruiser. "Help's here. I see them." She shifted back into Park and collapsed against her seat.

"Do you need me to stay on the phone?" the gentle lifeline asked.

"I'm fine. Thank you. For everything." She disconnected, and a need for the same comfort and strength Reid had given her the night before had her scrolling her contact list for his information. Before she could overthink it, she pressed Call.

"Hey, what's up? Miss me already?" The jovial tone of his voice sent a wave of emotion crashing over her.

Tears sprang to her eyes, and she struggled to speak.

"Eve? Are you all right? What's going on?" Panic washed away all hints of amusement.

"I got a flat tire and the man from last night appeared on the street. He's gone and a deputy just showed up, but…" She wasn't sure how to finish her sentence. But she was scared, and she wanted Reid.

"Where are you? I'm coming."

She rattled off her location and disconnected as the deputy approached her door. Help was here, Reid was on his way and she had no reason to still be frightened.

No amount of logic could stop her mind from racing and her gut from telling her that this nightmare was far from over.

Reid drove as fast as he could along the downtown streets to get to Eve. Damn it. He'd never imagined her attacker would come after her again in broad daylight. He'd hoped the man had moved on, never to be seen again, but his actions today told him otherwise.

This changed everything.

Screeching to a stop, he parked behind the deputy's cruiser and leaped out of the truck. Pain shot up his side, but he pushed it away. His comfort didn't matter right now. All that mattered was getting to Eve.

Eve stood on the sidewalk next to a young sheriff's deputy with her arms hugging her middle. She glanced up, and their eyes locked. The relief on her face almost undid him.

He jogged to her side and didn't even fight his instinct to wrap an arm securely around her shoulders. "You okay?"

She nodded, but the worry lines etched on her delicate face told him a different story.

Reid turned his attention to the young deputy in the well-pressed uniform. "You find the bastard?"

The man's grim expression answered the question before he spoke. "Not yet. My partner is canvassing the area. I just finished taking Ms. Tilly's statement."

Reid trailed his knuckles against the smooth material of her T-shirt encasing her bicep. "Did he get close to you? Say anything?" He didn't want to make her replay the whole miserable event again but had to know what happened.

"No. When I stepped out to look at the tire, I noticed him walking toward me. He was whistling, then waved after I locked myself in my car." A shudder shook her shoulders, and he pulled her even closer. "What are the odds he was in the area when I got a flat?"

Reid worked his jaw back and forth. "My thoughts exactly. Deputy, have you looked at the tire?"

"Not yet. Was about to do that when you showed up."

The deputy crouched beside the vehicle and studied the rubber. "Looks like a puncture. Maybe a nail or screw. You could have run over something while driving then it fell out. Gave you a slow leak."

Reid hated to leave Eve's side but knelt on the road to get a better look. His fingers itched to run along the jagged grooves.

"I was just in her car. Drove into town from the hospital. There was no sign of a leak at any point. And if she would have run over something that big that left this size of a hole, she would have felt it." He turned back to look up at her, grateful for the shade blocking the sun from his eyes. "Did you hit anything? Any giant potholes?"

She shook her head, eyes wide. "No. I'm sure I'd remember that."

"When you noticed something was wrong, did the car vibrate a little before popping or was it a sudden motion when it went flat?" Reid asked.

The V between her eyebrows deepened. "Um, it wasn't all of a sudden. More like the car vibrated a little and veered to the side. The pop came later. Once I'd already realized something was wrong."

Reid stood, his mind working over the information.

"What are you thinking?" Standing, the deputy hooked his thumbs in his belt loops.

"That coincidence is bullshit, and there's no way the guy who attacked Eve last night just happened to be walking down the street when she got a flat tire."

Eve returned to her guarded position—arms crossed over her stomach, shoulders hunched, deep frown. "I hate to say it, but I had the same thought. What does that mean?"

"Means we need to pull security video from more than just the people on this street," Reid said, dipping his chin toward the houses across the road. "I want to check any security cameras from the businesses near where you were parked. You were right in front of Sunrise Security. We should have a camera that gives us a good view of your vehicle."

"You think this man put a hole in the tire then pursued on foot?" the deputy asked.

A strangled sound escaped from Eve's lips, and she covered her mouth with her hand.

"It's a possibility." One that made a lot more sense in Reid's mind than a random string of bad luck.

The deputy nodded. "I agree. I'll get on it right away."

"I'll secure the footage from our office," Reid said. "I want to look at it. Meet me at Sunrise Security's office in thirty minutes."

"Ms. Tilly, I'll be in touch." The young deputy spoke into the communicator attached to his shoulder as he made his way back to his cruiser.

Eve stared at Reid with a world of uncertainty dancing in her eyes. "What do I do now?"

He hated the smallness of her voice, the way she shrank as if trying to hide away from the man who'd stormed into her life and turned it upside down. The need to spring into action pulsed through his body with every beat of his heart, but instead he rushed to her and pulled her into his arms.

Unable to stop himself, he placed a kiss on the top of her head. "We'll figure this out. I promise."

"I have a life to live. Things to do. How do I just head to work and act like everything's all right when I feel this guy's eyes on me? When I'm constantly looking over my shoulder, waiting for his next move?"

The truth of what he needed to do smashed him upside the head. "You act the same way you always would, because I'll be right by your side until this guy is caught."

Pulling back, she stared up at him. "Seriously?"

Screw it. Madden needed him to help with the case they'd just signed onto with the sheriff's department, but there was no way he could leave Eve's side. No way he could let her face the unknown alone.

"Yes, seriously. I'm with you for as long as you want me."

As he said the words, something shifted inside him. A part of him wanted to be with Eve long after the asshole who was after her was caught and behind bars. But that was a part of him that he needed to ignore at all costs.

Chapter 8

The crystal-clear images playing on the computer monitor in Reid's office tightened the muscles in Eve's stomach. She sat in the soft leather bucket seat, Reid and Madden standing beside her, with her hands clenched in her lap.

"There," Reid said, jabbing his index finger toward the screen. "That son of a bitch walked right up to her car, stabbed something into the tire, then walked away."

"Man's got balls," Madden said, his voice as rigid as his wide-legged stance.

Nausea sloshed in her gut. This man had followed her into town, knew which car was hers, then made sure she'd be stranded with him close by. "I can't believe it. Why? Why is he doing this?"

Reid and Madden shared a look before Reid knelt down so they were eye to eye. "He's doing this because he's a bad person. He's sick and taking all of his ugliness out on you. His boldness tells me this isn't the first time he's done something like this. But I'll keep you safe. We'll find him."

"We'll do whatever we can to make sure this guy doesn't bother you anymore," Madden said, echoing Reid's sentiments. A phone rang from Madden's pocket, and he snagged it to look at the screen. "I need to take this. I'll be right back."

Once Madden was out of the room, Eve refocused on Reid still in front of her. "None of this feels real, but in a blink of an eye my life is in jeopardy and I'm forced to constantly keep looking over my shoulder. I can't just hole up in my house until this guy's caught." Panic constricted her chest until her words came out high and tight.

Reid latched onto her hands with his. "You don't have to. Where you go, I go. I won't let him get anywhere near you."

The idea of Reid staying so close to her during all hours of the day and night created a heat flash so intense she thought she was in menopause. She swallowed hard, hating the tiny flutter of excitement stirring inside her.

"Thank you," she said, shoving aside ideas of how she and Reid could occupy their time.

Madden cleared his throat from the doorway. "Reid. Can I speak with you for a second in my office?"

Frowning, Reid stood. "Yeah. Sure. I'll be right back, Eve."

Watching them leave, she slumped against the chair and squeezed her eyes shut. Her brain sped along a jagged track of anxiety and fear until she thought she'd implode. She scrubbed her palms over her face. If she was going to survive the next however many hours of being with Reid, she needed to calm down. And with her nerves worn raw, the best way to calm down was to call Becca.

Besides, she needed to let her know she'd be even later coming in to work tonight.

"Hey, you on your way?" Becca asked when she answered the call on the first ring.

"Not exactly." Eve replayed the entire scary ordeal for her friend as quickly as possible, her hands shaking as she recalled each detail.

"Are okay? Do you need me stay with you? Or why don't you stay with me and Bobby until this guy is caught? There's no reason for you to be alone."

Eve cracked a small smile at the don't-argue-with-me tone her friend always used on Suzy. With Eve's parents traveling the country in their RV and no siblings, it'd be easy to feel lonely or as though she didn't have family nearby for support. Living in Cloud Valley meant always having people around to look out for her. Something she'd never take for granted.

"I appreciate the offer," she said. "But it's not necessary. Reid will stay close until this is all over."

"Oh, really?" Amusement practically oozed from Becca's voice.

Eve rolled her eyes. "It's not like that. I'm hiring someone from a security company to keep me safe. Period."

"Sure, whatever you have to tell yourself."

Frustration tightened her lips into a firm line. Fighting her growing feelings for Reid was hard enough without Becca adding gasoline to the fire. "All I'm telling myself now is to get my ass to work and help with the dinner shift. I don't have the capacity to think beyond that right now. We're still at Sunrise Security, but once we're done, I'll have Reid take me home so I can change, then I'll be right in."

"Absolutely not," Becca said.

"Becca, I can't put my life on hold. Tilly's has to be ready for tomorrow. I have to work."

"Honey, everything for tomorrow's event is all set.

There's nothing more for any of us to do. I'll call Bobby and have him come in to tend bar. My mom will watch Suzy. She missed her this morning, so she'll love a little extra time with her only grandchild. You've been through hell today. Go home, spend some time with that sexy bodyguard of yours and we'll reassess in the morning."

A part of Eve wanted to protest, but Becca was right. She'd made sure the band was set and the inventory stocked weeks ago. Besides, she was exhausted. She'd had little sleep and a hectic day filled with enough drama to push a teenage girl over the edge. Becca wouldn't say everything was handled if it wasn't, and they both knew Bobby secretly loved playing bartender.

"Okay. I won't come in tonight, but call if anything changes and you need me."

"We'll be fine. You take care of you."

Disconnecting the call, Eve felt a little lighter. She wouldn't have taken the night off if Becca hadn't pushed, but she hadn't realized how much she needed some downtime. At least one night to unwind and process her trauma.

Reid returned to the office, and an aura of heaviness clung to him. He scrubbed his hand over his jaw and darted his gaze around the room as if he didn't want to look at her.

Her insides twisted like a pretzel. "Is everything all right? I know you mentioned you guys are really busy. Does Madden need you to do a different job?" The thought of him not being with her sent her into a panic, but she refused to show it.

He finally met her eyes, and the flash of anger and fear would have knocked her on her ass if she'd been standing.

"Madden got a call from the sheriff regarding the woman who was killed. A witness came forward."

The urgency in his voice set her on the edge of her seat. "And? Did they catch the killer?"

Reid shook his head. "No, but someone got a good look at the last person seen going into the women's trailer last night. The man wore a dirty cowboy hat and jean jacket and had a big, bushy beard. He was there about forty minutes before you were attacked."

Dark spots penetrated her vision, and the world tilted around her. The man who was after her wasn't just some creep looking to scare her. He was a murderer.

Reid attached the sensor above the window in Eve's living room. Installing security systems wasn't difficult, but damn, was it tedious. People didn't realize how many means of entry they really had until they were forced to protect them all.

Eve stood watching him. "And that little white thing will help keep me safe?"

He stepped off the ladder and wiped his hands on the thighs of his jeans. "This will alert you, and me while I'm monitoring the system, if anyone opens the window or smashes the glass. The notification will pop right up on the app on your phone. We want to make sure we have eyes on all ways in and out of your house."

She nodded along with his words. "Makes sense. I never thought about getting a security system—never had a reason. But being proactive is calming my nerves. I like knowing I'm taking action and not just sitting around and waiting for something else to happen."

"There's a lot you can do to help yourself. Have you ever taken self-defense classes?"

"No," she said, wrinkling her nose. Her only form of exercise was hiking trails that weren't too strenuous. Anything more than that never sounded like much fun.

"Later I can show you a few moves that could prove beneficial. But first let's finish this installation." Fisting his hands on his hips, he glanced around the tidy room. "We've got all the windows in here and the kitchen. I already did the guest bathroom and bedroom. I think all that's left is your bedroom and en suite bathroom. Do you know how many windows you have in there?"

She swished her lips to the side. "Two in the bedroom. One in the bathroom."

He grabbed what he'd need then swept an arm through the air. "Lead the way."

Hesitation pinched her face. "Why don't you go ahead? You don't really need me in the way, and I can order pizza or something for dinner. I mean, I'd better at least feed you for all your work, right?" She chuckled, but it came out forced and a little awkward.

He bit back a smart-ass remark about her not wanting to be alone in her room with him. That type of comment would be typical for them, but not in this moment when she was so vulnerable. Besides, the idea of seeing her bedroom sent such an intense thrill through his body it was better to pretend it was all par for the course.

"Pizza sounds great," he said. "I'll be quick."

He headed down the short hallway and veered into her room. He flipped on the light and strode straight into the attached bathroom. If he took too much time, he'd get lost in a stupid fantasy about a more interesting reason to be in here. He made quick work of putting up the last sensors then crossed back into the bedroom.

He couldn't help but glance around the room. A blue-and-orange-swirled comforter neatly covered a four-post bed, and a ton of decorative pillows made it look comfortable as hell. Like he could dive right into a cloud. Two cherrywood nightstands flanked the bed, small lamps and stacked books on both. Framed photos stood on her long dresser along with an intricate jewelry box, and an ivory-colored chair nestled in the corner with a bright orange throw blanket tossed over the back.

A vibrant painting on the light gray wall caught his attention. He approached it slowly, studying the pops of pinks, purples and reds in a field of green. The jagged mountain peaks loomed in the distance with a smattering of lush trees filling out the perimeter, as if protecting the colorful flowers from intruders—preserving the essence of peace and calm.

"Doesn't look like you're getting too much work done in here."

Eve's amused tone turned him around. He shrugged then faced the painting again. "Just being nosy, I guess. I really like this picture. I'm not sure why. There's just something about it."

"It's my favorite spot," Eve said, moving to stand beside him. She stared at the framed art. "My dad had this commissioned for me before he and my mom left town. He wanted a way for me to feel close to him. This is actually where I picked those flowers from earlier."

He hooked a brow. "Really? I've tried most of the trails around here, but I don't think I've seen this spot."

"Not surprising. It's one of the easiest trails around.

This park is mostly used by parents with small kids who need fresh air and an excuse to get out of the house. I'm sure you like something a little more challenging. You know, more manly and rugged." Her expression was one of mock sincerity.

He chuckled. "You know me well. But I'd love to see this place someday. Looks beautiful." He stared down at her as he spoke, his words meaning so much more than a compliment for the picture. A few seconds of silence settled between them, and he wished he had the courage to say more. To stop using humor to disguise his emotions.

As if feeling his eyes on her, Eve tilted up her chin and their eyes locked.

Time stood still. Heat climbed the back of his neck and everything else around him disappeared. His throat went dry, and the overwhelming desire to finally discover how she tasted had him wetting his lips with his tongue.

She swallowed hard, a pretty blush staining her cheeks.

Screw it. He was tired of fighting his instincts, tired of holding back when all he wanted to do was jump in with both feet. His heart puttered in his chest and he leaned forward, the scent of her floral perfume invading his senses and making his world unsteady.

Her eyes widened for a beat before slowly closing.

He bent lower, her mouth so close. Her body so warm. He glided his palm around her neck, his thumb pressed against the sensual curve just below her lips. He'd waited months for this—held back out of respect for this woman who'd become his friend. Never wanting to lead her on or promise things he couldn't provide, but just one kiss would be all he'd need to douse his curiosity.

The doorbell rang and they jumped apart like two teenagers caught by their parents.

Eve's eyes flew open, and she flattened her hand to her chest. A forced laugh barked from her throat. "Got to love Luigi's. Delivery's always so dang fast. Ready to eat?"

What he was ready to do was stand under a bucket of cold water to erase the stupidity that had momentarily taken hold of him. He took a step backward, needing to get out of her intoxicating orbit. "I have two more sensors to install over the windows in here."

"Okay. I'll grab the pizza and set everything out." She turned to leave, and he reached for her forearm to stop her. She hesitated, staring at him as if waiting for him to finish what he'd started.

He dropped his hand to his side and cleared his throat. "Hold on one second. I want to make sure it's okay for you to answer the door." He hated the flash of disappointment that darkened her face as he grabbed his phone and pulled up the security app. A quick glance confirmed the young delivery girl standing on the porch, waiting with a pizza box in her hands. "Yep. Pizza's here."

She gave him a tight smile and hurried out of the room.

"Shit," he muttered, squeezing the back of his neck. Great job making things awkward from the very start of this assignment. He had no idea how much time he'd be spending with Eve over the next few days, but one thing was sure—if he didn't keep himself in check, he'd never survive.

Chapter 9

Stupid, stupid, stupid.

Eve mentally slammed her forehead against the cabinet door as she busied herself getting everything they needed for dinner.

Okay, dinner had been delivered in a box, so she really didn't have to do much to prepare, but in order not to scream out loud, she had to stay active. Not just sit idly waiting for Reid to appear, replaying their almost kiss over and over in her head.

She squeezed her eyes shut for a beat and willed herself to calm down, for the flash of heat to leave already.

"You feeling okay?"

She jumped at the sound of Reid's voice and slapped a hand over her rapidly beating heart. "Yeah. Sorry. Just taking a moment."

The smirk on Reid's face told her he knew exactly why she needed a moment, but at least he was gentleman enough not to comment.

Instead, he rounded the edge of the island and inhaled. "Gino's?"

She wrinkled her nose. The town of Cloud Valley was split in two very distinct camps—team Gino's pizza, or team Luigi's. Her allegiance would always fall in line with

Luigi's. "Not in this house." She flipped the lid closed and jabbed her index finger toward the bold red-and-green lettering scrawled across the top.

"Never tried pizza from this place," Reid said with a casual shrug. "When I moved here, Madden always ordered from Gino's. I liked it well enough so never bothered ordering anything else."

Her jaw dropped in mock outrage. "And I thought you were a man with impeccable taste. I hate to break it to you, but if you take a bite of this delicious meat lover's pizza and you don't agree that it's far superior to its competition, I'm not sure we can be friends anymore."

Reid grimaced. "Wow, I didn't understand how important this was. Now I'm afraid to try it, but it smells so damn good I don't think I can resist."

She grabbed a plate and placed a gooey slice on it. She kept all traces of humor from her face and handed it to him. "I'd say no pressure, but..."

He cracked a grin as he accepted her offering, and she was eternally grateful for the silly banter over something as innocuous as dinner. This back-and-forth was exactly what she needed to forget the way her toes had curled as his mouth leaned close to hers, as the smell of his cedar and citrus cologne turned her brain into a pile of mush.

"What's that look about?"

Well, crap. She was about to ruin the easygoing moment of delusion she needed because she couldn't stop replaying the almost kiss.

Clearing her throat, she turned back to the counter to get a plate for herself then loaded it with two slices of her favorite indulgence. "Nothing, still in shock about Madden leading you astray. I should have known. You needed someone with a little more finesse to show you the ropes around here." She shot him a wink then carried her plate to the small two-person table where she'd set bottles of water and napkins.

Reid's warm chuckle followed her to the table, and he took the seat beside her. "So really this is all your fault."

Grinning, she shrugged and lifted her pizza to her mouth. She stopped with it near her lips and arched her brows in challenge. "Ready to have your life changed forever?"

He mimicked her actions and let out a long breath. "I don't think I have a choice."

She ignored the ping of curiosity at his tone. Something deep down in her gut told her he wasn't just talking about their meal, but asking would go against the bury-her-head-in-the-sand mentality she was going for right now.

Biting into the warm, gooey cheese, she moaned. Spicy bits of sausage combined with the salty bacon and ham, creating the most beautiful symphony of explosions on her tongue. She felt the heat of Reid's gaze on her face, but she couldn't care less. No man would ever get in the way of enjoying her food.

Especially Luigi's.

Reid took his own bite then tilted his head from side to side as he chewed. "It's okay."

"What?" She practically screamed the question across the table. "You've got to be kidding, right?"

He grinned and held up his palms. "One hundred percent. I'll call Madden immediately and yell at him for leading me astray. Hell, this might be better than anything I've even had at Tilly's."

She wadded up a napkin and threw it at him.

Laughing, he ducked and let the cloth fall to the floor. "Joking, joking."

She chuckled and went in for another bite, enjoying the sense of normalcy after such a crazy day. "Speaking of Tilly's, I need to be there tomorrow. It's our busiest day of the year. I can't put that on my staff while I stay home."

"I'm not here to tell you what you can or can't do, but do you really think it's worth your safety?"

"I do," she said with no hesitation. "Besides, you can keep me just as safe at Tilly's as you can here."

He snorted out a humorless laugh. "I'm glad you think so. I wish I could pull some more manpower from Sunrise Security, but we're short-staffed. Madden hired Dax and our buddy Ben today so he could have more hands working with the sheriff's department."

Wincing, she placed the warm pizza back on her plate. "I'm sorry I'm taking you away when you're needed."

"Hey," he said, reaching to place a hand on top of hers. "What did I say about apologizing for things that aren't your fault? Besides, I'm needed here, and there's nowhere else I'd rather be."

He removed his hand, and a cool rush of air took its place, sending goose bumps up her arm. She hated how badly she liked having him around, in her home to share a casual meal. She had to keep reminding herself he was here because she was in danger, not because he chose to be in her company.

She forced a smile. "My house does smell much better than those dusty old fairgrounds."

He inched his finger and thumb apart. "A little."

If she'd had another napkin, she'd have tossed it again. She gave an exaggerated eye roll. "You're the worst."

He let loose a full belly laugh that melted away every last worry clinging to her brain like a cobweb. "Oh, you love having me around and you know it."

He'd hit the nail of truth with a giant hammer, but instead of commenting she smirked and rose with her empty plate. She didn't want to think about how much she enjoyed having him around, but she also didn't want to think about the chaos surrounding her life like a tornado, which left her two options.

Sleep or booze.

A quick glance at the clock on the stovetop told her it was too early for bed, so she opened the fridge and found two bottles of beer. She popped the tops off both then offered one to Reid. "Nothing goes better with pizza than cold beer."

Shutting the lid on the empty box, Reid carried it outside and placed it in the trash can behind the house. Darkness had fallen and a dusting of stars covered the inky sky. He stilled, listening to nature's calling card of critters and crickets, waiting to see if anything else pricked his ears.

He fought the instinct to walk a perimeter around the property. Most assignments since becoming a security specialist kept him outside, patrolling ranches or installing security systems to keep thieves away from large parcels of land. It wasn't until recently that he and Madden had expanded their business to include bodyguard and private investigator services.

But Eve's yard was small and there was no reason to stay in the cool night air, pacing around the lone maple tree in the center of the yard. He had a good visual of the space, and not many shadows provided coverage for someone waiting to ambush Eve.

Although he'd be lying if he told himself that was the only reason he lingered outside. Sharing an evening meal with Eve had given him more pleasure than he'd expected. Luckily his bonehead move in her room hadn't ruined anything. Neither had spoken of his blunder. In order to keep his focus on Eve's safety, he had to do a better job of keeping his feelings in check.

Breathing in one more breath of crisp air, he returned inside. The kitchen was tidy, all traces of their dinner cleared away. He followed the sound of televised laughter into the living room and found Eve sitting on the sofa with another beer in her hands.

She glanced up and offered a small smile. "I set another one for you on the end table." She nodded toward the brown bottle on the coaster.

He settled in beside her but ignored the drink. He didn't talk to anyone about his one-drink limit, and he didn't plan to start tonight. He'd just pour the beer down the drain when she wasn't looking. "What are we watching?"

"A sitcom I've seen a hundred times. It's a comfort show, but I can change it if you want to watch something else."

"I'm fine with anything."

She returned her gaze to the television and peeled the label from her bottle. Only the soundtrack from the show interrupted the silence. A dozen questions about Eve and her life tumbled around his head, but he held them back. A weird tension simmered between them, and he wasn't sure diving even deeper into their shifting dynamic was the best answer right now.

His phone buzzed against his thigh. He plucked it from his pocket and read the text sent by his sister, sighing as he shoved the phone back in place.

"Everything all right?" Eve asked, brow furrowed in concern.

"Yeah. Just Tara. I'll call her later." He winced at the familiar pinch of guilt. He hadn't touched base with his sister after their conversation the night before. He hated that she was struggling to deal with their father—again—but he also didn't want to get caught up in the mess. Not when he'd worked so hard to untangle himself from his father's bad decisions. Their father would never change, and Tara had to either accept that or move on.

"You sure? Don't feel like you have to stay up and babysit me. I'm fine and will probably head to bed soon. I'm actually pretty exhausted."

"It can wait. She wants to continue our conversation from last night, and I'm not really sure what all is left to say. I don't want to upset her more than she is, but I can't tell her what she wants to hear."

Eve tilted her head to the side and her soft auburn locks tumbled over her shoulder. "And how do you know what she wants you to tell her?"

He debated how much to divulge. Getting into his family dynamics was as low on his list as a getting a root canal, but he also didn't want to brush Eve's question aside. "Because she and I have been going around in the same circle for years. Like the most dysfunctional carousel ride. She wants me to keep riding, I want her to get the hell off the carousel, and neither of us can see the other's point of view."

Eve frowned. "I'm sorry. That sounds super frustrating. Especially with someone you care about so much."

The weight of a million burdens crushed down on his shoulders. "I want what's best for Tara, and Tara wants what's best for our dad. Unfortunately, there can only be one winner in that situation. If she stays and continues on the same path she's been on for years, he'll keep dragging her down with him."

His throat suddenly went dry, and he reached for his beer. He'd just take one drink and set it aside. Gripping the cool glass in his hand, he breathed in and out, hating the instant desire to battle his emotions with alcohol.

Like his dad.

Leaning forward, he set the drink on the coffee table and rested his elbows on his knees. Something on the floor caught his attention. He scooped a little wooden carving off the ground and rolled it around his fingers. "I never realized how much you like flowers. First the painting, now a little knickknack. This is pretty cool, though. Did someone make it, or did you buy it?"

Straightening, he settled it in his palm and lifted it for her to see.

All the color drained from her face, and she shot to her feet. "No. No way. I know I didn't drop that in the living room. How did it get in here?" Shaking her head back and forth, she patted the pockets of her jeans from front to back. "Where did I put the other one? Damn it, I was so upset by everything that happened I completely forgot about the stupid flowers."

Rising to his feet, he placed the wooden carving on the coffee table and held up his hands as if trying to calm a spooked horse. "Hold on a second. What are you talking about?"

"That." The word came out on a screech as she jabbed a finger toward the trinket. "He's leaving them for me. I know it. There was one at the bar last night, on that guy's plate. Then I saw one in my driveway and Suzy was holding one after I got her out of the car. I tried to tell myself it was all in my head. I must have accidently pocketed the one from the bar, which fell when I got home then somehow showed up in my car. But now this? In my house?" She continued shaking her head side to side, her motions quick and jerky.

He absorbed the truth of her statement like a physical blow and forced himself to stay calm. "Are you saying the man who attacked you is leaving you these little carvings?"

"I think so, yes."

"And where are the other ones?"

Closing her eyes, she pinched the bridge of her nose. "I put one in my jacket pocket earlier. If it's not the same one, one might be in my car. But my car's not here to check."

"Okay, then let's check your jacket."

She rushed across the living room to the entryway closet. Yanking open the door, she found the light coat and rummaged through the pocket. She pulled out a little wooden flower and a small groan leaked from her mouth. She turned wide eyes on Reid. "He's been here. He's been inside my house."

Chapter 10

Nervous energy combined with the pizza and beer, souring Eve's stomach. She'd *known* someone was watching her earlier, had felt eyes on her skin. She shouldn't have brushed away her intuition, because not only had her attacker stalked her, he'd forced his way into her private space—violated her yet again.

The wooden carving no longer sat on the coffee table, but she still visualized it where Reid had placed it thirty minutes before.

He'd insisted they call the sheriff's department to fill them in on the newest development. Deputy Silver had come by to take her statement as well as the creepy flower for evidence. Madden had arrived—Lily by his side—shorty after to discuss how to move forward.

Lily sat to her right on the overstuffed, cream-colored chair while Madden settled on the attached ottoman. Concern rippled across Lily's smooth brow. "How do you feel?"

Eve sank deeper into the sofa cushion and wrapped the bright red throw blanket around her shoulders. How could she possibly answer such a loaded question? Her mind was stuffed to the brim with possibilities of what could have happened as well as horrible memories of what already had. Her body shook, and the desire to drive right out of town and hide until the man terrorizing her was caught coiled every muscle tight, ready to spring into action.

"Eve?" Reid asked, his voice so close even though she wished his big, strong body was closer.

She glanced to her left. His presence steadied her, but she'd give anything for him to wrap her in his arms and tell her everything would be all right. That she was safe and he wouldn't let anyone near her.

"Are you okay?" he asked, dipping his chin so their eyes locked.

Clearing her throat, she forced herself back to the moment. "Sorry. I got lost in my thoughts, which isn't the best place for me to be right now. How do I feel?" She repeated Lily's question and struggled to pull forward the right response. "Scared, unsettled, creeped out that someone was in my house, in my personal space, and I didn't even realize it. I'm agonizing over every detail of the past twenty-four hours, searching for anything that stands out to give me some answers on how to move forward, but I'm coming up blank. I'm...overwhelmed."

"I know what you're going through is different than what I experienced after my father was attacked and someone came after me, but I understand those emotions plus about a hundred more," Lily said. "Nothing anyone says will make you feel better, so all I'll say is that I'm really sorry this is happening."

Eve tried to offer a smile but was afraid it came out more of a grimace.

"Are you all right to stay here?" Madden asked. "Reid has this place locked up tight and the security system is top-of-the-line, but that still doesn't mean you'll feel comfortable. You can always stay with me and Lily."

Reid stiffened beside her. "She's safe with me."

"I have no doubt," Madden said. "I just want Eve to have zero doubts as well."

She drew in a large breath, considering her options. "I won't feel like I'm out of harm's way until this guy is caught. Until then, I'd rather be in my own home—with Reid."

Madden nodded then stood. "All right. We'll get out of your hair. You've had a long day, and it's getting late. Call if you need anything at all. Both of you."

"I'll see you out." Reid stood and waited for Lily to give Eve a quick hug before walking them to the door.

The sound of the security system being armed was like nails on a chalkboard. She cringed, hating how each new ping was another weight placed on her chest, caging her inside her own home.

Reid strolled back into the living room and plunged his hands deep in the front pockets of his jeans. "Madden was right. It's getting late."

She sighed and stared up at him. She should take his lead and head to bed, but only nightmares waited to haunt her there.

Frowning, he took a step forward. "Not tired?"

"I am, but I'm not sure I can sleep."

"Okay," he said, crossing to sit back down beside her. "I get that. You've had a lot thrown at you, and your head's probably spinning. When I get like that, I like to write down everything clogging up my brain. Make a list of things to do the next day. Anything to help me feel like I'm being proactive."

She twisted on the couch to face him. "How would being proactive help me sleep? Wouldn't it just keep repeating everything in my mind?"

"Maybe, maybe not. For me, seeing everything written down helps me process. Helps me know exactly what I have to do, which takes away some of my anxiety. That helps me sleep. It's worth a shot."

She wanted to tell him that what would help her sleep was him holding her close until her eyelids finally snapped shut. Instead, she rummaged through the drawer of the end table and found a notepad and pen. She tapped the tip of the pen on the paper.

"Either you have a lot of thoughts or none at all."

She glanced up to find Reid's amused smirk. "Fine, smart-ass," she mumbled and scribbled the only thought that was sure to keep her from getting any rest.

He reached for the pad, and his fingertips brushed against hers.

Sucking in a breath, she stilled, afraid any movement would cause him to take back the soothing feel of his skin on hers.

He lingered for a few more beats before sliding the notepad onto his lap, leaving her deflated. He let out a low whistle. "You led with the big dog, huh?"

She looked down at the words she'd written. *Find my attacker.* "That's the only thing I want to do, and the last thing I know how to do. I know what this guy looks like, what he smells like, even the way a creepy light shines in his eyes when he sees my fear, but none of that helps me pinpoint who he is or where he's hiding."

"That's why sheriff's deputies are scouring the county right now. They're going to find him. He can't hide forever."

"And if they can't find him? Or it takes days, weeks? Then what? I want to do something to find this creep now. Will you help me?" She might have hired Reid to protect her, but that didn't mean they couldn't do more. Sitting in the house for hours, waiting for answers, wasn't an option. At least not for her. If he wanted her to be proactive, she would be. But she'd do a whole hell of a lot more than writing ideas down on a piece of paper.

Reid pressed his mouth in a firm line, gaze fixed on her messy handwriting. "Are you sure you want to jump down this rabbit hole? It might be safer to lay low and let the professionals do their job."

"You're a professional," she shot back.

A small smile poked through his gruff expression. "I guess I am. And if you want my help to figure out who this guy is so we can take him down, you've got it."

A sliver of excitement wedged itself through her fear. "Where do we start?"

Frowning, he scratched his chin. "Back to the first place your attacker was spotted. Tomorrow morning, we head to the rodeo."

Sleep eluded Reid as he lay on the bed in the guest room. The bright light of his phone screen intensified the ache in the middle of his forehead. He rubbed his eyes then refocused on the words he'd typed in his notes app.

Talk to Madden about finding Eve's attacker.
Get more information on the murdered woman.
Secure bar for Eve's event.

He paused with his thumb hovering above the keyboard. He wished he had more ideas of what to do tomorrow, but this was a start. He might not have a ton of investigative experience—hell, he'd thought Madden crazy when he'd suggested adding PI services to their business—but he'd learned one thing over the last few months.

He didn't have to reinvent the wheel.

If he wanted to uncover more information, he needed to go to the person who had the information. In this instance, that person was the witness who'd seen the man fitting Eve's attacker's description leaving the murdered woman's trailer. Hopefully she'd be easy enough to find and willing to talk.

Then he'd uncover as much as he could about the woman who was killed.

The light of his phone dimmed, and he swiped his thumb over the screen to bring it back to life. He had one more item left to write, but as much as he dreaded it, he couldn't put it off until the morning. He had to call his sister now.

Before he changed his mind, he found Tara's number and pressed Call. The line rang in his ear, and he sent up a silent prayer for her voice message to click over, before she finally answered.

"Hey," she said. "I wasn't expecting to hear from you tonight."

The heaviness in her usually upbeat voice had him sitting up in the unfamiliar bed. "Yeah, sorry. I was busy when you texted and I'm just getting a chance to reach out."

"New case?"

He rubbed a palm over his normally smooth face and thought back on the last twenty-four hours with Eve. This assignment was way different than just another job, but he didn't want to dive into that with his baby sister. "I'm keeping a local woman safe while some things get sorted. How you holdin' up?"

A beat of silence stretched into seconds, followed by the sound of Tara sniffing. "I'm okay. It's rough, you know?"

He bit back his frustration, knowing anything he said against their father would immediately raise his sister's hackles. "I'm sorry you're going through this again. You don't deserve to be treated this way."

"I don't know where Dad is," Tara continued. "I've called all his usual spots, searched the last shithole he stayed at and spoken with the degenerates he calls friends. He's nowhere. And now Richard is pissed he stole the money we've been saving for vacation. Just swept right into the house when no one was home and took it. Richard's threatening to leave me—claims he's over the drama—but what am I supposed to do? I can't abandon Dad and leave him for certain death like everyone else."

Reid's blood heated. He and Tara had argued over their respective positions on their father countless times. She claimed Reid was coldhearted and not willing to be there for family. He countered he'd learned how to have healthy boundaries and she needed to do the same or their father would ruin her life like he did everyone else's.

Neither could ever see the other's perspective, leaving them in an endless loop of resentment and frustration.

"Well, are you going to say anything?" Tara asked, cutting into his thoughts.

Sighing, he sat up and prepared for battle. "Do you want to hear what I really think?"

"Yes." The word came out clipped and defensive, all but guaranteeing another fight.

He chewed over how to lay out the same logic he spouted weekly, praying this time she'd finally hear him. "Dad doesn't want help. He wants a handout. He wants to live life on his terms. He wants to drink. Until that changes, nothing you do will help. He'll keep pushing you away until he shoves you over a cliff, just like he did with Mom. Just like he tried to do with me."

More sniffles sounded through the phone and tore at his heart.

"Tara, I love you. I don't want to see you hurt over and over again. Mom tried to fix him for years, and she was rewarded by him smashing their car into a tree, stealing the best years of her life. If she couldn't get through to him, no one can."

"I don't know how to say no to him. Mom would want me to stay. To keep trying."

The smallness of her voice reminded him of Tara as a little girl. Big blue eyes and dark curls, always wanting to please everyone.

But that was the problem. Tara lived her life to please others, to help others over helping herself. If she couldn't figure out how to escape their father's unhealthy clutches, she'd never be happy.

"Mom would hate for you to be stuck in the same pattern she was in for years. Hate to see you stuck catering to a man who loved booze more than anything else in this world—more than his family. The difference is Mom stayed for us. To try and protect us and provide us with stability the only way she knew how. You have a choice. A future away from him. But just like Dad's the only one who can choose sobriety, you're the only one who can decide when you've taken enough abuse and walk away."

"But what if I leave and he needs me?"

Reid tightened his grip on the phone and gritted his teeth. He hated the position Tara found herself in, and he hated himself for leaving her back in their small-ass town where she felt as though she was the only thing standing between Stan Sommers and death.

But he'd made the choice Tara faced daily. He'd walked out of his father's life and never looked back. He might share blood with that man, but he wouldn't sacrifice himself for the sake of someone who didn't deserve it.

"He's a grown man. If he needs help, he knows how to get it," he said. "Maybe he needs to fall on his face a few times before he can finally pick himself back up."

More silence. More crying. More guilt crushing down on Reid's chest, making it hard to breathe.

But at least Tara wasn't fighting him, wasn't hurling insults or making excuse after excuse for the horrible way their father treated her. Maybe she was finally ready to see reason.

"I'll think about it," she said. "Something has to change. I can't keep living like this."

She disconnected the call before he had a chance to respond, and he slumped back onto the comfortable bed in Eve's guest room. The sadness in her voice hit a familiar note he'd heard all his life. First from his mother and now his sister.

He fisted the cool blue sheets in his hand. A part of him wanted to drive back to Indiana, hunt down his dad and kick his ass for being such a jerk. For destroying the lives of everyone who loved him.

But the other part—the part he fought to listen to daily—told him if he ever went back, he'd fall into the same trap that ensnared every Sommers man. He'd become the person he hated most—he'd become just like his father.

Chapter 11

The smell of fresh coffee coaxed Eve out of her comfortable bed after a restless night. She'd tossed and turned, her brain unable to shut off and give her a moment's peace. But if she couldn't have peace, at least she could have caffeine.

Wrapping a plush robe over her pajamas, she padded out to the kitchen and found Reid hunched over his computer at the table, a steaming mug beside him.

His head snapped up, and he offered her a tight smile. Bags hung low under his eyes, and his shaggy hair stuck out as if he'd been recently pulled at the strands. "Morning. How'd you sleep?"

"Probably about as good as you." She made a beeline for the coffee machine and poured a giant cup, inhaling her first sip before facing him.

He snorted out a humorless laugh. "So, like shit?"

She grinned, taking another hit of the liquid gold. Leaning against the counter, she cradled the warm mug in her hands. "Pretty much. What are you working on?"

"Research. I spoke with Madden and got the contact information of the witness. I left her a message, and she agreed to meet with us. Said if we got there before the crowd started rolling in, she'd have more time to talk but isn't sure how much she has to say."

Eve's stomach revolted at the thought of diving into the muck surrounding her life, but this was what she'd asked for, and she wasn't about to turn back now. "Okay. I'll get ready and we can head over right away. The sooner we can speak with her, the better."

"Agreed." Reid took a sip from his mug then stood and placed it in the dishwasher. "You hungry? I can whip something up while you get dressed."

"I don't think I can eat." She studied the navy-blue T-shirt sculpted across his torso and crisp, clean jeans and realization struck her upside the head. "We never stopped by your place yesterday. Where'd you get a change of clothes?"

"I had a duffel in my truck," he said with a casual shrug. "Before I went to bed, I grabbed it. I keep a few essentials in there, but I'll need to get more if I stay another night."

She hid her face behind another sip. She'd be lying if she said the only thing that kept her awake the night before was fear. Knowing Reid was right across her hallway had her imagination getting the best of her more than once. If he stayed a few more nights, she might not survive.

"We can find time to stop by your place so you can get whatever you need," she said. "Hopefully you won't have to stay too much longer. I'm sure bunking in my guest room is the last thing you want."

An unknown emotion skittered across his face before he tucked in his lips and sat back down, avoiding her gaze. "Not a big deal. I've slept in worse places. Even though it was a little disconcerting to wake up under a frilly comforter surrounded by a mound of fancy pillows."

As much as she wished she could read what was really going on in his mind, she'd settle for the usual sarcasm that floated between them. "Not my fault you don't usu-ally sleep places with taste."

His eyes widened before a sly grin lifted the corner of his mouth. "What would you know about the places I sleep?"

She rolled her eyes at the impish smile, his words a gentle reminder of why she couldn't fall for a man like Reid. He flirted with his fair share of women. She didn't want to think about the beds he fell into and the women who slept beside him. "I wouldn't and don't need to. Give me ten minutes and I'll be ready to leave."

Fifteen minutes later she sat beside him in his truck. A crispness in the air promised an early arrival of fall, and Eve was glad she'd decided to throw her favorite red flannel over her gray T-shirt. Today she yearned for com-fort, even if that was her worn jeans and old sneakers.

She lost herself in her thoughts as they drove out of town. Houses dotted the landscape, their expansive yards showing off gentle slopes, until all that lay before them was an empty country road and the wide-open blue sky. Towering trees and thick brush clogged the side of the road, only allowing quick glimpses into what lay beyond.

A sign for the fairgrounds loomed ahead, and her in-sides coiled. Only five miles separated her from answers. As much as she was ready for those answers—whatever they may be—the idea of questioning someone about such a grisly act soured the coffee in her stomach.

Good thing she hadn't taken Reid up on breakfast. Any-thing more substantial surely would have come right back up.

Reid shot her a quick glance before returning his focus to the road. "You doing okay?"

She could lie. Tell him she was fine and mentally preparing for what lay ahead. But what was the point? No matter the weird tension between them or the mounting attraction she couldn't extinguish, Reid was still her friend. And right now, that's what she needed most.

"I wish I could tell you to keep driving. To ignore the signs to turn up ahead and go somewhere far away. Somewhere safe and serene, like the trail I took Suzy to yesterday that's just up ahead. Maybe a little cabin in the woods surrounded with wildflowers. Anywhere but to a dusty old fairground and the place a young woman died."

"You can tell me to do anything you want," Reid said, his voice low and tender. "This is your call."

She chewed her bottom lip, hating the unrest tormenting her insides. "If I left town, I'd be a coward."

A low growl rumbled from Reid, and he guided the truck to the side of the road, parking before turning on his hazard lights.

"What are you doing?" she asked, frowning.

Shifting to face her, he extended his arm to rest on the back of her seat. His fingers dangled down and brushed against the top of her shoulder. "You're no coward. You are strong and fierce and smart as hell. There's no one way to play this. If you want to get out of town, hell, I'll take you to a beach for the week and let someone else deal with this. Because this shouldn't be on your shoulders, none of it. All you have to do is listen to your gut. Follow your instincts."

An image of relaxing on a beach next to Reid heated her from the inside out. Maybe that wouldn't be such a horrible idea. Too bad she had responsibilities she couldn't ignore, people who depended on her.

"What's that look for?"

Not wanting to admit she liked the idea of him in a bathing suit, she tilted her head and studied him. "Would you wear that cowboy hat on the beach?"

Grinning, he tipped the front of the cream-colored hat that was like another limb. "Yes, ma'am."

"Then scratch that. Nobody wants to see a cowboy in the ocean. We better stick around here."

All hints of amusement left his face, and his kind brown eyes bored into hers. As if challenging her to be truthful. "You sure?"

She nodded, even if she wasn't sure of anything. "Yeah. I'll get through this."

He flashed a small smile and tapped his fist lightly against her shoulder before shifting back in his seat. "Yes, you will, and I'll be right beside you while you do."

Nerves tightened her gut as he glided back onto the road then made the turn toward the fairgrounds. Ready or not, it was time to go to the rodeo.

A sense of déjà vu warped Reid's reality. Only yesterday he'd trekked the same path past the same shut-down vendors, around the same grandstands, toward the mini campground that housed the rodeo workers.

The memory made him gingerly touch his side, the stitches causing a slight irritation under his shirt.

But today the stakes were even higher.

Eve walked beside him, her arms crossed over her chest as if blocking out any external force. He hated that she was feeling anxiety and fear and hoped they could get enough answers today to give her a little peace of mind.

The gravel pathway melted into a narrow, dusty trail that wound back under the trees. A few people stood outside their trailers, but most of the temporary homes were quiet, the owners either inside getting ready or already starting their day elsewhere.

"Do you know where we're going?" Eve asked, bouncing her gaze around the area.

Yellow tape still wove around the perimeter of the crime scene where he and Madden had spoken with the sheriff's deputies yesterday. He pointed to the camper across the way. "There. The woman's name is Sarah Campbell."

He led the way across the small patch of grass and stopped in front of the narrow door. "Ready?"

Standing beside him, Eve nodded.

He fisted his hand and tapped on the flimsy barrier.

The door cracked open to reveal a twentysomething woman with tanned skin and wide eyes. Her dark hair was swept into a low ponytail. She half hid behind the frame. "Hello?"

"Mornin', Ms. Campbell," Reid said, touching the brim of his hat. "We spoke earlier. I'm Reid Sommers, and this is Eve Tilly."

Eve gave a small wave. "Hi."

Sarah swallowed hard and darted her gaze around them as if afraid of what others would think of her speaking with them. "Hello. Like I said, I'm not sure how I can help, but I'll tell you anything you want to know."

"We appreciate that," Eve said. "Would you be more comfortable speaking inside?"

Sarah's pinched expression told Reid she wouldn't be comfortable anywhere, but she took a step backward in silent invitation.

He waited for Eve to enter before stepping inside. A small counter and mini fridge took up one wall of the trailer with a table jutting out the other side that divided the space in half. Browns and avocado greens gave a '70s vibe, but everything was clean and tidy.

"We can sit at the table," Sarah said, sliding onto the mud-colored bench cushion. "Can I get you anything? Water? Tea?"

Reid pressed his hand to the small of Eve's back and ushered her in the seat opposite Sarah then sat beside her.

"We're fine," Eve said. "Thank you for speaking with us. I'm sure it can't be easy."

Sarah wrapped her arms around her chest and moved her fingertips along her biceps, as if chasing away a chill. "It doesn't seem real. Dana was so young. So full of life. I still can't believe she's gone."

"You told the authorities you saw a man leave Dana's trailer the night before she was found," Reid said. "Did you know who he was?"

She shook her head. "No. I'd never seen him before, but he has to be the same guy who'd been bothering her."

"What do you mean by bothering?" Eve asked.

"A guy asked Dana out a few months ago. She said no, she'd just gotten out of a long relationship and wasn't interested in dating, but he didn't take her rejection well."

Reid tightened his jaw, hating that this predator had been on the loose for so long. "Did he get aggressive? Ever hurt her?"

Sarah scraped the tip of her fingernail against a groove on the laminate table. "Things escalated. At first, she laughed it off, but he kept showing up, kept asking. Over the last few weeks, he got angrier. He'd show up unexpectedly and try and intimidate her."

"Did she ever speak with the police?" Reid asked.

"No," Sarah said, shaking her head. "We're never in one place too long, and she hoped eventually he'd stop. And it's not like he overtly threatened her or laid hands on her. She didn't think it was something anyone would take seriously."

"Harassment and stalking are serious crimes," Eve said, her voice clipped and tight. "It's emotional and mental abuse. I hate that your friend didn't feel as though anyone would help her."

Tears filled Sarah's eyes. "Me, too."

"Did you ever meet this guy?" Reid asked. "Did she ever tell you his name?"

Again, she shook her head. "He always seemed to appear when no one else was around. When she was alone with the horses or coming home from a competition. She'd mention him in passing but didn't want to linger over the topic. Almost as though discussing him gave him more attention than he deserved."

Eve tilted her head to the side, eyes narrowed. "You said he'd appear when she'd get home. Did she have a home base or was she mainly on the road while traveling from rodeo to rodeo?"

"Always on the road, but that might just be because he didn't start pestering her until a couple months ago. We've been traveling ever since. We both live in Nashville, and there's been no time in between competitions for visits back there."

Disappointment pressed down on Reid's lungs, but he latched onto a piece of information. "Do you remember where you were when he first asked out Dana?"

Sarah scratched the spot on the table with more intention. "Denver. I remember because he said something crude about taking her higher in the mile-high city."

Eve cringed. "Classy."

Sarah sighed. "That's what we said. We laughed over what an idiot he sounded like—made some smart-ass comments about how if he was going to follow the rodeo around, he should get a job as a rodeo clown. I guess the joke's on us, though. He got what he wanted in the end."

Eve reached over the table and rested her hand on top of Sarah's. "Are you sure it was the same man?"

"Yes," she said, staring Eve straight in the eye. "Dana mentioned his long, bushy beard and this creepy look in his eyes. She said he always had on a dirty cowboy hat and worn jean jacket. The man who walked out of her trailer was an exact match. I should have known then something was off. Should have charged inside and asked what happened. But I was in a hurry, running late for the last barrel race of the night. Maybe if I'd stayed…" Sobs stole her voice and she hung her head, wiping her eyes with the backs of her hands.

"You couldn't have saved her," Reid said, not knowing if that was true but understanding this woman had done nothing wrong. There was no reason for her to carry around guilt for the rest of her life over the actions of a bad man. "And you're helping now. Helping to get justice for your friend and doing what you can to make sure this doesn't happen to another woman."

Sarah stared blankly back at him as if she didn't quite believe him. "I hope you're right."

So did he, because if the man she'd described got away with murder once, he'd stop at nothing to do it again. And this time, his sights were set on the one woman who meant more to him than any woman ever had.

Eve.

Chapter 12

Eve stepped out of the trailer and sucked in a large breath of cool, fresh air. Her gaze latched onto the yellow tape across the path, whipping in the wind. A shiver raced down her spine and she hurried to turn away from the reminder of death.

Reid plunged his hands in the front pockets of his jeans and walked beside her. His pinched expression broadcast his anger and irritation, a handsome mirror to a lot of what she was feeling.

They walked through a break in the trees and the morning chaos of the rodeo greeted her. The smells of frying oil and tempting sweets made her mouth water, reminding her she hadn't eaten. Although she still wasn't sure her stomach could handle food.

"How you holdin' up?" Reid asked, sidestepping a man hurrying through the growing crowd with a hay-filled wheelbarrow.

"My heart is broken for what Dana went through. How scared she must have felt and how lonely it must have been to feel like there was no one to help her. And I hate that I'm disappointed not to find out more. Sarah warned us she didn't have much to say, but I hoped for at least a name. Something to pinpoint who this guy is."

"We found out the first time he approached Dana was in Denver," Reid said. "That could be his hometown."

"Denver's a huge city. Odds of us finding a guy based on his appearance and first known location are pretty low."

"True, but I'm sure Dana spoke with more people than just her barrel-racing buddy about what was going on. Family, close friends, even other people working the rodeo. The more we uncover about Dana, the closer we might get to the truth."

His logic made sense and loosened some of the knots in her stomach. "Where do we start?"

"First, we'll talk to the sheriff's department. They've already begun an investigation and have probably spoken to plenty of people. No need to do the same job twice if we can help it."

"Do you think they'll tell us what they've learned?" She didn't know much about how police investigations worked, but loose lips were probably frowned upon.

Reid shrugged. "They might. Keeping you informed should be a priority. Not to mention Madden and I've been working closely with the sheriff's department lately. I'm not saying they'd divulge confidential information to a buddy, but I've established relationships that may help grease the wheels a bit."

The mention of grease brought her attention to a white-and-red-striped food cart straight ahead. A woman with gray hair braided down her back placed little balls of dough in a vat of boiling oil. As soon as she plopped a couple in, she fished others out with a slotted spoon, tossed them on a plate and dusted them with powdered sugar.

Eve couldn't stop the small groan from pouring out of her mouth.

Reid stilled and stared down at her.

Wrinkling her nose, she glanced up at him. Heat scorched her cheeks. "Sorry."

He widened his eyes. "Everything okay?"

She extended a finger toward the truck, where a small line had formed. "Fresh doughnut holes."

A slow grin spread across his mouth. "Would you like some?"

She nodded. "More than anything."

"Whatever you want," he said, sweeping his arm in a go-ahead gesture.

Jumping into line, she grabbed his hand and yanked him along beside her.

Instead of letting go, Reid laced their fingers together and squeezed. "How about this, I'll place a call with Madden and see if he knows anything. He's been in constant contact with the deputies, heading up security here while this guy is at large. He might already have some information. If not, he might make the call so we can focus on other things."

"Like what?"

He pulled her forward as the teenagers in front of them moved ahead. "Fried fair food. Now that everything's opening up, I want more than measly doughnuts."

Her jaw dropped. "Measly?"

"They're so small. I need something with a little more substance. I saw giant turkey legs when I was here yesterday, and I've been craving one ever since."

A wave of nostalgia hit like a sucker punch. "My dad always ate those things. He'd bring me and my mom to the rodeo every year as a way to say goodbye to summer. We'd stuff ourselves with food until we almost burst, and he'd let me pet every animal I could find. Except the bulls. Those always scared the bejesus out of me."

He winced and slid his hand from hers to rest on his side where the stiches lay beneath his shirt. "Good call. I don't think I'll ever look at one of those the same after yesterday."

Before she could comment, the woman at the counter called them forward.

Eve placed her order, her mouth watering as she watched the fresh dough bobbing in the oil. She focused on the sweet-smelling vanilla and hints of cinnamon instead of the fear that had swallowed her whole when she'd heard Reid had been injured. He wasn't the only one who'd never view a bull the same way.

"All right, darlin'," the woman said, holding out the giant paper plate. "Enjoy."

Reid took the plate. "I'll carry it, you eat. Let's walk toward those turkey legs."

She plucked a warm doughnut hole from the plate and popped it in her mouth. A burst of heat had her parting her lips and blowing out steam, but she refused to waste the delicious mound of flaky pastry. "So good."

He chuckled and led the way past colorful displays of homemade wares and trinkets.

It'd been years since she'd visited the rodeo, too concerned with preparing her bar for the annual line dancing to take time from her day to just enjoy the festivities. She'd forgotten how much she loved watching the people in traditional Western wear walking beside the younger generations with tattoos and piercings, coming together to celebrate traditions as old as the West itself.

But even when she'd visited the rodeo with her parents, she hadn't spent much time looking at the homemade candles or knickknacks. She'd been more excited by the livestock and action in the arenas.

Now she understood her mistake. Jars of jam and beautiful crafts that must have taken hours to create lined decorative shelves. If her fingers weren't covered in sugar, she'd be tempted to run them over the knitted blankets and Native American dream catchers. Each step took her mind further from her troubles, and she could almost pretend this was just a normal day with a handsome man and delicious food.

The path curved and a burly man who could be a professional lumberjack sat hunched over on a tree stump. He concentrated on something in his hand, his big brow furrowed. She stopped and watched, unable to see what he worked on.

Behind him was a trifold draped in burgundy fabric. Decorations of some kind hung on the display. She took a step closer, not wanting to disturb the man but eager to see what he was selling. The decorations were all shapes and sizes with intricate patterns and details.

Terror swelled in her chest, forcing the air from her lungs. The items might all be different, but they had one thing in common. They were all carved from wood.

Tugging on Reid's sleeve, she pointed to a small selection of carvings resting in a porcelain bowl on the table.

"What is it?"

"Look," she said. "Flowers." A flash of panic shook her hand and made the sweet treat revolt in her stomach.

Reid followed her sight line and frowned, shifting his focus back to the man on the stump. "That's not the same guy, is it?"

The man was sitting, but Eve had no doubt if he stood, he would have a good five inches on Reid. The man who'd attacked her had been a similar height to Reid. The man in front of her had a beard, but it wasn't as long, and the white whiskers blended with the black.

Eve shook her head. "No, but those flowers look so similar to the ones I keep finding."

"Excuse me," Reid said, stepping forward.

The man lifted his gaze, his hands stilling. "Can I help you?" His long drawl of each word spoke of a man who gave careful thought to what came out of his mouth.

"Those flowers." Reid flicked his wrist toward the bowl a few feet away. "Did you make those?"

"Sure did. I make everything you see here." He tipped his head in the direction of the display boasting his products.

"Do you mind if we take a closer look?" Eve asked, a pit forming in her stomach.

"That's fine. If you don't see anything you like, I can make most anything. The bigger the challenge, the better."

Reid approached the table, Eve right beside him, and picked up one of the flowers.

"These petals are more intricate," she said. "It's close, and standing farther back they look identical. But these aren't the same."

The man stood, placing the piece he'd been working on in a tan leather apron tied around his waist. "Not the same as what?"

"Someone has made flowers like yours and left them in her home," Reid said.

"Like a gift or forgot them or something?"

Clearing her voice, Eve stood a little straighter. "As in he broke in and left them there to scare me."

The man's features pinched, and he fisted his hands at his sides. "He did what?"

"Someone is stalking my friend here," Reid said, wrapping an arm around her shoulders and drawing her near. "He's using little wooden flowers as part of his weird mind games. Do you sell other whittled flowers that have less precise details on the petals?"

The carver scratched the back of his neck. "I make a lot of different kinds of things. Some are custom, some just little ideas I have. I'm sure there are flowers out there I've done that are less intricate, different shapes and size, completely different flowers."

"What about roses?" Eve asked. "The ones left for me have been roses in partial bloom."

A dark cloud passed over the woodworker's face. "About this big?" He indicated a length of about an inch with his thumb and forefinger.

"Yes, about that big."

"And all the same?"

"Pretty much. Has someone made an order from you recently including flowers of that description?"

"No, but I know someone who made the same damn flowers over and over again. He'd come by and talk to me about what I was working on. He had talent, and I always encouraged him to do something new. Try to make something different. He spouted nonsense about the simple and natural beauty of roses. How he didn't need to make anything more elaborate because he just liked using his hands."

A wave of excitement pushed her on her toes. "Do you know his name?"

"His first name, yeah. Tyson. He was a bull rider. We were on the circuit together for a while. When his marriage fell apart, he disappeared. Figured he went home to his old woman to make things right. At least that's what I'd do if my Edith put her foot down. I'd burn all this to the ground if it meant making her happy." A wistful smile showed beneath his beard, softening his edges to show the teddy bear he must be inside.

"Do you remember the last time you saw him?" Reid asked. "The last city you were in when he left?"

"It's been at least four, five months since I've heard from him. I can't pinpoint the exact location, but I can give you a few cities I was in around that time."

"That'd be really helpful," Reid said.

"Give me a second." The man rounded the corner of his booth and disappeared except a glimpse of his boots as he shuffled around.

Hope tripled her heart rate. "If we can figure out who this guy is, it could lead us right to him."

"It will help, that's for sure. Once we get a list of cities, I'll get ahold of Madden. He knows more about how this world works than I do. He might know who to contact to find more details about this guy."

"And the more details, the better. Then we can find him and lock him up and my life can go back to normal."

Reid flattened his lips in a tight smile, and a flash of disappointment mirrored the dread climbing up the back of her neck.

She didn't want to live in a constant state of fear, but she also didn't want to stop spending so much time with Reid. Peeling back his layers revealed he was more than a womanizing flirt, but that hadn't been easy. Once they returned to their normal lives, his shield would go right back up and he wouldn't be forced to be around her long enough to tear it back down.

And at the end of the day, she didn't want a man who wouldn't freely open up to her. She had too much on her plate to have any leftover energy for a relationship with a man who was anything less than supportive and willing to be what she needed.

Even if every fiber of her body told her what she needed—what she wanted—was Reid.

Chapter 13

A quick call to Madden pointed Reid in the right direction for information. He quickly verified the full name of the bull rider who had a penchant for whittling roses.

Tyson Brown.

Eve sat in the chair he'd dragged around his desk to sit beside his leather rolling chair. "I can't believe that was so quick."

Reid studied the face on the computer screen. The rugged cowboy with the full beard and dirty hat leaned against a split-rail fence with a piece of hay between his lips. He stared at the camera as if issuing some kind of silent challenge. "Wasn't hard once Madden told me where to find the registered riders from all the rodeos in the cities we were given."

"I think we should alert the authorities," Eve said, gaze fixed on the screen. "If he's a murderer as well as my stalker, he might already have a rap sheet or at least a way to pinpoint where he is."

Agreeing, he grabbed his phone and made the call directly to Deputy Silver. She'd given him her card the night Eve was attacked.

"Deputy Silver," she answered in a clipped tone after the first ring.

He activated the speaker option and set the phone on the desk between them. "Hi, Deputy. It's Reid Sommers. I'm here with Eve and we wanted to touch base. We've got a name for the man stalking Eve. Wanted to pass it along."

"Oh," she said, shock clear in her voice. "What's the name?"

"Tyson Brown. He was a bull rider until five months ago. Rumor has it he was having marital issues and disappeared. He matches the description given by the witness who was questioned about the murdered barrel racer. I'm staring at his picture on my computer. Eve and I are both convinced it's the same man who attacked her."

"And how did you come across this information? Deputy Hill and I spoke with the witness. She didn't know the name of the man she saw. Claimed Dana never told her."

"Eve and I walked around the rodeo a bit, and she noticed one of the vendors selling whittled pieces of wood." He stopped to shoot her a small smile. Stumbling upon such an important piece of the puzzle was all because of her keen eye. "Some of the flowers he sold were similar to the ones left at her house, so we asked him a few questions. He gave us some information, and we traced it back to our man."

"I'll run this right away and see what pops," Deputy Silver said. "I'll be in touch," she said before disconnecting.

Eve let out a long breath. "A part of me thought she'd be pissed for some reason. Like we were stepping on her toes."

"She's good at her job, which means she listens and acts when needed. She'll let us know if the name leads them anywhere."

"Until then…" Eve leaned over him and brought up another tab on his internet browser. "We keep digging."

The slight touch of her skin against his arm set his

nerve endings on fire. He stilled, his body tight and eager to have her so damn close. Lust clogged his throat, and he coughed to clear it. "And how do you propose we do that?"

She shot him a quick grin then returned her focus to the computer. "Social media. People tend to share way too much about themselves on there. We can hope Tyson Brown is one of them."

Her fingers flew across the keyboard, and a list of people littered the screen.

"Popular name," he said, scanning the photos for the right man. "There. That looks like him."

She moved the cursor to the small picture and clicked, taking them to Tyson Brown's profile page. "Says here he's from Denver. He must have been back home when he ran into Dana."

"Bring up his 'about' information," Reid said. She did as he asked, and he scanned the data, shoving bits and pieces into his brain. "Doesn't mention a wife. Either she carried through on her threats and left him or he never posted about his marriage."

"My money's on the former. Anyone who has no problem telling the world he was the beer pong champion of his graduating class as well as giving way too many details about where he shops isn't going to shy away from talking about his life."

Returning to the main profile page, she sat back in her seat but scooched forward just enough to keep her in his personal space.

He gritted his teeth against his automatic reaction to her nearness. This was ridiculous. He'd been in much more intimate situations with other women and he'd remained in control of his body and his emotions. The outpouring of need and longing pulsing through his veins made his head spin—gave him conflicting impulses to both jump in with two feet and stay far away from Eve.

"Nothing on here says anything about being in Cloud Valley," she said, snapping him back to reality. "I hoped he'd have pictures or something so we could figure out where he's spending his time or, hell, even where's he's staying."

Reid leaned back in his chair. "That's a good point."

"What is?"

"He has to be sleeping somewhere. There aren't many options for lodging in town, and most of the people working the rodeo are camping at the fairgrounds."

"Now that the police have his name, I'm sure they'll poke around for a credit card trail."

He bobbed his head along with her words. "True, but that's only if he's actually paying for a hotel room."

She frowned, her brow rippling with confusion. "What do you mean? We just said he has to be staying somewhere."

"True," he said. "But people are creatures of habit who tend to stick with what they know. What does Tyson Brown know?"

"The rodeo."

"And where do they tend to sleep?"

"In trailers at the fairgrounds." She swished her lips back and forth as if giving it considerable thought. "You think he has a trailer?"

He nodded. "Either that or camping gear. Something in the woods or tucked away where nobody sees him. Maybe he's friends with the other rodeo workers—hell, my money is that he stuck close to keep an eye on Dana.

Stalking. Planning. Executing. And now that she's dead, he'd move on to where his attention is fixed."

"He's sticking close to me."

She spoke with certainty, a statement rather than a question. Because like him, she was starting to understand who Tyson Brown was.

A dangerous man who'd keep his prey in his sights until he could go in for the kill.

"He may be as close as he can get, but I'm closer, and I won't let him hurt you."

She blew out a long, shaky breath. "I know."

Her belief in him constricted his chest. He hated making promises he couldn't keep, but there was one thing he knew with one hundred percent certainty—he'd keep Eve safe or die trying.

A constant chill had crept into Eve's bones. The sun was out but the wind blew, announcing the coming of the changing seasons.

But that wasn't the only reason for the goose bumps cascading up her arms. Fear had a way of making her look over her shoulder, even when riding in the passenger seat of Reid's truck as he turned into the parking lot of his apartment complex.

Gliding into a spot near the front of the lot, Reid shut off the engine. "I'll be quick. I want to toss a few things in a bag then we can head to Tilly's. I know you're anxious to get to work."

The knots in her stomach had more to do with the dangerous man stalking her than the busy night ahead. Being outside heightened her anxiety, and she couldn't wait to be safely inside the building. She forced a tight smile. He didn't need to hear about her worries again. They both understood where things stood, and dissecting every little thing would only make her more paranoid.

"Take your time," she said. "Becca can handle things until I get there. Heck, everything's already handled. The control freak in me just needs to see the restaurant to believe there's not something waiting for me to fix."

He opened his door and had one booted foot out when he stared back at her with a smirk. "Control freak, huh? Go figure."

She couldn't tell if he was kidding or not, so she just rolled her eyes then met him at the hood of his truck. She stared at the building with its scalloped-edged windows and pitched roof. The dark brown siding mimicked a log cabin while vines of ivy snaked up the corner, bleeding into a massive oak tree. "I don't know why, but I never imagined you living in an apartment. I pictured you tucked away on a large plot of land and a generous view of the mountains."

He dug his keys from his pocket. "You've thought about where I live a lot?"

This time his teasing was evident, and she grinned, enjoying the playfulness. "Mostly when I want to close down the bar and you won't leave."

The warmth of his booming chuckle chased away a bit of that lingering chill. Reid could always make her troubles melt away—even if only for a minute or two. A part of her wanted to skip work, hide out at his place and find some more creative ways for Reid to occupy her thoughts.

The memory of their almost kiss crashed back with the force of a hurricane, and heat slammed into her cheeks. He'd made it clear he wasn't interested in pursuing her romantically or, hell, even physically. She had to shove all those feelings he evoked to the far corner of her mind and never let them see the light of day again.

"You okay?"

She blinked at the curiosity in his voice, surprised he'd made it to the entrance and held the door open, waiting for her to enter.

"Yeah. I'm fine. Just anxious to get to work." The lie tasted bitter on her tongue but was better than admitting where her mind had taken her for a few seconds.

She stepped into the small foyer that displayed a cluster of mailboxes on one wall, a door marked Maintenance and a stairwell. The area wasn't flashy, but fresh paint and a lemony smell made it clean and well-kept. She followed him up two flights of stairs and down a wide, carpeted hallway.

Reid stopped in front of the last door on the right and lifted his keys to the dead-bolt lock. His hand wavered, the lines on his face tightening.

The shift of energy heightened her awareness. The buzzing of the overhead lights intensified, and she glanced up and down the hallway, searching for the source of Reid's hesitation. "What's wrong?"

"The door's ajar." His voice was clipped. "Stay in the hall. I'll check it out."

"No way I'm staying out here. What if it's a trap? A ploy to get me alone while you're inside. I stay with you. Always."

Grim-faced, he nodded and grabbed a gun tucked in his waistband, hidden by his T-shirt. He pushed open the door and tiptoed inside.

She stayed close, her heart beating so loudly in her

ears she had no doubt Reid could hear. Anxiety twisted her gut, and each step felt as though she moved through a minefield. No one waited to ambush them in the living room, which bled into the small kitchen, but that didn't mean the rest of the place was empty.

"Down the hall is a bathroom and two bedrooms. We'll move slowly, making sure they're all clear before I call this in to the authorities."

She swallowed past the ball of fear wedged at the base of her throat. "Could it just be a break-in?" She knew the answer before asking the question. The space was neat and tidy, everything seemingly in its place, down to the perfectly placed blue pillows on each end of the gray sofa.

"Hard to know for sure," he whispered. He kept his gun in front of him, both hands around the handle and the barrel aimed at the ground. "But unlikely."

A loud thump sounded from the hallway, and she jumped. Her muscles coiled and she gripped the back of Reid's shirt like a lifeline. "Any chance you have a really fat cat?"

He snorted but shook his head. "I wish. I want you to go back out in the hallway. Someone is back there. I want to know you're safe."

"No." The word came out on a hiss of air. "I don't want to be without you."

The statement struck a chord in her soul, but she didn't have time to stop and really consider what that meant. Not now.

"Eve, I nee—"

Footsteps pounded on the floor. Reid faced the hallway, gun raised.

A woman emerged, her bright grin falling, and she

threw her palms in the air. "What the actual hell, Reid. Are you trying to give me a freaking heart attack? Not exactly the warm welcome I'd hoped for."

Muttered curses poured from Reid's mouth, and he shoved the gun back in place. "Damn it, Tara. What are you doing here?"

The sudden shift of energy made Eve's head spin. "Tara? As in your sister? I didn't know she was coming to town."

"Neither did I." Reid rubbed the back of his neck, his scowl slowly melting into a smile. "Why didn't you tell me?"

Tara scrunched her freckled nose. "I didn't want you to talk me out of it. I made the decision, booked the first flight I could get on and showed up. I see now that was a mistake."

"Never, although a little heads-up would have been nice." He opened his arms, waiting until Tara got close to wrap in her a quick hug. "It's so good to see you."

He shifted so one arm hooked around Tara's shoulders and he turned her to face Eve. "Eve, I'd like to officially introduce you to my little sister, Tara. Tara, this is Eve."

Interest lit Tara's blue eyes. "Nice to meet you, Eve. Do you hang out with my brother in his apartment a lot?"

Before she could answer, Reid nudged Tara with his elbow. "Don't start. Eve's a good friend, and she's hired me to help her with some things."

"Nice to meet you, Tara." His answer was like a punch in the gut, but Eve managed to keep what she hoped was a natural-looking smile on her face. She'd needed that reminder to keep her mind out of fantasyland and firmly in reality where it belonged.

Chapter 14

An hour later, Reid still couldn't wrap his mind around the fact that Tara was sitting at a table with him at Tilly's. He'd lived in Cloud Valley for a little over a year, and not once had she left their hometown in Indiana to visit.

Not once had she felt comfortable enough to put that much distance between her and their toxic father.

A hundred questions spun around his brain like a tornado, but a chance to discuss what had caused her to act so impulsively hadn't presented itself.

Tara bobbed her straw up and down in her cola and took in the atmosphere. "This place is awesome. I feel like I stepped onto some movie set with rugged cowboys waiting to sweep me off my feet."

"I'm sure Richard would love that." Tara's tortured expression made him wish he could take back the words as soon as he said them. But now that the happy-go-lucky mask had slipped, he might as well push through the rest of her walls. "Why are you here?"

She tapped the tip of her finger against the table, her gaze fixed on a trio of giggling women about her age taking shots at the crowded bar. "After we talked last night, I really took a hard look at my life. I'm exhausted, Reid. Completely overwhelmed and miserable. Every time my phone rings I'm terrified of who's on the other end. If it's Dad, he'll want money or to pour on the guilt or tell me about the latest stupid mess I have to clean up. If it's Robert, he's pissed about something. I'm constantly walking on eggshells. I can't do it anymore. I'm afraid of what I'll turn into if I do."

Reaching across the table, he rested his hand on top of hers and squeezed. Leaving his hometown had been what he'd needed for his own mental health, but he regretted how much it had placed on her shoulders. "I'm sorry. I hate that you've been the one dealing with this for so long. You deserve better. And if you need me to kick Richard's ass, just say the word. It'd be pretty damn satisfying."

The side of her mouth ticked up. "He's not worth the trouble. Not yours and definitely not mine."

"So you two are done for good?"

Tears misted her eyes, and she wiped them away. "Yeah. What a waste of time. I guess I should be grateful he never got around to proposing."

"Well, for what it's worth, the reason you're here sucks, but I'm happy to see you." He was even happier he'd given her a key and open invitation to visit the last time he saw her. He lifted his own soda in cheers then took a sip, his gaze seeking Eve as she bustled from table to table.

After his initial shock at finding Tara in his apartment, she'd been excited to tag along with him and Eve to Tilly's. As much as he wished he could stay glued to Eve's side as she hustled around the crowded bar and grill, there was no way to keep up with her. She'd agreed to stay behind the bar, coming out only to help deliver a drink or two.

He and Tara set up at a table where he could get to Eve

in a second's notice. His senses were on high alert, but with everything he'd learned about Tyson Brown, he understood the bastard was a coward at heart—he waited to pounce on his prey when they were alone or vulnerable.

He had to hang on to the hope that he wouldn't break pattern tonight when Tilly's was packed with locals and tourists waiting to dance along with the live band. At least Madden planned to join him once he was done keeping guard at the rodeo.

"So what's going on with you and Eve?" Tara asked.

He tracked Eve as she moved behind the bar and filled two pints with the local ale before giving them to Becca to serve. "She's a client. Some shit's happened the last couple of days. I'm keeping an eye on her until things settle down."

"You don't look at her like she's just a client. You look at her the same way you looked at Gabby Shaffer when you were in high school." Tara wiggled her eyebrows and grinned.

He couldn't help but laugh at the memory of his high school crush. "Big difference between Eve and Gabby. Eve and I are friends. Gabby wouldn't give me the time of day."

"Not from lack of trying."

He wadded up the paper from the straw and tossed it at her. "Nobody here knows about my tragic past with Gabby Shaffer. I'd like to keep it that way."

A heavy hand on his shoulder had him whipping his attention up to Madden's wide grin. "I want to know about your tragic past. Hi, Tara. Didn't know you were visiting."

"Hey, Madden. Long time no see."

"Yeah, it's been a while. Good to see you again." Madden skirted the side of the table to give her a quick hug then placed his hand on the small of Lily's back. "This is my fiancée, Lily. Lily, Tara is Reid's sister. She lives in Indiana, and I believe this is her first time to Cloud Valley."

Lily offered a wave. "Nice to meet you."

"You as well. And yes, first time here and I'm loving the vibe. Is this place always so packed?"

Reid continued his constant perusal of the room. Every table was filled, and the crowd at the bar grew. Music blasted from the jukebox, competing with the sound of pool balls bouncing off each other and the constant stream of chatter.

"Not like this. The rodeo's in town, and tonight's the annual line dancing. A band will play soon and there are a ton of tourists. Speaking of which," he said, eyes on Madden. "I'm surprised you're here. Figured you'd be with Dax and Ben for a little longer."

Madden pulled out a chair and waited for Lily to take a seat before settling in the one beside her. "As you can see, people were shifting their focus. Wanting to get here early. Ben and Dax are finishing up at the fairgrounds and will be on their way here soon, so I figured you could use an extra pair of eyes here sooner rather than later."

"Appreciate it," Reid said. "I don't like Eve being so far from my side, and the more the crowd grows, the more anxious I get."

Lily clicked her tongue then smoothed her hand over her blond ponytail. "Can't say I blame you. Maybe we can convince her to sit with us and grab dinner before things really get crazy."

"You think she'll sit and eat while her staff is busting their asses?" Reid asked, eyebrows raised high.

Lily scrunched her nose. "Absolutely not."

Another group of women wearing short dresses with cowboy boots walked through the door, catching the attention of the two men playing pool. A man in a tan cowboy hat stalked in behind them, his head angled toward the floor.

Reid shot to his feet and pushed through the crowd toward the man. "Madden, go to Eve. Now."

Without further explanation, Madden jumped up and moved toward the bar.

Reid wove between tables and shimmied past laughing partiers, his eyes never wavering from the tan hat that stormed forward. The worn jean jacket disappeared around a pillar, and Reid's heart jumped to his throat. He shoved past anyone who stood in his way, ignoring shouts and curses in his wake.

Rounding the pillar, the jean jacket reappeared, the man within arm's reach as he approached the bar. Reid lunged forward, gripped the collar of the jacket, and yanked the man backward.

The man's arms flailed out before he spun around, escaping Reid's grasp. His blue eyes were wide, his clean-shaven face pinched in anger. "What the hell, man?"

Relief seeped into every pore in Reid's body, and he held up his palms. "Sorry, dude. I thought you were someone else. Enjoy your night."

Muttering under his breath, the man shook his head and continued to the bar.

With his pulse still racing, he made his way to where Eve stood with Madden, her fear louder than the old country song blasting through the room. Tara's unexpected arrival had thrown him off his game.

He couldn't let that happen. Eve's life was on the line. He didn't care if she was working and didn't want him to hover. Didn't care if she'd rather he sit in the corner and watch from a distance. For the rest of the night, he'd be by her side.

And if he was being honest with himself, there was nowhere else he'd rather be.

The steady beat of the drums and crisp notes of the guitar cut through the noise in the room. The singer behind the microphone tipped his cowboy hat at a jaunty angle and moved his hips along with the words about women and whiskey. The temporary dance floor was filled with couples swaying and laughing, leaving empty plates to be bussed on the deserted tables.

Eve stayed behind the bar, filling glasses and pouring whiskey faster than she thought possible. Thank God Reid had stayed close as the crowd had grown. She'd put him to work on the tap to free Becca and Nellie to ferry food from the slammed kitchen.

A lull hit, and she leaned against the long counter that displayed bottles of liquor. Her feet ached and her stomach growled as she watched her patrons enjoying the live music.

This was one of her favorite nights of the year. Yes, the hours were longer and bar busier, but there was nothing like the joy of seeing the place she loved packed and thriving. Even if her world outside these walls was in chaos, everything inside was perfect.

Reid tilted a pint glass and filled it with amber liquid from the tap. He handed it over to an older man who preferred a bar stool to the dance floor but tapped his foot along with the beat. Reid wiped his palms on the thighs of his jeans then shot her a grin. "This is fun."

She snorted out a laugh. "Glad you're enjoying yourself."

He leaned against the counter beside her, his shoulder resting against hers. "Don't get me wrong, I'm exhausted. I don't know how you do this every day."

Keeping her eyes on the dance floor, she shrugged. "It's not always like this, but it's always hard work. It is fun, though. And we aren't the only ones enjoying ourselves."

He followed her sight line to where Tara danced with Dax in the middle of the crush of people. "Dude better watch where he puts his hands."

"So, you're the protective type, huh?" She bumped against him, gaze fixed on his sister. Tara laughed at something Dax said before playfully slapping his arm.

"With Tara, not as much as I should have been. I'm glad she's here. She deserves to have some fun."

The wistful note in his voice piqued her curiosity. "Is she having a rough time? Is that why she's here?"

"I don't want to get into that now." He grabbed another empty glass to fill. "You deserve some fun, too. You ever go out there and dance?"

She wrinkled her nose, irritated he'd evaded her question. "Nah. I've got two left feet. Besides, this is the part I love. Standing and watching people having fun in my bar. Knowing I'm carrying on traditions that have been passed down since before I was born."

"Really?" he asked, frowning down at her.

Memories washed over her, of all the times she stood there in front of a similar scene, as well as memories passed down to her that she hadn't experienced but wished she had. "Yep. To me, this night is almost as special as Christmas."

"Why's that? Does Honky-Tonk Santa make an appearance at some point?"

She grinned at the picture he painted but shook her head. "Nothing so eclectic."

"Then what?"

"My parents met on a night just like tonight," she said, wishing they were both with her in this moment. "This bar belonged to my grandparents. They were the ones who insisted on having an annual line dancing event when the rodeo was in town. My dad was working one night when my mom came with friends from a few towns over. He asked her to dance, and the rest is history. They've been happy and in love for close to thirty years."

"So your parents fell in love at a dance and gave you two left feet? Damn shame," he said, clicking his tongue.

She burst into laughter then smacked him with a nearby dishcloth. "Are you ever serious?"

"Only when I need to be." He winked at her then returned his focus to Tara. "Dax will see that side of me if he doesn't take Tara back to her seat soon."

"Dax is harmless. A lot like you, really. Too busy having fun to cause any real trouble."

Something in Reid's eyes made her stomach drop, but it left before she could figure out its meaning.

"Sometimes it's the ones you think are joking through life who have the least to laugh about."

Before she could ask more questions he'd probably ignore, he pushed away from the counter and helped a man with scruff covering his jawline and a baseball hat

pulled low over his eyes. After he poured a double whiskey neat, he glanced over his shoulder. "Eve, have you
met Ben yet?"

She hadn't, but the man's hunched shoulders and scowl
didn't make her want to change that. She forced a smile
and busied herself by wiping down the bar. "Don't believe I have. Nice to meet you."

Ben grunted something that sounded a little like *you
too* then sipped his drink.

"His bark's worse than his bite," Reid said.

"Does he bite a lot?"

A deep, husky chuckle rumbled from Ben's chest, and
she swore a hint of a smile lifted the corner of his mouth.

Okay, so he wasn't as scary as she first thought.

"Not as much as he used to. He's helping me and Madden out with some security work. Might make it permanent if it goes well."

"Hope you enjoy Cloud Valley," she said. "I'm sure
I'll see you around."

He gave a brief nod then shifted to face the band.

Hooking a brow, she glanced at Reid.

He gave a tiny shake of his head.

Frustration simmered in her veins. She couldn't ask
about Ben, couldn't ask about Reid's cryptic statement,
couldn't step outside and scream, because God forbid she
go anywhere alone.

As if sensing she needed a break, Becca hurried over
and lifted two fingers. "Need two more local ales. Kitch-
en's closed, so things will start to slow down. We're going
to survive another year."

Eve poured the drinks and passed them to her best
friend. The band would wind down in another ten min-

utes then they could start the lengthy process of cleaning up and getting the place ready to open for brunch the next day.

Exhaustion and the lingering fear tightened her muscles and threatened to steal her joy.

No. She'd worked too damn hard for the success of this night. For once she wanted to step out on the dance floor and experience every part of the evening.

She poured herself a shot of her favorite whiskey, taking it in one quick swallow. The liquor burned her throat and warmed her belly as well as bolstered her courage. Before she could chicken out, she rounded the bar and grabbed Ben's hand, yanking him to his feet. "You come to my bar, you can't just sit and watch. Let's go, cowboy. Show me what you've got."

Ben's eyes flew wide, but she refused to take no for an answer. She led him to the dance floor, linking their hands and facing him with a grin. "Don't worry. I suck at this."

He flashed a small smile before spinning her in a smooth circle then resting a palm on her waist. "Don't worry," he echoed her words. "I'll take the lead."

Closing her eyes, she gave in to the music and the stranger who twirled her around and made her feel like she knew what she was doing. Stress melted away, and for a few minutes all her worries floated far away, as if they belonged to someone else.

When the song ended, she opened her eyes, thanked her surprising partner and found herself face-to-face with Reid, who stood on the edge of the dance floor.

She swallowed hard. If looks could kill, Ben would be a dead man.

Chapter 15

A swift, crippling rage swept through Reid like a downpour. Not jealously, not protectiveness—rage.

Seeing Eve laughing and carefree in his buddy's arms was like pouring a gallon of salt on a gunshot wound. As much as he wanted Eve to let her hair down and have fun, he didn't want her to choose Ben to have the fun with.

Damn it, it should have been him.

He'd mentioned her dancing. She'd shot down that idea before he could even ask. And then she asked Ben? *Ben?*

He'd never considered himself the jealous type, but he'd never had a reason to be. All that had changed the second he saw Ben's hand settle on Eve's hip. Screw being professional. Forget keeping her at a distance out of self-preservation and fear. He wanted her, at least for the next five minutes, when he could hold her in his arms and no one would bat an eye.

When he could pretend all he wanted was to join in on the fun.

Ben gave a brief nod as he passed by and returned to his seat at the bar. He finished his drink then gave Reid a mock salute. "G'night."

"You're right," Eve said. "Not much of a bite at all."

She made a move to step past him, and he hooked his arm around her waist, locking her in place.

"He's not the one you've got to worry about," Reid said.

Her eyes flew wide, and her already flushed cheeks turned a deeper shade of red. "And who is?"

"Me if you don't let me spin you around this dance floor."

She swallowed hard, eyes locked on his, and slipped her hand into his.

All the air leaked from his lungs and his mouth went dry. The commotion around them disappeared, and Eve was the only thing in his world. "Is that a yes?"

"Can you make me look as good as Ben did?"

"Honey, you have no idea."

She grinned and took a step closer, erasing the distance between them.

The music stopped. The crowd erupted into applause as the band bowed and wished everyone a good night.

Disappointment pressed down on his chest.

Eve stepped out of his hold and shrugged. "Maybe next time. I need to get back behind the bar. People with open tabs will start cashing out. It'll get a little busy then we'll need to close up."

Deflated, he followed her and ignored the stab of pain that had nothing to do with his stitched-up side. Seeing Eve in the arms of another man had woken him up, and now he'd missed his chance.

He wouldn't make that mistake again.

Figuring out his next move, he stalked back to where Eve stood at the register, quickly ringing out customers on the old-fashioned machine. He lost himself in the rhythm of washing dishes and replacing bottles. Wiping sticky residue from the scarred bar and refilling garnishes for the drinks he didn't know how to make.

Tara approached, with Dax attached to her side. "Hey, big brother, when are you heading to your place?"

"Yeah, big brother. What's the plan?" Dax tipped the brim of his hat and laughed. Mischief lit his blue eyes, and the dark stubble lining his jaw was longer than usual.

Reid glared at Madden's younger brother. "The only plan you should be concerned with is the one that involves getting yourself home. Alone."

Tara rolled her eyes and shoved a strand of hair off her face, tucking it behind her ear. "Stop. Dax was nice enough to hang out with me while you were busy."

"Yeah," Dax said. "I'm just being a good guy."

Madden approached and rested his palms on Dax's shoulders. He squeezed, applying enough pressure to make Dax wince. "Good guy? You? Don't think so, my man."

Lily rested her hands on top of Madden's and eased him away. "Leave him be."

"Yeah, listen to Lil so I can continue my conversation with Reid about his sister."

A growl rumbled deep in Reid's chest, and he struggled to keep it trapped inside. He wasn't in the mood to deal with Dax's smart-ass comments, and he didn't have much experience looking out for Tara. She was a grown woman who could make her own decisions, but he'd be damned if going home with Dax was one of them.

Tara gave Dax a playful slap upside his head. "I don't need anyone to have a conversation with anyone about me." She turned her attention to Reid. "I do need to know if we plan to head back to your apartment once you're done helping Eve."

He flicked a quick glance at Eve, still swiping credit cards. "I have to stay with Eve until this thing blows over."

"Oh," she said, drawing out the word into three syllables.

"It's a good thing I stuck around to drive you to Reid's place safely." Dax puffed out his chest, his grin slippery as a wet dog.

"How about Lily and I take Tara to your place?" Madden asked. "No need for Dax to suffer rejection again."

Dax threw up his palms, but his grin stayed in place. "Only trying to help."

"My hero," Tara said. "But I'll ride with Madden and Lily."

Relief loosened Reid's muscles. He wasn't used to watching Tara interact with men. Hell, when he'd left town, she was just entering high school. By the time he'd enlisted in the service, she was already with Richard—whom he'd hated. Standing by and watching Dax drool over her was giving him a glimpse of himself he hadn't known existed.

The protective side of himself that saw blood when Ben danced with Eve.

"Does that work?" Tara asked, breaking into his thoughts.

"Yeah. Everything you need should be there. The sheets on the guest bed are clean. Call if there're any issues. Just…make sure to lock up."

A small slice of guilt gnawed at his conscious. A dangerous man was on the loose. Maybe Tara shouldn't be alone, but saying that out loud would only upset her and bait Dax into saying something else to piss him off.

As if reading his thoughts, Lily hooked her arm through Tara's. "She'll be fine. We'll make sure she has everything she needs before we leave her for the night. She'll be safe."

"Thanks, Lily." He leaned over the bar to give Tara a quick hug. "I'll talk to you tomorrow."

"Sounds good. You two have fun." Tara's laugh lingered behind her as she waved goodbye to Eve then walked with Lily and Madden out the door, Dax following.

The sound of the cash register continued to chime, and he returned to work. He wanted the place sparkling and Eve's mind clear of any more chores. Then, when the bar was empty except him and Eve, he'd find a way to finally discover how Eve felt in his arms.

Exhaustion seeped into Eve's muscles. Fatigue made her eyes heavy, but she finished poring over the revenue for the night. Normally she'd sit in her small office after closing time and ready the deposit for the next day. Tonight she opted to sit on a stool beside the register. She didn't want to be tucked away, out of sight of the staff bustling around the restaurant.

And hell, she wasn't sure her feet would carry her that far.

Becca slid a plate in front of her. "Hungry?"

"God bless you. How did you get this?" A colorful salad topped with grilled chicken and a side of Italian dressing stared up at her. "The kitchen's been closed for a while. I was mentally going through the contents of my refrigerator to figure out what I could make really quickly when I got home."

"I made sure to set aside some chicken and threw together the salad." She set down another plate.

"You joining me?"

"No." Becca twirled her braid around her finger then wound it on top of her head, wrapping it in place with a hair tie to make a messy bun. "I've got a foot rub and a comfy bed waiting for me at home."

"Suzy's waiting up to give you a foot rub?" Eve stabbed a cherry tomato and popped it in her mouth.

"Ha-ha," Becca said. "Her cute little butt better be fast asleep."

"Who's the extra salad for?" Eve asked. "Think I'm hungry enough to eat two?"

Becca flicked her wrist toward Reid, who was placing turned-up chairs on top of tables. "Figured he'd be hungry, too. He worked for his supper tonight."

Reid grabbed a broom and tidied the floor, making her smile. "He sure did. Nellie already left. Why don't you let him know he has food waiting then take off?"

"You sure? I can finish sweeping while you two eat. That's the last of what needs done tonight."

"I've got it. You've been here longer than you should have been tonight. I appreciate you."

Becca wrapped her in a side hug. "I'll call you tomorrow."

Eve attacked her salad again, cutting into the grilled chicken. Notes of garlic and pepper exploded on her tongue. She closed her eyes to savor the taste and sent a silent prayer of gratitude for her best friend.

"Must be a damn good salad."

Reid's amused voice lifted her lips and opened her eyes. He stood next to her, one arm hooked behind the back of her stool while the other leaned against the bar.

"You have no idea." She nudged his plate. "Becca made one for you, too. Take a seat. We'll finish cleaning after we eat."

"Everything's done."

"Floors are mopped?"

"Yep. I did that a little earlier, after Nellie swept. I just noticed a few crumbs and wanted to get them out of the way." He sat next to her but kept his arm behind her. "How'd we do tonight?"

She beamed, liking the way *we* sounded a little too much. "Best night of the year, as always. The next two days will still be a little busy, but then we'll slow down. Thanks for all your help."

"I was here. Might as well be useful." He speared his fork into the chicken and took a bite. "Holy hell. This is amazing. Make sure to tell Becca I said thanks."

She took another few bites then asked, "Did Tara go to your place?"

"Yeah. Madden and Lily drove her. She had a ball tonight. It was nice to see her happy." He took another couple of bites.

Setting down her fork, she considered her next words. He'd made it clear he didn't want to talk about his family, but damn it, she wanted to know. She wanted him to open up to her. "Has she not been happy lately? Is that why she came?"

Reid stared down at his half-empty plate. "Tara's life hasn't been easy. Especially with my living so far away. A lot falls on her shoulders that shouldn't, and she's tired of carrying the burden. I hope being here for a while will show her it's time for her to live her own life. To pursue her own passions."

"I'm sure she will. If she's made the first steps toward that, you'll help her make the second. She's lucky to have you as a brother. I wish I would have had one like you growing up."

Disgust pinched his features. "You wish I was your brother?"

Heat snaked up the back of her neck. "No. I didn't mean it like that. I just meant, you two are lucky to have each other. My parents are great, but I always envied all my friends who had siblings. Built-in partners in crime. It'd be nice to know someone is watching out for you, standing in the shadows to help things go your way."

"As far as Tara's concerned, I've been in the shadows for too long. I plan to change that." He set his fork down and pushed away his plate. Rising to his feet, he captured her hand in his. "And that's not the only thing I need to change."

He tugged her to her feet and led her to the corner of the room.

If her curiosity wasn't so strong, she'd complain about how late it was or how much her feet hurt. Instead, she followed along, curiosity growing when they stopped in front of the jukebox. With the lights low, the neon signs and colors from the jukebox cast a rainbow glow around the room. "What are you doing?"

Snagging a quarter from the front pocket of his jeans, he fed it into the machine and pressed a button. A familiar song filled the air. The music was slow, and a woman's voice belted out words of love and longing. He held out a hand. "Have time for that dance?"

A smile blossomed on her lips, and she stared down at his palm before returning her focus to his handsome face. "Seriously?"

He nodded. "I missed my chance earlier. I don't want that to happen again. Just one dance then we can head home. I know you're probably exhausted."

With her mouth suddenly dry, she nestled her palm into his and electricity shot all the way down to her toes. Her heart raced so loud she could barely make out the words to the song, but they didn't matter. All that mattered was Reid and his charming grin and the look in his eyes that told her she was in big trouble.

Wrapping his arm around her waist, he pulled her close. "Here we go."

A rush of excitement threatened to steal all coherent thoughts from her brain. A hint of his sweat mixed with the cedar and citrus cologne holding on strong, making her head swim. He spun her around the dance floor, never taking his eyes off her.

She moved her body impossibly closer to him and got lost in the moment. Lost in his arms. Lost in a fantasy that this wasn't just one dance but a promise of wonderful things to come.

The music faded. The song ended. She stared up at him, her heart lodged in her throat. A sense of déjà vu struck her. They'd been in this moment once before. With her gaze fixed on his mouth and a need to know how he tasted consuming every inch of her being.

"Eve?"

The question may have been filled with a hundred words with all the meaning put into it.

She forced her dry throat to swallow her apprehension. "Yes?"

"A dance like that deserves one hell of a finale, don't you think?"

Unable to speak, she nodded.

"I'm glad we're on the same page." His smirk melted away as he leaned down and placed his lips on hers.

Chapter 16

Fireworks.

Goddamn fireworks.

Nothing else could describe the eruption of desire and emotions uncapped as Reid held Eve in his arms and kissed her. Not wanting it to end, he held her tighter and molded her body against his. The feel of her breasts pressed to his chest and the way she slid one hand up to thread her fingers through his hair threatened to make his heart explode.

Why had he resisted this? Why had he struggled against the feelings he had for Eve for so long? Everything about her—about this moment—was pure perfection.

A moan purred from her throat, and she opened her mouth just enough for him to slip his tongue inside. She tasted sweet and tangy and tempting as hell. He deepened the kiss and glided one palm up her spine to rest at the nape of her neck.

She shivered and moved her lips in a slow rhythm with his.

He wanted more. Wanted to feel her warm, silky skin and to show her how crazy she made him.

Framing her face with his hands, he broke the kiss and his breath came out in sharp gasps. He stared into her kind hazel eyes. Damn, he could get lost in those eyes.

She blinked and her tongue swiped against her swollen lips. She didn't say a word, but he could read the questions in her expression like a freaking book.

"I didn't like watching you dance with another man." He didn't know where the confession came from, but he couldn't keep it tucked inside. Hell, he didn't want to. Not anymore. "Seeing you in Ben's arms shook some sense into me."

She frowned. "That wasn't my intention."

He couldn't help but smile. "I know that. It was a me problem, not a you problem."

"So, what's your problem now?" She tilted her head to the side, her auburn ponytail spilling over her shoulder.

He could open up all the way, really confide in her the problems he faced in his life—in his past. But something held him back. He wanted this thing with Eve to be real, solid. Exposing all his scars too soon might scare her. Hell, might remind him of all the reasons he should stay far away.

"Right now, I have no problems at all. What about you?"

She twisted her lips to the side as if giving the question serious thought. "Right now, my biggest problem is that you stopped kissing me."

"I can fix that." Leaning down, he caught her mouth in his once more.

Her arms slid around his neck, and she nipped playfully at his bottom lip.

Chuckling, he rested his forehead on hers and breathed in the subtle floral notes clinging to her skin. "I like this side of you."

"If you take me back home, there might be more of that to see."

His breath stuttered in his chest, and he gripped her hips in his hands. All he'd wanted was a dance and one little kiss.

Okay, scratch that, he hadn't known how his world would be turned upside down after his lips met hers. Now he wanted anything she was willing to give him. "Are you sure?"

She took a step back and linked their hands together. She kept her gaze locked on his. "Positive. Take me home."

"You don't have to tell me twice," he said, grinning wide. "Grab your stuff and let's lock this place up tight."

He waited by the door as she hurried around the room, flipping off lights and snatching her purse from behind the bar. By the time she met him, his body was vibrating with lust. If he didn't want their first time to be special, to really take his time and show her what she meant to him, he'd carry her into the back room and make love to her against the wall.

The thought of her legs wrapped around him as he pushed inside her made him groan.

"You all right?" she asked.

He placed kisses up her jawline until he reached her ear. "Just thinking of all the things I want to do to you tonight. I hope you're ready."

She gasped, eyes wide. "I've been ready for longer than you know. Let's go."

Stepping outside, cool night air did nothing to calm the raging fire building in his core. Only one thing could put that out, and if all went as planned, it'd take hours for that to happen. He'd waited a lifetime for Eve, and he wanted to take all the time in the world to give her everything she deserved.

With the door locked, he captured her hand and led her to his truck parked on the street in front of the bar and grill. He kept vigilant, glancing in all directions to make sure no one waited in the shadows to attack. Once he got Eve settled in the passenger seat, he jogged around the front of his vehicle and hopped inside.

Eve slid closer on the bench seat, twining her arm through his and joining their palms. She used her free palm to lazily run her finger up and down the inside of his forearm.

The energy inside the truck was filled with anxious anticipation. He struggled not to push the gas pedal all the way to the floor for the two-block drive to her house.

Turning in to her driveway, he shut off the engine and pressed a kiss to her forehead. As much as he wanted to sweep her out of the truck and carry her straight into her bedroom, he needed her to understand she was more to him than a quick lay. "Eve, before we head inside, there's some things I want you to know."

Concern rippled her brow. "Okay."

"Since I've moved to Cloud Valley, you've become one of my favorite people. I look forward to seeing you all day long. You have this way of smoothing my edges when they're all out of whack. Of making me feel better after the shittiest day. Besides Madden, you're my best friend."

She squirmed in her seat. "Is that how you want to keep things? Friends? I mean, I know you don't like to get serious with anyone. I respect that, I really do. I don't want to change you. I just want...heck, I don't know. I just want to forget all the craziness of the last couple days with someone I trust."

Well, hell. He hadn't expressed himself the way he'd wanted, but maybe it was better not to admit that. He didn't want to stay just friends with her. Even if right now, all she was looking for was someone to take her mind off her troubles.

He could be that person. And then he could figure out if there was a way to open Eve up to the possibility of taking their relationship past the friend zone.

"I'm glad you trust me," he said. "Now let's get inside."

He jumped down and met her at her side. He pressed his hand to the small of her back and ushered her up the porch steps.

She dug in her purse for her keys and pushed open her door.

The overwhelming smell of flowers slammed against Reid like a punch in the gut seconds before he registered that the security system didn't sound. Alarm bells went off in his brain, and he grabbed Eve's elbow to lock her in place.

He flipped on the hallway light and anger slammed against him with more force than a charging bull. Hundreds of flower petals filled the living room, as if someone had tossed handfuls of colorful blooms in the air and let them rain down. Clumps of dirt dangled from stems torn from the ground, and ripped petals were ground into the carpet.

Eve shrieked and turned to bury her face in his neck. He held her tight and vowed to destroy the man who refused to leave her alone.

* * *

Panic mixed with the suffocating scent of flowers, stealing the air from Eve's lungs. She clung to Reid, refusing to believe this was happening.

Refusing to believe Tyson Brown had invaded her home once again, taking her sense of security with him.

Reid skimmed his knuckles up and down her arms. "Listen. I know you're scared, but I need to make sure no one is in the house·then call the authorities. Okay?"

She nodded then took a step away from his protective embrace. The last thing she wanted to do was walk through every room of her house to see if someone had been there—to see if more terrifying surprises waited.

But Reid was right. They couldn't just stand in the hallway and pretend like the rug hadn't been pulled out from under her again.

"Stay close. Just like at my place."

Again, she nodded.

Reid grabbed the gun she knew he kept tucked in the back of his waistband and inched through the house.

She'd been terrified at Reid's apartment earlier, but that didn't even begin to describe the almost paralyzing emotions circling through her nervous system. Her body jerked with every groan of the house, every shift of the floor beneath her feet. At the entry of each room, she held her breath and waited for Reid to tell her everything was all right.

He approached her bedroom door, and her heart broke a little. This was not how she'd thought this night would end. With fear and questions and the nauseating scent of flowers permeating her psyche. She'd looked forward to kisses and passion and hopefully the beginning of something more with a man she'd never imagined was in her reach.

Reid pushed open the door and flipped on the light. The sight of red flower petals sprinkled on her bed made bile shoot up the back of her throat. Wind lifted the ends of her curtains, glass shattered on the floor, giving a glimpse into how Tyson had entered her home without the alarm going off.

She stood in the doorway while Reid crept around her space. She pressed her hand to her mouth to keep from getting sick. Her gaze found the painting on her wall she'd always cherished. Now the colorful blooms in the photo would forever remind her of her worst nightmare.

"All clear." Reid crossed to her and dug his phone from his pocket. He swiped the screen and made a call before placing the device to his ear and ushering her out of the room. "Deputy Silver, it's Reid. Eve and I need you at her house. There's been another break-in."

Disconnecting, he slipped his phone back in his pocket and steered her into the kitchen.

She marched along beside him, her body numb, her senses both dulled and extra sensitive at the same time. Her legs were wooden and stiff as she moved, her mind blank.

"Why don't you sit down?" Reid pulled out a chair from the kitchen table.

She lowered herself onto the hard seat and stared up at him. "The alarm didn't go off. We had no idea he'd been in here. Doing that." She flung her wrist toward the sick offering left for her in the living room.

The familiar wildflowers she'd loved since childhood stared back at her from the attached room, taunting her.

Cracking her heart down the middle. Frustrated tears spilled from her eyes.

"Hey, now." Reid dropped to his knees and gripped her hands. "It's going to be okay. I promise."

"He's tarnishing everything I love. Everything I treasure. My home. My memories. How can I live here, knowing he's been inside? Been in my bedroom!"

Reid picked up her hands and kissed her knuckles. "You don't have to stay anywhere you don't want. I'll take you as far away as you want to go. But honey, don't let him win. Don't let him ruin all the things you've spent a lifetime building. He's not worth it. And when he gets caught and thrown in jail where he belongs, you'll take back what's yours. However that looks for you."

She wanted to believe him. Wanted to truly believe that this nightmare would end and she could go back to her life the way it had always been.

But was that really what she wanted? Yes, she wanted to live without fear and stop constantly looking over her shoulder. What she didn't want to do was return to a world where she didn't see Reid every single day. She didn't want to go back to being friends who relied on flirty banter and surface-level conversation.

That was a discussion for another time. There was no need to think about what a future together could look like when she didn't know what the next couple of hours would bring. Besides, he'd given her a nice little speech in the truck about how she was one of his best friends. Maybe that was as far as he wanted things to go.

"Eve," Reid said softly, breaking into her spiraling thoughts. "Are you okay? The look on your face tells me you're thinking of either sprinting out of here or passing out."

"Sorry. My mind is spinning a million miles a minute. I'm not sure what the next right thing is. All I know is I can't stay here tonight."

He squeezed her hands. "We'll stay at my place. I'll call Tara and let her know we'll head that way after we speak with the deputies."

As if summoning the authorities with his words, the doorbell rang.

Reid stood. "I'm sure that's them now. Give me a second."

She stayed glued to her seat. Her legs probably couldn't carry her too far now even if she'd wanted to walk with him. Low murmurs reached her ears seconds before Deputies Silver and Hill entered the kitchen with matching frowns.

Deputy Hill held his hat in his hands. "Sorry for your troubles, Eve. We just need to take your statement then we'll look at the house. Figure out how this guy got in and out without being detected."

Nodding, she crossed her arms over her chest. "The window in my bedroom is broken. He must have gotten in that way."

Deputy Silver arched a thin brow and glanced at Reid, who stood at Eve's side. "No alarms on the windows?"

He rubbed the back of his neck. "The alarms go off if the glass is smashed. Looks like he cut the window, making a cleaner break. My guess, he knew Eve wasn't here, or that would have been loud enough to alert her to his presence. He got in, then tampered with the alarm from the inside. I checked the panel by the door, and the power is cut and backup batteries disabled."

She gaped. "Can nothing keep me safe from this man?"

Reid rested a hand on her shoulder. "I can, and I will."

His firm conviction chased away a bit of her apprehension.

"The more chances he takes, the more likely he'll slip up," Deputy Hill said. "And when he does, we'll catch him. Just stay close to Reid until this is all over."

She almost laughed at the advice, because with or without a madman after her, there was nowhere else she'd rather be.

Chapter 17

His sister's worried eyes were the last thing Reid had thought he'd see tonight. Hell, he'd planned to spend the night in Eve's bed, losing sleep and exploring every inch of her beautiful body. Instead, after a tough conversation with the deputies in charge of finding Eve's stalker, he could barely stay awake as exhaustion ate away at his muscles.

"Oh my God, are you two okay?" Tara let them inside, then quickly closed and locked the door. A blue robe hid her slight frame and her dark hair fell down her back in messy waves.

"We're fine," Eve said. "Sorry if we woke you. I know it's late."

Tara threw her arms around Eve and hugged her tight. "Don't be silly. I'm just glad no one was hurt."

His sister's empathy warmed the cold pit in Reid's stomach a fraction, but nothing could make it disappear. At least not when Tyson Brown was still on the loose.

"Do you need anything? Tea? Warm milk? Chocolate?" Tara kept one arm hooked around Eve and faced him. "You have that stuff, right?"

He couldn't help but grin at her need to do something to help. So like Tara to jump in and worry about how to make others feel better in their time of need. It was one of her best attributes, even if it was the same personality trait that kept her chained to toxic relationships.

"Yes, I have those things, but I think we both want some sleep. It's been a long day." Eve's pale face and the circles under her eyes told him he'd made the right call, but just in case he asked, "Is that all right with you, or did you need anything before bed?"

"I'd like to sleep for a hundred years if that's an option," Eve said.

"I understand that feeling," Tara said. "I already put linens on the sofa for me. You take the guest room."

If everyone in the world was more like his sister, it'd be a much better place. "Appreciate that, Tara, but you stay in the guest room. Eve can have my room. I'll take the couch. I doubt I'll get much sleep anyway."

Tara frowned. "Can you even fit on that thing?"

"I'll be fine. Now, it's late, and you've had a long day, too. We'll see you in the morning."

She hesitated as if unsure if she should relent so quickly, but he'd used the stern voice that he only brought out in the rare moments when he needed Tara not to argue. It usually didn't work, but something on his face must have caused her to reconsider.

"Let me know if you change your mind. Good night." She gave Eve another squeeze then padded over to Reid. "I want more details tomorrow. I should know what's going on if I plan to stay." She kissed his cheek then disappeared down the hall and into the guest room.

"Sorry about that," he said to Eve. He picked up the bag she'd set down after Tara grabbed her and led the way to his room. "She's a mother hen. Always clucking, wanting to help."

"Are you kidding me? She's wonderful. It was nice having such a lovely welcome waiting."

He flipped up the light switch, illuminating his small room. He didn't spend much time in his apartment, so size and amenities weren't a priority. He was more concerned with something close to work and cheap enough that he could sock away a big part of his income to buy his own place. He never brought women home, so he'd never given much thought to how others might see things.

He hoped Eve wasn't put off by the simple gray blanket on the queen-size bed. A tall dresser and cabinet that his grandma had passed down to him completed the sparse collection of furniture. One framed photo of him and his sister with their mother was the only decoration.

"The bathroom is through that door." He set her bag by his feet then pointed in the direction of the en suite. "The sheets were just washed, so no need to worry."

The side of her mouth hitched up. "I wasn't worried about your bedding."

He scrubbed his palm over the whiskers on his cheeks, not wanting to leave the room but needing to let her rest. "I'll grab clothes to sleep and then head to the living room. If you can't find something, come out and ask. Like I said, I probably won't get much sleep."

Sighing, Eve closed the sliver of space separating them and slid her palm up to rest on his chest. "I really don't think you'll fit on that couch."

"I'm not making you sleep out there."

"That wasn't what I was thinking."

His breath caught at the base of his throat. "And what were you thinking?"

"I'm shaken. Badly shaken. All I want is to slip under those covers and have you hold me tight so I can close my eyes and know I'm safe. I know that's not—"

He covered her hand with his, trapping the heat between them. "That sounds perfect."

She snorted out a humorless laugh. "After what we had planned, I doubt your sincerity."

"You can doubt a lot of things, but never my sincerity." Lifting their joined hands to his lips, he pressed a kiss to her knuckles. "I hate what brought you to my room, but I'm glad you're here. I'll do whatever you want to make you feel better. To make you feel safe."

"Then hold me."

Her whispered words had him lowering his mouth to hers for a quick kiss. "You don't have to tell me twice."

"Good. Give me a second." Rummaging through her bag, she grabbed clothes and a toothbrush then hurried into the bathroom.

While he waited, he slid out of his jeans and pulled on a pair of gym shorts, then yanked off his shirt.

She slinked out of the bathroom and his mouth went dry. A gray sleep tank molded against her breasts and revealed more skin than it concealed. Black-and-red-checked shorts showed off toned legs. She'd twisted her long auburn hair into a braid that hung over one shoulder.

Needing a minute to collect himself, he cleared his throat. "Go ahead and get in bed. I need to brush my teeth."

While she climbed under his sheets, he locked himself in the bathroom and splashed cold water on his face before scrubbing the day's grime from his teeth. With fresh breath and a better grasp on his self-control, he returned to the room and shut off the light before easing down on the mattress.

Eve was curled on her side, and he hooked an arm around her waist to pull her against the curve of his body. Her contented sigh had him gritting his teeth. His palm itched to inch lower to her thigh, and his lips ached to touch the crook of her neck.

Instead, he kissed her cheek and snuggled her close. "Good night, Eve."

"Good night," she echoed.

With his head on his pillow and the woman of his dreams in his arms, he closed his eyes and drifted off to sleep.

Trickles of awareness dripped through Eve's deep slumber. She struggled against the instinct to open her eyes. Her body wasn't used to waking so early—but not even sleep could shut off her brain.

A strong arm snagged her across her middle, and she snuggled against the hard curve of a warm body.

Reid.

"Wiggling too much might be dangerous for you right now." Reid kissed the sensitive spot behind her ear. "Waking up with a beautiful woman in my arms is tempting enough. Moving your ass against my groin is like throwing a live grenade in the damn bed."

If she'd been ready to test the waters with Reid once he'd kissed her senseless at Tilly's, after sleeping in the comfort of his arms she was ready to dive headfirst into raging rapids. But as much as her body yearned to give in to temptation, a part of her was glad they hadn't taken that step.

Spending the night in his bed had created a different

kind of intimacy. Intimacy that cemented a truth she held deep inside of her but that she was scared as hell to voice. She didn't want to be just another woman in Reid's life, didn't want to be a casual fling or friends with benefits.

She wanted all of him.

And until she held his whole heart, she needed to find a way to slow things back down. Because if she fell into bed with him and was crushed in the end, their friendship wouldn't survive.

"I better stop then," she said, regret heavy in her voice. "Wouldn't want to catch the bed on fire."

"Are you sure about that?" He slipped his palm under her tank top and flattened it on her stomach.

Sucking in a breath, she reconsidered her stance but was determined to stand strong.

"Knock, knock." Tara's singsong voice accompanied her tapping on the door. "Are you awake? I need some help out here."

"I'm going to kill her." Reid growled and buried his head under her wisps of hair that had escaped her braid, his whiskers scratching her skin. "Maybe if we're really quiet she'll go away."

Giggling, Eve loosened his hold on her and wiggled out of his embrace. "One second, Tara," she called then turned to rest a palm on the hard line of his jaw. "You just said last night you wanted to step up for your sister. What better time than now?"

"I can think of much better times," he growled and lunged after her, snagging her at the waist and flipping her on her back as he hovered over her.

Lust sparked in his brown eyes and his shaggy hair framed his handsome face, making her heart sputter. She threaded her fingers through his locks, brushing them off his forehead. "Even if we stayed in bed all morning, would we have much fun with your sister waiting on the other side of the door?"

"Good point. I'll get rid of her." He jumped out of bed and made a show for stretching toward the door.

Her mouth watered at the defined ridges of his abdomen, and even with the white bandage covering his stitches, it took all her strength to climb out of the bed before he could jump back under the covers. "No, you'll see what she needs and help her. I have to use the restroom. I'll be out in a minute."

He heaved a dramatic sigh but cracked a grin. "Fine. I'm coming." The last words were thrown out loud enough for Tara to hear.

"Thank you!" Tara called out.

Reid yanked a gray T-shirt over his head, shot her a wink, then left the room.

"Dear Lord, help me." Eve rested a hand over her heart and steadied herself then hustled into the restroom. After washing her face and brushing her teeth, she added a touch of mascara. She didn't want to look like she'd tried too hard, so she threw her hair in a high ponytail then dressed in a pair of yoga pants and a long-sleeved shirt.

By the time she found Reid and Tara in the kitchen, her pulse was back to a normal speed. Tara was dressed in jeans and a blue sweater that matched her eyes, her dark hair falling in long waves down her back. She leaned against the counter while sipping a steaming mug of coffee.

Reid sat at the small island with a mug of his own in front of him.

"Good morning," Tara said. "Sorry if I woke you. I had an issue with the bathroom sink."

"I'm still not sure how you got all that hair stuck in there after one day," Reid grumbled.

Tara rolled her eyes. "It wasn't mine, dummy."

The implication made Eve's stomach dip. How many women had been in this apartment? Woken up in Reid's arms in his bed?

She couldn't think about that now. Besides, the past was behind them. She wanted Reid's future.

"You didn't wake me," she said, aiming what she hoped was a sincere smile at Tara. "Any more coffee in that pot?"

"Sure is. Let me get that for you." Tara grabbed a black coffee cup from the cabinet and filled it near to the top before handing it over. "There's cream and sugar if you want some. I couldn't find any good creamer, but if you tell me what you like, I'll pick some up when I run out."

Eve doctored her morning brew and savored her first sip before settling on the backless stool beside Reid. The small island faced the lone window above the sink. Flecks of brown ran through the white marble countertop at Tara's back. The white tiled backsplash highlighted the navy-blue cabinets.

"This is perfect," she said. "No need to run out on my account."

"Well, I've been informed I was quite the pest this morning, so I thought I'd make amends by running out and grabbing some breakfast." Tara shot Reid a sickeningly sweet smile. "Least I can do to apologize."

"You weren't a pest." Eve swatted Reid's arm. "Don't listen to your brother."

"I rarely do." Tara chuckled. "But I'm still leaving

for a bit. I want to check out the cute little coffee shop I saw downtown. It's just a quick walk from here, and I'm craving some pastries. Do either of you want anything?"

"Nah," Reid said. "I planned on frying up some bacon and eggs. Something a little heartier."

"Bacon and eggs sound good," Eve said.

"More chocolate croissants for me." Tara set her mug in the sink then walked to the front door to slip on her shoes. "I won't be gone long."

"Keep your phone on you," Reid said. "Pay attention to your surroundings."

"Yes, sir." Tara gave him a two-finger salute then disappeared out the door.

Eve studied the hard lines of his face. "You're worried about her."

He lifted a shoulder. "Hard not to be with everything going on. I told her you'd hired me to help with some issues, and she knows someone broke into your house last night. Other than that, I've been vague about the details so I didn't freak her out. I should have filled her all the way in so she'd be more careful."

"I'm sure she'll be fine."

"Not much I can do about it now." He hopped to his feet and rubbed his palms together. "What about that breakfast?"

Unable to stop herself, she asked, "Do you cook for all the women who stay at your place?"

His expression crumpled. "Is that what you think?"

She wished she could joke off the question and act like the answer didn't bother her, but she couldn't. It was time to find out what kind of man Reid really was.

Chapter 18

His question hung in the air like a giant, ugly elephant. A pit lodged in Reid's gut. He hated that Eve assumed he was some pig who had a rotating lineup of women coming into his home. She'd be shocked to learn he'd been with no woman since he'd moved to Cloud Valley. Sure, he loved to charm his way into an enjoyable evening with interesting company. But after he'd set eyes on Eve, no one else in town held a candle to her.

Which was exactly why he'd never asked her out. Whatever this feeling was could crash and burn, and he'd not only lose the prettiest thing to ever steal his heart, but his friend as well. He'd rather die alone than hurt her, the fear of repeating the same mistakes as his father a constant flashing caution sign in the back of his head.

Eve avoided eye contact and traced the pad of her finger around the rim of the coffee mug. "I don't know what to think. I see you at the bar, laughing and flirting with women. As much as it pains me to think of what happens once I turn on that closed sign, I can only assume how your nights end. I just want to know if I'm one of many."

The hesitancy in her voice crushed him. "Honey, you're one of a kind in every single way."

"I'm not sure if I buy that," she said with an indelicate snort.

Reclaiming his stool, he widened his legs so her slim thighs fit between them. He rested his hands on her knees. "I need you to. Because trust me when I tell you that I've never met a woman like you. Not here. Not in Indiana. Not anyone in this whole damn world. I might smile and laugh and look like I'm the jolly freaking giant, but none of that means a thing."

Frowning, she narrowed her gaze. "What does it mean then?"

The question made him squirm a little, but he wouldn't evade it. Not this time. "It's easier for me to joke around and keep things casual than let anyone in. I don't open myself up often, which is why I've never brought a woman back to this apartment. Ever. I don't like letting people see the other parts of me. Parts of me that are ugly and scarred and better left in the dark."

She sucked in a sharp breath, eyes wide. "No part of you is ugly, Reid."

Scrunching his nose, he tunneled his hand through his hair. He'd gotten a little off topic. He wanted Eve to be secure in the knowledge that bringing her into his home was a first for him, not confess all his deepest secrets. "I don't agree, and honestly, that's a big discussion to have at another time. But for right now, I need you to know I'm not the guy you think I am."

A shy smile finally settled on her face. "You've really never brought anyone here?"

"You and Tara. That's it." Something she'd said crept back to the forefront of his mind. "What did you mean, it pained you when you saw me leave the bar?"

Now it was her time to squirm. A light blush spread over her cheeks, but she held his gaze. "Watching you flirt sucks. When you come into the bar, it always makes my day better. My night more enjoyable. But when other women set their sights on you and you'd give them that handsome smile or some witty banter, it's like a knife in the heart."

"Why didn't you ever tell me?" He had his own reasons for not giving in to his feelings for Eve. Reasons that grew more and more insignificant with each minute he spent with her. He'd never considered she had her reservations about considering a relationship with him. He'd always figured she preferred to keep their friendship as it was because she didn't look at him as anything more than that.

"I value your friendship. I didn't want to do anything to jeopardize it. And besides, I work long hours and most guys aren't a fan of that. I've tried it before, and it doesn't work."

The way her focus shifted back to her coffee made him guess she wasn't being completely transparent. "Is that it? You don't want to risk our friendship?"

"I don't think I could go back to the way things were, and it scares me to death."

He tucked his thumb under her chin and gently shifted her to face him. "Does it make you feel better to know I'm scared, too?"

"Not really."

He barked out a laugh. "Listen, we can both be scared and unsure of what the future holds. But just know this, you are not one of many. You're the only one I've been looking at for a long while, and it's about damn time we see if this thing between us could work."

"Are you sure you won't get sick of me?" she asked. "Maybe it's the danger we're running from that's exciting you."

"Honey, trust me. As far as I'm considered, you're downright dangerous." He placed a kiss on the tip of her nose. "Now, how about that breakfast?"

"I say you better get cooking. I'm starving." She grinned up at him, and all the tension in the room evaporated. "What's the plan after we eat?"

Making his way to the stove, he gathered everything he needed to start breakfast. He settled two frying pans on the burners and cracked eggs into a bowl. "Scrambled okay?"

She nodded.

"We should talk to Deputy Silver and Deputy Hill. Last night we were exhausted, so I didn't ask many questions about what they've uncovered about Tyson Brown. I want to know if they have any more information that could be beneficial." He found a whisk in a drawer and beat the eggs, adding milk and a little shredded mozzarella before pouring the mixture into a pan.

"Do you think anyone else working the rodeo circuit knows this guy? If so, they might have an idea where he's hiding." Eve sipped her coffee, her eyes following along with his every motion.

"Another question for the deputies. I'll ask Madden as well. He's been out there the last couple of days."

She winced. "That's right. I forgot you're supposed to be helping with guarding things while the events are underway."

He waved off her comment with his spatula. "You're my priority. Sticking close and keeping you safe is all that matters. Besides, Dax and Ben are lending a hand. They should have things covered." An image of Eve spinning around the dance floor sprang into his mind, and he tightened his grip on the utensil. "Of course, I've had my share of problems with Ben's hands and where they've been."

Laughing, Eve shook her head. "A girl dances with one handsome stranger and it causes all sorts of drama."

"You think he's handsome, huh?"

She rolled her eyes. "Stop. I came home with you, didn't I?"

"And don't you forget it." He grinned, enjoying having her in his kitchen.

"I'm working the lunch shift today. Things will still be busy, and I don't want to leave my staff shorthanded. Will that be a problem?"

"Not at all." He stirred the eggs then laid strips of bacon on the larger of the two pans. "Once you taste my cookin', you might want to put me to work in the kitchen today instead of sticking me behind the bar."

The door swung open, and Tara bounced inside. "I'm back! Man, I love this town. The shops are so cute, and I can't wait to explore them all. Everyone is so nice, and if the rest of the food is as good as what I had at Tilly's last night and the pastry I had this morning, I better find a gym to join."

He had a hard time keeping up with the rapid-fire words coming out of his sister's mouth, but her happiness practically oozed from her pores. "You plan on staying awhile then?"

She slipped out of her shoes and carried her haul to the island. She set down a white paper bag and a bundle of flowers wrapped in brown paper. Heaving out a large puff of air, she anchored a fist on her hip and grinned. "I'm thinking about it."

"I love that," Eve said. "And I see you stopped by Sweet Stems. Don't they have the best selection? It's one of my favorite spots in town. The owner even keeps jars full of fresh flowers in the cutest stand by her house."

"Actually," Tara said, grin growing, "I ran into a man at the coffee shop who asked me to give these to you. How sweet is that? Seems like you have your share of admirers in town."

Wide-eyed, Eve rose to her feet and backed away from the explosion of colorful blooms.

Raw, hot anger mixed with ice-cold fear, causing spikes of adrenaline to pump through Reid's body. "What did the man look like?"

Oblivious to the shift in energy, Tara chuckled and shook her head in an aren't-you-jealous way. "Don't worry, he wasn't nearly as handsome as you, Reid. Not unless Eve has a thing for long bushy beards and dirty jean jackets."

"He knows I'm here," Eve said, her voice breathless. "He knows Tara was coming back and would see me."

Tara frowned. "What are you talking about?"

Gritting his teeth, Reid fought the urge to throw the flowers in the trash can. "The man who gave these to you isn't Eve's admirer. He's her stalker, and he's dangerous. And now he knows you're both here."

As much as Eve loved visiting Lily at her family's ranch, showing up at her and Madden's doorstep to discuss a murdering asshole wasn't exactly how she'd wanted to start her day. The sound of horses playing in the pasture turned her toward the frolicking animals.

She wished it was just another day. That she was here to enjoy a morning off work with her friend. Maybe sit in one of the rocking chairs on the wide porch and stare at the mountains over girl talk. Or take a walk through the meadows down to the creek behind the barn.

Anything other than creating a plan to evade the man desperate to terrorize her.

Tara stood close to Eve's side, her arms wrapped around her middle. She hadn't said much since she'd learned exactly how close to danger she'd been.

Reid knocked on the door, standing in front of them, gaze darting all around as if someone waited to jump out and grab her.

Hell, for all she knew, someone *was* there. Waiting. Watching. Ready to finally take what he wanted.

Her.

The door swung open and Madden stood in the doorway, a scowl on his chiseled jaw. "Come on in."

Reid waited for her and Tara to step inside before entering behind them and closing the door.

Lily stood in the foyer, hands clasped in front of her. She hurried to welcome Eve and Tara with hugs then walked them to the tan leather couch in the middle of the living room.

"Thank you so much for letting us come over," Eve said, sitting next to Tara.

"Are you kidding?" Lily took a seat on the overstuffed chair beside the large stone fireplace. "You're always welcome here."

Madden and Reid spoke in hushed whispers as they stepped into the room.

"With this guy strolling around town like he doesn't have a care in the world, I'm not sure how I'll ever be safe." Eve trusted Reid and knew he'd do everything possible to protect her, but she'd underestimated just what they were dealing with.

Reid shook his head. "I still can't believe he's just walking around town. If I'd gone to the coffee shop with Tara, I could have put a stop to this once and for all." He crossed to stand beside where Eve sat on the couch and anchored his arms over his chest.

She reached up to grab his hand. "He's not stupid. If you'd been around, he wouldn't have shown his face."

"He shouldn't be able to show his face anywhere around here without the cops grabbing his ass and throwing him in a cell," Reid said.

"That's something I plan to speak with the sheriff about," Madden said. "We know who this guy is. Know his face, his name, his target. His picture should be plastered all over. The town is swimming with people right now, which makes it easier for him to blend in, but if his photo was out there, it'd also make it easier for people to spot him."

"People don't always pay attention," Lily said. "I agree, there's more that could be done, but the sheriff's department is short-staffed right now as it is. That's why Sunrise Security is helping with crowd control at the rodeo and needed to hire more specialists. That's a tough enough gig, but with the parade tomorrow, I'm not sure what else can be done besides keeping Eve out of sight."

"Damn, I forgot about the parade." Reid slipped his hand from hers and pinched the bridge of his nose.

Tara bounced her gaze between them all. "What parade?"

Eve sighed, hating that she'd forgotten for a second about another tradition she looked forward to every year. "At the end of the rodeo, the town puts on a parade. Everyone dresses in historical costumes and puts together floats. There are awards for fan favorites, and people take it very seriously. It's usually one of the most fun activities to close out the summer."

"And one of the most hectic," Reid added. "Sunrise Security already committed to working the event. We'd started discussing hiring Ben and Dax to prepare for that, and now they're needed elsewhere."

"That's a problem for later," Madden said. "I'm more concerned with finding Tyson and throwing him in jail. Are you working today, Eve? It might be best if you keep a low profile until he's caught."

Eve sighed. "I'll talk to Becca about closing the restaurant for a couple of days starting tomorrow. I hate losing the revenue, but I don't want anyone else to come into the line of fire."

"I think that's a good idea," Reid said. "Maybe we should head out of town for the day. Find something to keep us busy while the sheriff's department focuses their attention on Tyson."

She nodded, unsure what they could find to do that would keep her hands busy and her mind off her troubles.

"What about me?" Tara asked. "Maybe I should book a ticket for the next flight out of here. Come back when things settle down."

The tortured expression on Reid's face announced his uncertainty about Tara going back home. He hadn't told her the details of what brought his sister to Cloud Valley, but Eve understood it was important for her to stay. "I'd hate for you to leave so soon. You just got here."

"What if Tara stays with us?" Lily asked. "I can give you the full dude ranch experience, and you can stick close to Eve until this is over."

"Seriously?" Tara asked. "I don't want to impose."

A smile finally cracked through Madden's gruff expression. "Lily's favorite thing is to show out-of-towners what our part of the world has to offer. There's plenty of space, and if I know my fiancée, she'll have no trouble putting you to work."

Tara straightened. "Really? I could do like chores and stuff?"

Chuckling, Reid shook his head. "Don't get too excited. Mucking stalls gets old fast."

"I'm no stranger to getting my hands dirty. Dad had me helping on the farm since I was old enough to walk. A dairy farm might be a little different than a dude ranch, but I bet I can handle my own. As long as I'm not putting anyone out. I mean, I really would hate to go home."

Something in Tara's voice as well as the look she shot Reid twisted Eve's stomach. He'd told her parts of his past made him ugly. Curiosity gnawed at her, but now wasn't the time for questions.

"We'd love to have you." Lily beamed. "Did you bring your stuff?"

"I can head back to the apartment and grab it," Reid said.

Madden gave a subtle nod. "Problem solved. What are you two going to do?"

A tiny smile lifting the corner of Reid's mouth piqued Eve's curiosity even more. "I have a couple of ideas." He held out a hand to Eve. "Ready?"

"Yeah." She laced her fingers with his and stood. She was ready to follow Reid anywhere he wanted to go. She just hoped that once things settled, he'd still want her with him.

Chapter 19

An hour later, Reid drove down the tree-lined lane to the cabin tucked in the woods. As much as he hated the reason for being here, his pulse picked up at the sight of Sunrise Security's latest purchase.

Tall evergreens surrounded the log cabin fronted by a narrow porch. Nothing sprawling like Lily and Madden's place, just big enough to fit a couple of chairs and maybe a little table to set in between. The flowerbeds were edged out, but only dirt and weeds surrounded the house. Bags of mulch lay in a heap in front of the garage door, the unhung shutters freshly painted a deep red beside them.

"Home, sweet home." Reid turned off the engine. "Well, not really. Madden and I bought this place to use as a safe house for our clients. It's a work in progress. I figured I could show you around, spend some time here. It's one of my favorite places."

A slight frown caused the skin on her forehead to pinch in the middle. "How did it take us so long to get here? You took so many turns, I couldn't keep track of our location. But I swear we shouldn't be that far from town."

He grinned then grabbed the handles of their duffel bags. "We're only about twenty miles north of Cloud Valley. After we stopped at the store, I took the scenic route. Wanted to make sure no one followed us."

"Tricky. Here, I'll take my stuff."

Normally he'd insist on carrying her things, but he had a truck bed filled with reusable totes to gather. Once she hooked her duffel over her shoulder and stepped down from the vehicle, he hopped out and grabbed everything else.

The midmorning sun beat through the clearing of trees. Birds sang nearby. As he walked toward the porch, he filled his lungs with the fresh mountain air. This was a large part of why he'd moved to Wyoming—for peace and nature, to carve out a place beside the mountains where he could appreciate the quiet.

One day he'd carve out a place that belonged only to him. But for now, he'd take refuge in the little cabin and the woman beside him. The reason they were there sucked, but that didn't mean they couldn't find ways to enjoy their time together. He'd even made sure they both brought enough stuff for the night in case they decided to stay.

Eve followed him up the two steps and waited while he disarmed the security system and unlocked the door. When she crossed the threshold, he held his breath. She wasn't the high-maintenance type, but that didn't mean unfinished floors and fresh drywall in the kitchen wouldn't turn up her nose.

Setting her bag on the ground, Eve walked into the living room and spun in a slow circle. "This place is adorable."

The tightness in his chest loosened. The cabin was

special to him, and he wanted Eve to appreciate it as much as he did.

"It will be." He crossed through the living room to the attached kitchen and plopped the bags on the long island. "Madden and I keep trying to find time to get the work done. It's taking a little longer than we thought."

"You're doing the work yourselves? That's impressive." She strolled around the perimeter of the space until she met him in the kitchen. "I didn't know you had that skill set."

"Oh, I have a lot of skills you don't know about."

"Oh, really?"

He unpacked the refrigerated items from the bags. "Yep. You've already eaten my cooking." He shot her a wink before placing the items in the fridge then turning back around to grab a box of microwave popcorn.

"You're a man of many talents. Maybe I can show you some of my own."

He almost choked as his mind went to every dirty innuendo she could possibly mean.

Rounding the island, she plucked the box from his hand and kissed his cheek. "I mean around the cabin. I'm pretty handy myself. While we're here, I might as well be useful."

Her comment was a reminder of something he'd picked up at the store that was still in the back of his truck. He hoped she'd view his offering as something special and not be put off by his idea. "I'm glad to hear you say that, because I have something in mind." He laughed at the dubious furrow of her brow. "Okay, we'll talk about that after we get settled."

"Does it matter where I put this?" She shook the box in her hand.

"Not really. As you can tell, things aren't exactly organized around here."

She stuck the popcorn in a cabinet then zeroed in on swatches of paint colors lying on the granite counter. "Are these paint choices for the kitchen?"

He finished unloading the groceries then leaned against the counter beside her. Now that they'd opened the gates to this new part of their relationship, he couldn't stand having any space between them. "Yeah. We're leaning toward this dark blue. Something deep and rich, soothing for people in rough situations who find themselves here."

Smoothing her fingertip over the color he'd selected, she grinned up at him. "I like it—the color and the reason behind it. You and Madden are a great team. You put detail into the small things, which goes a long way with people. Can I see the rest of the cabin?"

"Of course." He snatched her hand and took her back through the living room. "There're three bedrooms and one bathroom. We didn't want anything too big, but enough space in case someone has a kid or something."

Her hand tightened in his. "I can't imagine being in danger and having a child to worry about. You should make sure to have some games and stuffed animals around."

He pushed open one of the closed doors, showing off the room they'd designated for a younger guest. "Already thought of that."

The walls were painted a light gray. A cream-colored blanket covered the queen-size bed and a bookcase filled with puzzles, books and games was pressed against the far wall.

"Oh, wow. I didn't expect the rooms to be complete."

He closed the door and shifted to the other room across the hall, revealing a similar space but with a long dresser instead of a bookcase. "We thought it was wise to have the rooms done first. People can stay here without cabinet doors in the kitchen. It'd be harder without beds and a quiet place to rest."

"Smart."

He padded down the hall and ushered her into the primary bedroom. "And this is my favorite space in the house."

With wide eyes, Eve strolled through the cozy room. She passed the fireplace that blended into the log wall and tapped her fingers on the circular table flanked by matching bucket chairs. Her gaze landed on the large bed with the pale blue quilt topped with a mound of coordinated pillows. "This room was ripped out of my dreams. Who did this?"

He stood in the doorway, enjoying watching her. "Me."

She faced him with the prettiest smile. "I think I could stay here forever."

Her words tightened his chest, making him somehow grateful for this chance to whisk her away, regardless of the reason.

Hopefully they could dig into that deeper a little later, because if he didn't get her out of this room right now, they'd never leave.

Curiosity urged Eve another step farther outside. Reid stood in front of her with one of the tote bags slung over his shoulder. "I'm afraid to ask what you have in mind."

"Come sit with me for a second and I'll explain." He sat on the first step and patted the wooden planks beside him.

Eyeing him carefully, she lowered herself onto the step. She leaned over to peer into the bag, but he scooted it away. "Why can't I just see what's inside?"

"Because I want to talk first. How are you holding up?"

Leaning her forearms on her knees, she stared out into her beautiful surroundings. "Right now, in this moment, I'm good. I can almost forget all the craziness that's consumed my life the last few days. I'm glad we came here. It's taken my mind off my troubles for a little while."

"I'm glad you like it as much as I do."

"I'm just sorry Tara didn't come with us. I know how happy you are to have her in town."

"She's probably having the time of her life. You and I both know Lily is giving her the VIP treatment, which Tara will eat up with a freaking spoon."

"I hope so," Eve said. "I wish I had some horses to ride or a trail to hike. Something to keep my focus off everything."

Her mind went back to standing in the cozy bedroom. She hadn't exaggerated when she'd said she could stay there forever. What she hadn't mentioned was wanting Reid to be there with her. A part of her had wanted him to sweep her off her feet and keep her occupied in that bed for the rest of the day.

The other part warned it was still too soon. There were still too many layers to Reid she needed to peel back.

"If you have paint, I'm good with a brush. Maybe you and I could knock out that kitchen while we're here." She'd much rather be outside, soaking up the last bits of summer sun while the breeze filtered through the trees. But sitting and thinking were her enemies right now.

"I have a better idea." Reid scooped up the bag he'd been hiding and set it between them. "Last night, the things you said about Tyson Brown stealing so much from you really stuck with me. I hate that he has that power. I meant what I said about taking back that power—about rebuilding your life. If you're up to it, I'd like to help you take baby steps to do that now."

She tried to make sense of his words but couldn't.

Her silence must have spurred him on, so he continued. "You told me about your dad. About how he'd take you to pick flowers. Hell, you even brought me some to thank me. I don't know if I ever told you how much that meant. You've used your love of flowers to bring joy to others as well as to make yourself happy. I want you to start reclaiming what you love."

A shiver tap-danced down her spine and the scent of hundreds of petals invaded her senses. She pressed the heels of her hands against her closed eyes and tried to block out the image of rose petals left on her bed like some kind of sick offering.

A gentle touch on her back opened her eyes and she sucked in a large breath. "I want that, I really do, but I don't know how. Especially with this guy still out there, threatening to show up and send me right back into a tailspin."

"I understand your misgivings. But that's where these come in." He opened the top of the bag and shifted it so she could see inside.

Her heart melted like butter. "Are those flower bulbs?"

"Yeah. I snuck some at the store when you weren't

looking. Luckily, in these parts, you can find steaks to grill and garden supplies in the same place. I grabbed tulips and daffodils and peonies. As you can see, we need to make the outside of the cabin look a little more presentable. If you're up for it, we could plant these. Knowing that it'll take some time for growth. Some time for the beauty of these plants to shine through."

Tears stung her eyes. She dipped her hand inside the bag and touched the rough surface of the dirt-covered bulbs. These weren't just flowers waiting to be planted. These were promises of a brighter future.

Promises of hope.

"This is the most thoughtful thing anyone has ever done for me," she said, awe filling her voice. "You're not just giving me a chance to use my hands and lose myself in something besides my own fear. You're giving me an opportunity to bury seeds and allow them time and space to bloom. To thrive."

"Maybe I just want free help to fix up this cabin?"

Laughing, she bumped her shoulder against his. "Maybe, but I doubt it. Thank you. This means the world to me. Do you have gardening tools?"

He shook the bag. "Best damn store around."

"Then let's get started." Standing, she took the bag and walked over to the overgrown flowerbed in front of the picture window. "Do you have a plan for where you want these? A layout for what you want the garden to look like?"

"Nope. Madden and I have been so busy on the inside, we haven't given much thought to outside. Not to mention I have two black thumbs."

She studied the curve of the flowerbed, the width of

the space and how best to utilize it. "At my house, I plant things in clusters to give a more English cottage feel. It's organized chaos, like my life. We could do the same here."

"Perfect. Just tell me what to do."

She grinned. "It's that easy? I just tell you what to do and you'll do it?"

He returned her smile and shrugged, his cowboy hat hiding the crinkles she knew surrounded his eyes. "I'll do whatever I can to make you happy."

Her heart leaped as high as the birds whistling their song above her. She had plenty of ideas for how he could make her happy, but for now, she'd stick with the necessities at hand. Tilting her head to the side, she planted her fists on her hips and schooled her face into the best don't-mess-with-me expression she could muster. "All right then. I need you on your knees."

His Adam's apple bobbed on a hard swallow. "Excuse me."

She pointed to the flowerbed. "Before we plant the bulbs, we need to pull the weeds. We can't do that standing up."

Growling, he hooked an arm around her waist and yanked her against him. "That's all you want from me, huh? Weed pulling?"

Now it was her time to swallow past the ball of desire lodged in her throat. She tipped up the brim of his hat so she could look into his eyes then rested a palm on his chest. "For now, yes. I can't make any promise for later."

"Oh, I can. I promise you what I have planned will be a hell of a lot more fun than playing in the dirt."

Chapter 20

Midmorning bled into late afternoon, and relief seeped through Reid's sore muscles. Tending the flowerbeds might have given Eve some comfort, but his dirt-caked fingers and throbbing side were glad to be done for the day. Scrubbing his hands in the kitchen sink, he tried to block out the splatter of water rushing from the shower in the next room.

Because if his mind drifted to the shower, it'd create a vision of the woman currently standing under that spray of warm water.

His stomach muscles clenched, and he shut off the faucet. If he washed his hands until he stopped thinking about Eve, his skin would crack and bleed. He located a towel to dry off his palms and was sidetracked by his ringing phone.

A quick glance at the screen before answering showed Madden's name. "Hey, man. What's up?"

"Just checking in," Madden said. "How are things going?"

Reid grabbed the towel and dried his hands before tossing it on the island and walking into the living room. The furniture was sparse—a large gray sectional in the middle of the room and a television balanced on a stand too small for its size—but it was enough for now. He sank onto the oversize cushion of the sofa and leaned back with the phone pressed to his ear. "Things are good. I might even see if she wants to crash here for the night. She likes it here. I even put her to work."

Madden chuckled. "Oh yeah? She hanging backsplash in the kitchen?"

"Not quite. We cleaned up the front flowerbed and planted some bulbs for spring. Put down some mulch. I thought it'd be good for her." He didn't dive into detail as to why he'd wanted Eve to lend a hand in cultivating the garden and appreciated Madden's lack of questions.

"Tell her I said thanks for the help."

The padding of footsteps on the wooden floors reached Reid's ears seconds before Eve emerged from the hallway. Her wet hair hung down her back and her face was free of makeup. Black yoga pants showed off her toned legs, and her fitted long-sleeved shirt made his imagination go wild. "She's here now. You can tell her yourself."

As she sat beside him, Reid activated the speaker function.

"Hi, Eve," Madden said. "Heard you and Reid did some work outside. Appreciate it, but don't let Reid boss you around."

"Ha!" Reid said. "You must not know Eve very well if you think that's possible."

Eve jabbed him with her elbow. "Watch yourself."

Madden's chuckle rumbled through the line. "Trust me, I've known Eve a long time. She only does what she wants. But other than the gardening, you guys holding up okay?"

Reid hooked an arm around Eve, letting his fingers dangle along her bicep. He wouldn't let Madden know just how well he was doing here with Eve. "We're good."

Eve grinned, gaze latched on him. "Yeah. No complaints."

"Glad to hear, but I didn't just call to check in. I spoke with the sheriff's department about Tyson Brown."

Eve's body tensed, and Reid pulled her closer.

"They watched video from town this morning and were able to catch the plate number off a truck that a man matching his description drove away from the coffee shop. The vehicle is registered to his former father-in-law. Law enforcement all over the county is on the lookout for the vehicle as well as Tyson. His photo is being circulated online and posted in local businesses."

"It's about damn time," Reid grumbled. "So now we have his name and know what his vehicle looks like. Any news on where he's been staying?"

"No." Madden heaved out a long sigh. "Deputies haven't seen any activity on a credit card, and they've spoken with the proprietors of all the local hotels. No one recognizes the guy. Deputy Silver said they're going to look farther out of town. See if they can nail down his location. He's got to be holed up somewhere."

"Unless he's sleeping in his truck," Eve said.

"Definitely a possibility," Madden said. "But at least now we know what kind of vehicle to be on the lookout for. Deputies are also digging into his past, talking to friends and family. They showed me a picture of his ex-wife. It's a little disconcerting."

Reid frowned. "What do you mean?"

"She looks a hell of a lot like Eve. And Dana Fishel, the barrel racer."

Eve shrank against the cushion as if trying to hide. "I was a sitting duck. There was no reason for him to target me except my auburn hair and hazel eyes. And for what? To punish the wife who left him?"

Anger beat against Reid's temples as the color drained from her face. They'd spent hours attacking the garden to keep her mind off her troubles, to help her take back some control and joy. All it took was one phone call to wash that all away. To bring her right back to this place of fear. "Bad people do bad things for all sorts of reasons that seldom make sense."

"And we will find him," Madden said. "While Reid is making sure you're safe, the rest of Sunrise Security is doing everything we can to aid the sheriff's department. You're our main priority, Eve."

She summoned a smile that Reid didn't quite believe.

She was close to reaching the breaking point, and as much as he wanted to get details from Madden, there wasn't anything else Eve needed to know.

"How's Tara liking the grand tour of Tremont Ranch?" he asked, switching gears.

"Lily's keeping her busy. They took Queenie and Ace on a trail ride, and Lily's giving her an inside look at how we run our weddings. Tara seems to be enjoying herself, and they've stayed close. I don't think Tara's at risk, but we're not taking any chances. I'm here, doing what I can from the phone and computer."

"Thanks for watching out for her, but I don't want you getting an earful from the sheriff for not being at the rodeo keeping an eye on things."

"It's apparent at this point Tyson's goal is getting to Eve, not terrorizing anyone at the rodeo. Showing his face there will only hurt his chances of getting what he wants.

Dax and Ben are still at the fairgrounds, just in case, but like I said, my priority is doing what I can for Eve."

"Thanks, Madden," she said.

"Anything for you, Eve," Madden said. "You two take it easy. I'll let you know if I find out any more information."

Reid disconnected and tossed his phone on the cushion. He leaned back, shifted to hook his knee on the sofa and face Eve.

"What now?" she asked.

"Whatever you want."

"What I want is to pinpoint Tyson Brown and finish this mess, but I don't think that's an option."

He gave a little tug on a strand of her hair. "I wish it was. We just have to wait and trust everyone to do their job."

"I hate being in limbo." She heaved out a long sigh. "Time to paint?"

Laughing, he shook his head. "I have something else in mind. We worked through lunch, and I'm starving. It's early, but if I grill the steaks now, we can enjoy dinner on the back deck. The view is amazing."

She glanced at her watch. "Early-bird special it is. Do you need help?"

"Can you handle baked potatoes and salad?"

Tipping her chin, she aimed raised brows his way. "I own a restaurant, remember?"

He lifted his palms. "No insult intended. I'll grill, you bake and toss, and we'll spend the evening enjoying each other's company."

Leaning forward, she gave him a quick peck on the cheek. "Deal."

Strolling to the kitchen, a lightness lifted his steps despite the seriousness of their situation. A cozy cabin, a good meal and a beautiful woman—things almost couldn't be better.

The twangy voice of Eve's favorite country singer boomed through her phone speaker. The garden might be where she found her peace, but the kitchen was where she found her purpose. As far back as she could remember, she'd helped her parents at Tilly's. Her mom would set her up in the corner of the kitchen with a tiny bowl and whisk, letting her make her own creations.

Okay, so that might not have actually helped her parents, but at the time, she'd assumed she was the number-one employee.

Later on, she'd waited tables and learned how to prepare dishes. Once she reached twenty-one, she tended bar and took on more managerial responsibilities. Now that the bar and grill was hers, she didn't get her hands as dirty as she liked, but she hadn't lost her touch with a couple of potatoes and a bowl full of vegetables.

And just like at Tilly's, she lost herself in the mundane and familiar tasks. Her voice cracked along with the melody, but she didn't care. She swayed her hips as she prepared her part of the meal.

The French doors to the deck opened, and Reid strolled in with a platter of meat. Scents of garlic and butter wafted in the air. "What's going on in here? A cat dying?"

Laughing, she grabbed a nearby towel and tossed it at him. "Are you saying I'm a bad singer?"

"I'm saying you were born with more faults than two left feet."

She anchored one fist on her hip. "I didn't hear any complaints about my dancing last night."

His expression turned serious, and he lessened the space between them with three long strides. Setting the platter of meat onto the counter, he cradled her jaw in his palm. "Trust me, there wasn't a damn thing wrong with that dance or what came after it."

Heat splashed against her cheek, but she didn't break their eye contact—didn't break the connection tethering her to him. "Well, if there wasn't anything wrong with how my feet move, I guess that means my voice is great, too."

His smile took over his face, and he pressed his lips to hers. "Everything about you is great. Ready to eat?"

"Mmm-hmm. Want some wine? I know you're more of a beer guy, but I grabbed a bottle of red at the store."

"Uh, sure. Just a little, though. I'm on the clock." He winked, but the usually playful gesture didn't cover the weird dip in his voice that told her something more was lurking behind his words.

She had all night to figure out where his head was. For now, she rummaged through the doorless cabinets until she found a stack of red plastic cups then unscrewed the cap. She filled both cups then handed one to Reid. "Cheers."

Reid accepted the cup and tapped it against hers. "Cheers." He took a small sip then set the drink on the counter. "The plastic cups go perfectly with paper plates. You might want to double them up to make them a little sturdier."

Taking his advice, she stacked two plates and topped them with a small filet, a potato and salad. "Is there a table on the deck?"

He lifted his hand and tilted it from side to side. "Kind of. I got a little creative, but it should work."

She waited for him to fill his plate then followed him

outside onto a square deck that jutted off the kitchen. Two five-gallon buckets propped up a piece of plywood, and a couple of lawn chairs, offered seating at the make-shift table.

But it was the pristine lake behind the house with the meadow beyond touching the mountains that stole her attention.

"This is gorgeous." Her voice came out in a whisper as she stood and took in the beauty around her. "I'd love to wake up to this view every single morning."

"I know the feeling."

She turned to see him watching her, and something told her that he wasn't talking about the view.

He dipped his head toward her plate. "You better set that down before you lose your steak."

"Good call." She studied the thin plywood. "You sure this thing will hold up?"

"Only one way to find out." He slid his full plate and cup onto the table then pumped his fist in triumph. "Perfect."

Laughing, she followed suit—sans fist pumping—and settled into the chair. "You were right. You're a man with many skills. Let's just hope grilling is one of them." Slicing off a piece of meat, she slid it into her mouth and moaned. "Dear God in heaven. I wasted you behind the bar last night."

He cut off his own chunk and skewered it with his fork, pointing in her direction for a beat before popping it in his mouth. "Told you."

They ate in silence, attacking their food while enjoying the peacefulness of the green meadow and sightings of furry creatures. Each bite was better than the last, the juices sinking into the tender cut of meat to create an explosion of flavor in her mouth.

With his food almost finished, Reid pushed it away and leaned back in the chair. "So why don't you have a house like this?"

"One that needs painting, with no cabinet doors?"

"Funny. No, I mean you said you could wake up to this view every morning. Why do you live in town instead of finding a place with some land?"

She took the last bite of her baked potato then sipped her wine. "Land takes time to maintain. It's hard enough to find time to mow my little yard. Heck, I don't have time for much of anything beyond keeping Tilly's afloat."

"Do you love spending so many hours working at the restaurant? Or is there a part of you that wants something different for your life?"

Thinking over the questions, she took another drink. "Honestly, I've never really thought about doing anything else. I grew up in Tilly's. I loved watching my parents feed the town. They built relationships and provided more than just meals. I can't imagine not carrying on the traditions they put so much love into."

"Like the line dancing."

She grinned. "Exactly. Those nights create magic."

He linked his fingers with hers. "They sure do."

Warmth spread down to her bare toes. "I love knowing I play a part in working that magic in the lives of others. That I'm feeding a community of hardworking people and maybe giving them something to look forward to. So no, I don't want something different. I guess what I want is something more."

"More than owning Tilly's?" he asked. "I don't think there's enough hours in the day."

"Not that." She scrunched her nose, preparing to unload the burden she'd trapped inside her heart for so many years. Becca was the only one she'd ever discussed her dreams with, but no man had ever cared enough to ask. "I wish I had more outside of work."

He frowned. "And you don't think you can?"

She shrugged. "I haven't been able to so far. I go in early. I get home late. The men I've come across don't like playing second fiddle to my job."

"Maybe you just haven't met the right man. As far as I'm concerned, a hardworking woman is worth her weight in gold."

As much as she appreciated the sentiment, sweet words were easy to say at the beginning of a relationship. When things were shiny and new. It didn't take long for the shine to fade and long hours to get old.

A familiar sadness crushed her lungs. "Maybe it's not finding the right man. Maybe it's my fault. Either way, as the years tick by, so do my hopes of getting everything I want."

Reid leaned forward, as if enraptured by her voice. "And what exactly is it you want, besides the house and the land you can't maintain?"

She may have lived in fear for her life the last few days, but it was a different kind of terror that seized her vocal cords. But if she wanted Reid to open up to her, she had to do the same. "A husband. Children. A family. Someone to pass down my legacy to like my parents did to me. I mean, isn't that what everyone wants?"

Chapter 21

Sweat dotted the space between Reid's shoulder blades, and he rubbed the back of his neck. Eve's wide, earnest eyes bored into his, waiting for a response. He'd gotten so caught up in the fantasy of being with Eve, he hadn't stopped to think about what she'd expect from a future together.

Continue a legacy?

Hell no, he didn't want to pass on his family's legacy to children. He'd run as fast and as far as he could to make sure that legacy didn't stick with him—drown him in a sea of addiction and bad choices.

He needed some space. Some distance. Some air to breathe that wasn't clouded with his intense feelings for Eve. Standing, he grabbed his plate and cup then forced a tight smile. "That sounds nice, and I'm sure if it's what you really want, you'll find a way to get it."

Her face fell, but he couldn't let her disappointment stop him from escaping this conversation faster than a striking rattlesnake. He rushed into the kitchen, tossed his paper plate in the trash can and shot back the rest of his wine in one big gulp. The bitter liquid burned his throat and he winced.

He shoved the empty cup aside and gripped the edge

of the counter. Inhaling deep breaths through his nose, he struggled to center himself. To smooth the rough edges of his life that had plagued him for years.

"Everything all right?" Eve asked.

Working his jaw back and forth, he spun around to face her. "Yeah. Fine. Just cleaning up."

"That's not what it looks like."

"And what does it look like?" He regretted the harsh snap of his words the moment he spoke.

Eve stood her ground. "Like you're running away. Did what I said scare you?"

"Yes," he said, tunneling his hand through his hair. "Just not in the way you think."

She snorted. "You mean not in the 'oh, shit, I'm scared of commitment and need out of here' kind of way?"

Her smart-ass remark coaxed a smile. "Exactly."

"Then what? If it's not a fear of commitment, is it me? I mean, maybe I've misread what's been happening between us, and if I did, I'm sorry. But I thought after last night...after this morning..." Her voice cracked, and she pressed the back of her hand to her mouth as if to keep her emotions from leaking out.

Eve's tears twisted his gut and reminded him why he'd stayed away from her for so long in the first place. No matter how hard he tried, he was bound to hurt her. He couldn't give her what she wanted, so why start a journey that was doomed to fail?

"You didn't misread anything, Eve. The time we've spent together has been amazing. It's only reinforced everything I've tried so hard to fight since meeting you."

"Then what's wrong?"

He let out a long, frustrated breath. "I'm a casual guy.

I like to keep things nice and simple, and things between me and you can never be simple. We're too good of friends for this not to end up messy, and I don't want that. Do you?"

"God forbid things get *messy*. I mean, how could two consenting adults who have strong feelings for each other ever deal with cleaning up a mess?"

He winced at the sarcasm dripping from her words, masking her anger. "That's not what I—"

"Mean? Seriously, I'm tired of the excuses and the bullshit. I can help you clean up whatever mess is pinning you in this god-awful place of fear."

He squeezed his eyes shut as the need to fully confide in her clawed at his chest. But he couldn't speak, couldn't make himself unload the ugliness that had been his life.

The sound of something falling to the floor snapped open his eyes. "What the hell are you doing?"

Eve stood behind her plate, which she'd tossed on the floor. Food splattered off the side, bits of potato clinging to her pant leg. "Life's never tidy. Not the bad parts, not the good parts." She strolled over to the tub of butter sitting on the counter and dipped her finger inside.

"Eve, stop."

"Stop what?" She smeared the butter on her forehead and down her nose then crossed to him and dotted what was left on his chin. "Stop being messy?"

"Damn it, Eve. This isn't funny. My life isn't something to laugh at and make light of. If I say I can't handle this—" He waved a hand between them. "Then just walk away and know I'm trying to do the right thing."

"So chivalrous, but you don't get to tell me to stop or to walk away or to forget all the beautiful things you said to me. Because if there's one thing I know, it's that you're not a liar. And you wouldn't have told me we should see if we could make things work if you didn't mean it."

He wanted to argue, to push back, to claim he'd spouted nonsense earlier to make her happy, but he couldn't get past the butter smeared across her cute little nose. Snagging the dishrag, he wiped her face clean. "You really want messy?"

"I really want you."

An internal war waged inside him, but he was tired of fighting. Tired of holding back. And more than anything, he didn't want to hurt Eve. Not ever, and certainly not like this—by hiding the broken pieces of himself.

"What brought me to Cloud Valley isn't pretty. You're right. Running away is something I've done for years. Not because I'm scared, but for survival. I don't want to run anymore."

She took the cloth from him and wiped off his chin then set it back on the counter. "I don't want you to run, either. I'm here waiting for you, Reid. That doesn't mean you have to tell me everything you've buried, but I hope you know you can."

The kindness in her tone cracked his last walls of resistance. A lump lodged in his throat, and he rubbed the base of his neck in an attempt to loosen it.

"Are you okay?" she asked, frowning. "Do you need something to drink?"

"Water'd be nice."

She reached behind him for a clean plastic cup and hurried to the faucet. "For this conversation, maybe we should stick with the wine."

He winced, the silly joke another twist of the knife that never left.

Eve stilled, the sound of the water echoing off the sink. "You never have more than one drink, do you?"

"No."

Shutting off the water, she carried the cup to him and waited until he drained the water to speak again. "I assumed you didn't want to overdo it in public, not when you were trying to establish your business. But even at my house, you didn't touch that second beer."

He set the cup down and took her hand, leading her past the mess on the floor to the sofa. He'd deal with cleanup later. For now, this wasn't a conversation he wanted to have standing in middle of the kitchen.

Once settled, he kept ahold of her hand. She grounded him, soothed those rough edges with her nearness. Made him want to unload his burdens so maybe, if he was lucky, he could finally set them aside and move past them.

"You're right," he said. "I never have more than one drink. Ever. My dad is an alcoholic."

She rested her free palm on his thigh. "I'm sorry."

The side of his mouth ticked up. His father's disease was just the tip of the damn iceberg. "Thanks, so am I. He's battled with his addiction for as long as I can remember. Well, *battled* isn't the right word. More like ignored. Refused to acknowledge he has a problem."

"That had to be tough on you and Tara."

He nodded and steadied his nerves. "My mom tried to shield us from most of his issues. She took the brunt of his anger when he was drunk or would take us to stay at our grandparents' when he'd disappear on a binge. For us, it was just normal. That was life. He gave me my first beer at thirteen. I thought he was so cool. We'd sneak into the garage and toss a few back. He'd laugh at me when I had too much."

Memories of his father's harsh words and quick fists attacked him, and nausea swam in his gut.

Clearing his throat, he forced himself to keep speaking. "As I got older, it got worse. I tried to intercept his anger, always stepped in the way if he went after my mom or Tara. I tried to protect them. Tried to keep them safe. I failed."

Emotion welled up, misting his eyes and constricting his airway. All the pain and fear and guilt crashed over him, threatening to pull him under a wave of despair. This was why he kept his past buried. Kept everything under lock and key, refusing to let it see the light of day. Because it was too much to relive. Too much to remember.

Eve wrapped her arms around his middle and held him. "I'm sure you did everything you knew how to do, and I'm sure your mom and Tara would agree."

"He killed her. He killed my mom and never even paid for it." The words fell out of his mouth along with all the pent-up tears and sadness he'd held inside. And now that they were out, he couldn't hide them any longer. "I tried to stop him from hitting Tara one night, and my mom intervened. He screamed. Raged like I'd never seen. My mom begged him to leave us alone and to just go. He got behind the wheel—dragging my mom into the passenger seat—and ran into a tree."

Rawness scraped against his throat, and his heart shattered all over again. The ache he'd carried around since his mother's death grew into a gaping hole. Trapped sobs stole his breath, causing his chest to heave as he struggled not to choke on his sorrow. "I couldn't save my own mother, couldn't stop my father from hurting everyone he claimed to love. I don't want to fail again. I wouldn't survive failing Tara, failing you. Every single day is a battle against control. Controlling my choices, my decisions, my actions. If I slip up, if I do the wrong thing, there's no telling who could get hurt."

She held him tighter, and he crumpled against her. He was wrong. Unleashing this burden didn't lighten the load, it clarified what he needed to do. He had to keep his distance from Eve. She was too important to risk.

A heaviness settled on Eve's shoulders like a two-ton weighted blanket. She wrapped her arms as tight around Reid's strong, muscular body as she could, wanting to absorb his pain. But deep down, she understood that nothing she said or did could take away his trauma. She couldn't fix or heal him.

All she could do was support him and offer encouragement while hoping he could see himself the same way everyone else in his life did.

Tears fell down her face. She couldn't pretend to understand what he'd been through. Her childhood hadn't been perfect—nobody's was—but she'd never doubted her parents loved her. She'd never doubted they'd always had her best interest at heart and tried their hardest to provide the best life possible.

A jolt of reality stole her breath.

Legacy.

That's what she'd said that'd freaked him out so bad. A fresh set of tears filled her eyes. Refusing to let Reid believe he was to blame for his father's sins, she dashed them away and pulled back just enough to see his face. "I hate that this happened to you. I hate that you grew up with so much turmoil and that your mother lost her life protecting you and your sister. You deserved better. You all did."

He shook his head. "I should have done more. I should have stopped her from getting in that truck."

She flattened her palm on his face and forced him to see her, to hear her. "It doesn't sound like you could have stopped what happened."

"How can you say that?" He yanked back as if trying to escape her touch, but she wouldn't let him.

"You tried as hard as you could. And as much as you wanted to protect her, she was doing the same."

He closed his eyes and breathed in deep through his nose. "I tell Tara that, but I'm not sure I really believe it."

"I do, and I believe your mom's so proud of the man you are. You aren't your father, Reid. You've been so worried about becoming the man he is, you haven't accepted the fact that you're the man your mother raised. You have carried on *her* legacy."

His eyes flew open, and the mixture of doubt and hope that shone through devastated her. "What do you mean?"

"She was your protector. Your champion. She instilled in you a need to serve others. Hell, you put your life on hold to serve and protect the citizens of this country. You've chosen a career where you keep others safe. I'm sure if you asked Tara, she'd share countless memories of when you stood up for her. Kept her from being on the opposite end of your father's wrath. You might think you have to maintain strict control in order to save others from yourself, but honey, your actions are continually putting other people's needs before your own. You are your mother's son."

A small smile cracked through his despair. "I want to believe that. I want so bad to think she's proud of me. But I left Tara behind. I ran away from my dad and all his issues and just left her stuck."

"No, you set healthy boundaries for your own sake and, from what I understand, tried for years to get Tara to do the same. And all that trying has paid off. She's here now, and maybe with you both across the country, your father will finally get the help he needs."

He huffed out a derisive snort. "I doubt it, and honestly, I don't care. I wasted so much time consumed with wanting him to get better. I can't spend any more energy on someone who's hell-bent on destroying himself and everyone around him."

She wasn't sure if he was being honest with himself, but right now, that didn't matter. "Sounds like your dad has a lot of demons, and it's up to him to fix them. Just like you're the only one who can decide if you're going to let your past dictate your future."

His jaw tightened, and he dropped his gaze to his lap. "I don't know how to not let the mess of my past get in the way."

Smiling, she lifted a shoulder. "The mess will always get in the way. Sometimes it's about finding the right person to help you clean it up."

Apprehension pinched his expression. He reached for her then pulled back. "I don't want to hurt you, Eve. I'd never forgive myself."

"We can't promise that we'll never hurt each other. Even if we walk into the sunset, hand in hand, determined to face the future together. Life happens, mistakes are made and people get hurt. That's just the way the world works. But we can promise to try our hardest, to keep open and honest communication, and to be the best versions of ourselves every day."

Swishing his lips to the side, he finally met her gaze. "I don't know if I want kids. I'm not sure if I can risk passing down all the issues I've battled to some innocent little baby. If that's something you need to complete you, I can't promise that's something I can give."

"Just because I may want a baby one day, or even a husband, doesn't mean I need either to complete me. My life is filled with so much joy and friendship and happiness that I've created. That I've nurtured. No matter where I end up, or who comes into my life, it will all be extra. That delicious icing on what I hope is a chocolate cake."

"I want to believe you. I want to believe that everything you said is the truth." He squeezed the bridge of his nose. "I've spent so long in this dark place, I'm not sure how to leave it behind."

"I'm not sure you can. I think it's about learning to let in a little bit of light every day until those places don't seem as dark anymore."

He drew in a shuddering breath. "Anyone ever tell you how smart you are?"

"All the time," she said, grinning.

Hooking an arm around her waist, he pulled her onto his lap and pressed his lips to hers. "Thank you for listening. Thank you for being you."

"No matter what, I'm always here for you, Reid." She rested her head on his chest and closed her eyes.

His heart beat a steady rhythm against her ear. His

breathing evened. "Can we just sit like this for a little a while?"

"You can hold me for as long as you want." She'd stay cuddled against him for the rest of her life if he'd let her, but this wasn't the time to say it. She didn't expect one conversation to shift his entire way of thinking. He'd taken a huge step by sharing so much with her, and hopefully each day would bring another baby step for him on his path to healing.

And if he let her, she'd be by his side for every single one of them.

Chapter 22

If Reid could choose one moment to freeze forever, it'd be this one. Sitting on the couch with Eve in his arms, a feeling of peace and contentment slicing through the turmoil that had eaten him up for so many years.

She was right. This was just the first, very big step. One that he'd needed more than he realized.

One that he prayed would take him to a better place, where he could truly believe in a future with Eve.

He rested his forehead on hers and breathed her in. Filled every fiber of his being with her essence, her kindness, her compassion. "I needed this. Needed you to drag it out of me. Tara's the only one I talk about this shit with, and that's mostly trying to convince her to let our dad pay for his mistakes. She means well, and I know she loves him, but part of her help just turns into enabling, leaving her the one screwed in the end."

"It's hard not to help the ones we love, even if that help ends up doing more bad than good. What led to Tara's breaking point?" As she spoke, she traced her fingertips against his arm, twisting the tiny hairs with the motion.

But he didn't mind. She could touch him anywhere and he'd be happy. "Dad was in rehab—again—and left early. He showed up at her place, stole money, then split."

"Poor Tara."

"And if that's not bad enough, her jackass boyfriend gave her a hard time and their relationship ended. The guy's a dick, always has been, but I can't blame him for getting fed up with my dad's toxic bullshit. I just hate that Tara was hurt."

"She's strong and has you for support," Eve said. "Maybe we can all help her see Cloud Valley would be a great place to live."

His heart sputtered and his already intense feelings for Eve grew higher than the mountain in the backyard. "I'd love nothing more. But no more talk about Tara or my dad or my childhood."

She cupped the back of his neck with her palm and drew herself closer. "What do you have in mind?"

Capturing her mouth, he slid his hand down her slender thigh, his body tingling with every curve and dip he explored. And hell, it was just her leg. Excitement beat triple time in his veins at what else was left to uncover.

His fingers smashed against something cold and lumpy. "Um, we might have to put this on pause."

Frowning, she pulled back and studied his face. "Absolutely. We can take things as slow as you need."

He chuckled and showed her the bits of potatoes he'd found clinging to her pants. "The timing isn't the issue."

Clapping a hand to her mouth, she burst into laughter. "Oh my gosh. I completely forgot I made a mess in the kitchen."

"You made your point, that's for sure. But we should pick that up before we forget and rodents scamper inside to eat your leftovers." With more regret than he could express, he unfolded himself from Eve and stood then pulled her to her feet. "Why don't you clean the potatoes off yourself, and I'll handle the kitchen."

"I'm the one who tossed my plate on the floor. I can handle it," she said. "There's still dishes to wash, too. You shouldn't have to deal with it all yourself."

He pulled her close, framing her face with his hands. "You've done more than you'll ever know. Let me do this. It's a small way to say thank you."

She scrunched her nose as if uncomfortable with the praise. "Fine. I might take another shower. I can still smell that butter. Not my best decision."

"I disagree," he said, tapping the tip of her nose with his finger. "Go. Enjoy."

"If you say so," she said in a singsong voice then gave him a peck on the cheek and strolled toward the hall.

He watched the subtle sway of her hips, and desire tightened his gut. Damn it, he should say screw the dishes and march after her into that shower. He'd barely survived knowing she was in there earlier. He wasn't sure if he was strong enough to do it again.

Ignoring his instinct to run after her, he walked into the kitchen and grinned at the forgotten paper plate on the floor. Who'd have guessed that tossing food around would result in cracking open the vault of emotions and memories he'd kept locked up for so long.

Luckily Eve had eaten most of her dinner, so the cleanup was easy. He hustled around the room, washing serving ware and wiping down counters. He dipped outside to make sure they'd left nothing behind on the deck then returned to the tidy kitchen.

A quick glance at his watch told him the evening was still young. An early dinner and baring his soul left them with a few hours to kill before bedtime. He debated checking in with Tara, but he didn't want to hover—didn't want her to think that if she decided to make her stay in Cloud Valley permanent, he'd be in her business all the time.

If she needed him, she'd call. He'd touch base with her in the morning.

Pipes groaned from the rush of water flowing into the bathtub. He groaned along with them as images of Eve came back. She could take all the hot water she needed, because once she was done, he'd need a shower cold as ice to cool his blood.

Maybe he could take Eve for a walk. A quick hike around the lake until the sun went down. That could chew up enough time, leaving them to watch a movie before calling it a night. He'd grab a hoodie from his bag and ask if she'd be interested in his plan.

Hurrying down the hall, he made a beeline past the closed bathroom door and stepped inside the primary bedroom. His bag lay untouched at the end of the bed. Zipping it open, he dug inside and found his favorite black sweatshirt. He shook out the wrinkles then tugged it over his head.

"Oh, sorry. I didn't know you were in here."

He stared at Eve, who stood in the doorway with a white cotton towel wrapped around her body. Unspoken words stuck in his dry throat.

"I forgot to grab my clothes," she said. "Are you cold?"

He smoothed a hand over the soft material of his sweatshirt. "No, I, ah, thought about taking a walk. How was your shower?"

"Good. All clean, but I'm not sure if I want to head outside. Can we take a walk in the morning instead?"

"Sure. Whatever you want."

She padded into the room and gave a gentle yank on the string dangling from his hood. "Anything, huh?"

An insatiable hunger roared through him. He didn't want to fight it anymore. Skimming the backs of his knuckles along the soft curve of her cheek, he stared down at her beautiful face. "Anything."

He bent down and pressed his lips to hers. Lust stirred in his core. He had taken a giant step earlier, and now it was time to take another one. But this time, it was a step for both him and Eve.

The heat of Reid's body against hers combined with the fire raging inside Eve and threatened to explode. She'd hoped standing under the spray of cool water for a second time would wash away the desire climbing up her body.

But all it took was one look, one touch, one taste to weaken her resolve and have her ready to drop to her knees and beg for more.

She broke the kiss, needing to know Reid was okay. That he was ready to take their relationship to this level and things weren't moving too fast after exposing so much of his past—of his fears.

"You okay?" he asked, tucking a strand of her wet hair behind her ear.

She smiled. "I was about to ask you the same thing."

Puzzlement creased his forehead. "How could I not be? I'm holding a beautiful woman who's dressed only in a towel."

"I'm being serious." She yanked on the strings of his hoodie again. "We talked about a lot of heavy stuff earlier. If you're not ready for this…for any of this…that's fine. I don't want you to feel pressured."

He grinned, melting her insides. "I don't think I've ever been on this side of the I-don't-want-to-pressure-you talk."

"What can I tell you," she said, shrugging. "I'm a modern woman."

Snaking his hand around the back of her neck, he lowered his head so they were eye to eye. "I appreciate your concern, but I'm ready. Ready to move forward. Ready to try. Ready to toss your ass in this bed and finally show you how much you mean to me."

She held her arms open. "Go for it."

Chuckling, he hauled her into his arms then playfully threw her on the bed before lunging after her. Lying on her back, she propped herself on her elbows, enjoying the view as he stalked forward like a panther about to devour his prey.

Hooking an arm around her waist, he shifted her to her side then lay in front of her so they were face-to-face. His fingers inched up her hip, creeping toward the knotted towel at her chest. "You have no idea how long I've wanted to do this."

She swallowed hard, her body humming with anticipation. A part of her wanted to yank the towel off herself and get started, stripping him naked to see the hard, chiseled muscles she knew lay under his clothes.

The other part of her wanted to be cherished, to savor the moment and everything that came with it.

"You could have fooled me," she said, her voice quivering.

He dipped the pad of his finger into the shallow dent of her cleavage, toying the with sensitive skin at the top of her breast. "Trust me, no more pretending. No more hiding."

As if speaking about her, he flicked the knot apart and smoothed his hand down between her breasts.

Squirming, she wiggled the towel free and threw it on the floor. She didn't want anything separating them—secrets, fears or clothes.

He stilled, his gaze flicking to her body for a few seconds before he tucked his head and captured one nipple between his teeth. His tongue took over, and the gentle movement of his mouth pushed her to lie on her back.

She gasped, her body thrusting forward as anticipation tingled between her legs.

His hand slid down to her stomach then stopped. He stared up at her, hunger lighting his eyes. "Are you sure this is what you want?"

Her hips bucked up in a desperate attempt to meet his fingers, the need for release of the unrelenting pressure enough to drive her mad. She shoved her hand into his shaggy hair, gripping the long strands. "Hmm-mm."

He kept his focus on her face as he slipped his fingers inside her.

Her breath caught in her throat, moisture clinging to her thighs as he moved his fingers in and out, his thumb gently swiping over her most sensitive spot.

"You're so damn beautiful, Eve," he said, his warm breath skimming over her skin. "Come on, baby. Just let yourself go."

She closed her eyes, listening to his voice and fisting the sheets in her hands as her body moved closer and closer to ultimate pleasure. Stars exploded and she screamed out his name, sweet release finally coming, replaced by a stronger, urgent need for more.

The feel of Reid's mouth on hers made her purr. She opened her eyes to find him hovering over her. Sweat dotted his hairline and tenderness filled his wide brown eyes. "You're amazing, Eve. Every single part of you."

She grinned, not even close to being done with their fun. "You've seen every part of me. I think it's time to even the score."

His grin matched hers, and he pushed up to sit on his knees as he straddled her. He yanked his hoodie and T-shirt over his head, making his already tousled hair messier.

The white bandage on his side caught her attention, and she frowned. Gingerly, she touched the area around the bandage. "Does it hurt?"

"Changing the bandage isn't much fun, but it doesn't hurt much now," he said with a small, husky laugh.

"I was terrified when I heard you were in the hospital. Even before I admitted to myself—to anyone—how much you meant to me, I knew if something happened to you, I wouldn't survive it."

Reid swiped the pad of his thumb across her cheek, leaving it to linger as he stared deep into her eyes. "I'm fine. Just a little bruise. I'm not going anywhere."

The implied promise lingered between them and misted Eve's eyes. She didn't expect a lifelong commitment or an expression of love. But he'd given her exactly what she needed—hope that they might figure out a future together.

"Neither am I," she said, the words catching on the emotion lodged in her throat.

He reclaimed her mouth, his body covering hers.

Her heart soared and she maneuvered her hands to slip under the soft material of his joggers, shoving them down as far as she could without breaking their kiss.

He severed their connection, his ragged breaths coming out in short puffs. "Give me a second." Jumping out of the bed, he finished the job and kicked out of his pants and boxers.

Her eyes bulged at the magnificent sight of him. All hard, lean muscles and the size of his erection enough to send a tiny bit of trepidation through her excitement. She kept her gaze locked on him as he moved to his bag, rummaging through it until he pulled out a condom. He ripped it open then rolled the rubber over his long, stiff shaft.

Her heart rate tripled. Good lord.

With everything in place, he reclaimed his spot beside her. "Are you sure you're ready for this?"

"I've been ready for you my whole life."

Her words lifted the side of his mouth, and he rolled on top of her, resting an arm above her head while his free hand positioned himself at her center. He pushed inside her and groaned. As he moved, he pressed kisses against her neck, her throat, then along her jawline until his lips found hers.

She deepened the kiss, each thrust inside her stretching her to fit him until any discomfort vanished, leaving behind only blinding pleasure. She moved her hips, meeting his demands on instinct, her body craving more and more as he went deeper and deeper.

As she teetered on the precipice of earth-shattering release, he pulled out and flipped her on her stomach. He roamed his hands along her back before linking their fingers, caging her palms with his and pinning them to the bed above her head.

Her ass reared back, the emptiness of not having him inside her too much to handle. "Reid." She said his name like a plea, like a prayer.

He entered her from behind, the shock wave of pleasure echoing through her soul. She cried out, grinding against him until an explosion of desire burst inside her. She squeezed his hands, the lack of control taking her to a level she'd never reached.

Reid kept moving, kept thrusting. His breaths became grunts and moans until his body jerked and dropped down, his lips placing hot bursts of kisses along her spine before he rolled to her side and pulled her to rest against him.

She loved the feel of him wrapped around her, but she turned in his arms to see his face. "Why did we wait so long to do that?"

"Because I'm an idiot." He grinned and swept her hair over her shoulder, kissing the shallow dent beside her neck. "I could kiss every inch of your body."

She chuckled, tilting her head to the side to give him more room to explore. How was it possible for her body to react to his every touch? She should be exhausted, spent after what they'd just experienced. Instead, her nerve endings hummed, her body craving more of him. "I think you already have."

His grin grew. "Baby, I'm just getting started."

Chapter 23

Streams of morning sunlight poured through the uncovered window, assaulting Reid's closed eyes and yanking him from sleep. He reached for Eve, his body already responding to the thought of continuing where they'd left off late into the night.

Finding the space beside him empty, he sat up and glanced around the room. Eve was nowhere in sight.

"Eve?"

When she didn't answer, he groaned and rolled out of the warm bed. He'd hoped they could stay tucked under the covers until midmorning at least, but that wasn't an option now. Maybe he could find her and drag her ass right back there. No doubt he could come up with some imaginative ways to keep her happy and staying put. Dressing quickly, he grabbed his phone off the nightstand, shoved it in his pocket and hurried from the room.

Scents of fresh coffee and vanilla lured him into the kitchen. Eve stood in front of the stove with her auburn hair piled on top of her head. A long T-shirt skimmed the top of her thighs. She sang a song he didn't recognize in her adorable out-of-tune voice while dipping bread in an egg mixture then tossing it on a flat pan.

She spun around and spied him. "Good morning. I

hope I didn't wake you. I planned to surprise you with breakfast in bed."

Grinning, he padded across the kitchen to pull her into his arms and kiss her. "Morning. I'd hoped to welcome the day in a different way, but this is the next best thing. What are you making?"

"French toast." She went up on her tiptoes to give him a peck on the tip of his nose then turned to flip the bread in the pan.

He kept his arms looped around her waist as she cooked. He flattened his palm on her stomach and nuzzled her neck. "I don't know which smells better, you or breakfast."

Laughing, she swatted his knuckles with the spatula. "I hope it's the breakfast."

"I'm not so sure." He pressed kisses along her neck. Hell, he couldn't get enough of this woman. Each taste only left him wanting more. "Looks delicious. We can still take it back to the bedroom. Then once we're done eating, we can enjoy some other activities to make this an even better morning."

She tipped back her head to rest against him, exposing the long column of her neck. "I never knew you were so impatient."

"Only with things I really, really want."

She faced him again and caught his chin in between her thumb and forefinger. "But when we wait, it makes things so much sweeter. Besides, didn't you get enough last night?" She wiggled her eyebrows and grinned.

He opened his mouth to argue, but his phone rang and stole his attention. He plucked it from his pocket and read Madden's name on the screen. "Just so you know, I could never get enough of you, but we'll finish this conversation after I talk to Madden."

Spinning back around, she flipped the bread then got another piece ready.

Tearing himself away from her, he answered the call. "Hey, man. What's up? Aren't you at the parade?"

The annual parade had a midmorning start time, but it took hours to get everything in place for the festivities. If Sunrise Security was in charge of crowd control, Madden and the rest of the crew would have shown up close to when the sun rose.

"I'm here with Lily and Tara. I wasn't sure if I should call you about this, but it seems like the right thing to do."

The hesitancy in his best friend's voice set him on high alert. "What's wrong?"

"Tara got a phone call from your dad last night," Madden said. "She was upset and spoke with Lily about it. Lily didn't tell me everything, but Tara's planning on flying home this afternoon. Something about your dad needing a place to stay or money. I guess he laid it on pretty thick, really made Tara feel guilty for leaving town."

Anger tightened his grip on the phone. "Son of a bitch."

"Lily told Tara she should let you know about the call, but she didn't want you to try and talk her out of leaving."

"Damn right I'd try to convince her to stay. I thought she finally figured out her help is wasted on him. She said she was finished with his bullshit, ready to put her own life first for once." Irritation swirled to life inside him like a dust storm, and he paced the length of the kitchen.

Eve removed the pan from the stove and shut off the burner. Her concerned gaze followed his every move.

"You and I both know it's not that easy," Madden said.

"Your dad has manipulated her for years, knows what buttons to press to get what he wants. Tara severing that tie isn't as simple as leaving town."

Head pounding, he pinched the bridge of his nose. "When's her flight?"

"Not until later this afternoon. She said she wanted to see a little of the parade, then asked if Lily would drive her."

"I'll call her. Thanks for letting me know."

"She's going to be so pissed," Madden said.

"Better her than me. Thanks again, man." Disconnecting, he didn't even a spare a second to let Eve know what had happened before he dialed Tara. The line rang in his ear, raising his blood pressure when her voicemail picked up. "Answer your phone, Tara. We need to talk."

Disconnecting, he hung his head. "Shit."

Eve rushed to him and slid her palm up and down his back. "What's going on?"

He brought up his text app and pounded out a message for his sister. "Dad called Tara last night and apparently guilted her enough to make her want to go back home. She booked a flight for later today. I need to talk to her before she goes. I'm afraid if she leaves, she'll get stuck in the same vicious cycle."

"And she's not answering your calls?"

He tossed his useless phone on the counter. "Nope."

"Well, then, let's head to Madden and Lily's place. You can talk to her there. Have a conversation about how both of you are feeling. Because the last thing she needs is for you to jump in and tell her what to do. She should see you are supporting her and encouraging her to do what's best for her."

He wrinkled his nose, hating that she was right. "Can't I just bring her here and lock her in a closet or something?"

She grinned. "I don't think so. I can clean this up and toss it in the freezer. We can always reheat it later. That way we can leave right away."

"Slight snag in your plan," he said.

Arching her brows, she waited.

"Tara's downtown with Madden while he manages security for the parade. She wanted to see some of the festivities before she left."

"Ok," Eve said, lifting her shoulders. "Then we'll head downtown."

He grimaced. "As much as I want to talk to Tara, I don't think that's a good idea. Taking you to a crowded event feels irresponsible."

Even as he spoke, his stomach tied in knots. He'd vowed to be a better brother, to help Tara see that her attempts at helping their father were fruitless. Now as soon as she was faced with a tough decision, she was too afraid of his reaction to talk to him.

And he couldn't even go find her to let her know he'd be there for her no matter what.

"I don't see any harm in taking a little field trip," she said, continuing the steady motion on his back. "There will be so many people around, he wouldn't dare make a move. Not when he's only ever tried when I've been completely alone. We can find Tara, you can talk, then we'll head right back here to spend the rest of the day however you want."

"*However* I want?"

She nodded. "This is important to you, so it's important to me. You'll regret it if you don't try."

Deep down, he knew she was right. He had to make Tara see their father had to fix his own mistakes. Then he'd haul Eve back to the cabin in the woods, where he could keep her safe—and hopefully in bed for the rest of the day.

With the parade only thirty minutes away from start time, the parking was scarce and the streets packed around downtown Cloud Valley. The warmth of the sun combated the subtle breeze stirring the leaves in the trees. Green grass and blue skies created the perfect backdrop for a day that promised fun and festivities.

"You might as well park at my house and we can walk from there," Eve said.

Reid flexed his hands around the steering wheel. "You're probably right. No way I'll find a spot much closer."

Trepidation did a tap dance in Eve's stomach as Reid pulled into her driveway and shut off the engine. "Do you know where Tara is?" As much as she wanted to catch a glimpse of the extravagance that came along with the annual parade, the idea of being around so many people had fear creeping up the back of her neck.

"Madden told me they're on Main Street, a few blocks south of Tilly's. He'll stay put until we get there. Lily knows we're coming, but he hasn't said a word to Tara, which is probably a good thing. She'd take off quick if she knew."

"She might still. You have to be prepared for that." She kept her voice low, not wanting to upset him.

He blew out a long breath. "I know."

"You're a good brother." She leaned over the seat to give him a quick kiss then hopped out of the truck.

"I don't think she'll see it that way, but I'm trying." He met her on her side of the vehicle then took her hand. "Stay close. I don't want to take any chances."

She squeezed his hand. "I don't think that will be too hard."

The closer they got to town, the more eclectic the crowd became. Little boys dressed like cowboys and girls wearing long prairie dresses paired with braided pigtails skipped beside their parents. Dogs with red bandannas tied around their necks pulled their pet parents down the road.

She smiled, the excitement infectious. "Becca talked about dressing Suzy up this year. Good luck getting that little girl to put on anything she didn't like."

"Maybe we'll see them down here."

"I thought about texting Becca, but I don't want to spend more time here than necessary. I'll have plenty of years to see her dressed like a bull rider or prairie princess." Her heart ached. The chaos of the last few nights had kept her from her regular check-ins with her favorite little girl. Once things settled down, she'd have to finally cash in on her slumber party with Suzy.

"Next year we'll bring Suzy ourselves." Reid pressed a kiss to her temple then steered her onto the sidewalk of Main Street.

Tingles of happiness beat back her fear. They hadn't made promises during their night of passion, but she didn't need them. Not yet. She knew where her heart stood and what she wanted. But Reid's casual mention of them doing something together next year gave her hope that his intentions were very much aligned with her own.

"At least we get to see some of the extravaganza." She gestured toward the line of floats waiting for the parade to begin. "I can't believe how much work people put into these. My mom used to tease my dad about putting something together for Tilly's when I was younger, but my parents knew they were useless with this kind of stuff."

"I could help if you want a float. I've got all those skills, remember?" Reid winked.

"If you can do that," she said, pointing at a large float decked out with a faux mountain that looked like it'd been ripped from the earth, surrounded by a miniature Old West town, "then we've got a deal."

He scrunched his nose and dipped his chin toward the float behind the one she'd indicated. "I was thinking more like that."

She laughed when she saw the pickup truck pulling a wagon filled with hay. Local children dressed in creative costumes bounced around, impatiently waiting for the parade to start.

"I'm not sure how that would represent Tilly's, but it'd be a start."

The farther up the sidewalk they walked, the more congested it became. People closed in on them, trapping Eve between Reid and a wall of bodies. She tightened her grip on Reid's hand, terrified of severing the connection and being swept away in a sea of people.

"You okay?" he asked.

She nodded, gaze fixed straight ahead. She used her free hand to wave at friendly faces and flashed what she hoped looked like genuine smiles to people she'd known most her life. But unease skittered around her skin in angry circles, refusing to leave.

"There's Madden." Reid wove through the crowd, keeping her close.

When Madden noticed their approach, he leaned to whisper in Lily's ear. Tara stood with her back to them, unaware of what was happening.

"Here we go," Reid whispered under his breath.

His nerves were as loud to Eve's ear as the pack of giggling children darting around with sticks of cotton candy. "You've got this."

They stopped right behind Tara, and Reid cleared his throat.

Tara glanced over her shoulder, and her eyes widened for a beat before her mouth settled into a tight line. "What are you doing here?"

Eve winced at Tara's harsh tone.

"I just want to talk to you for a minute," Reid said.

"You mean you want to tell me what to do. That my choices are stupid," she snapped.

"Tara," Eve said, slipping her hand from Reid's and placing it on his sister's arm. "Please. He's here because he loves you. All he wants you to do is listen. To have a conversation."

Lily snaked an arm around Madden's waist. "Why don't we give them some privacy? Besides, honey, you're supposed to be working. Not standing around chatting with friends."

Tara waited for Madden and Lily to disappear down the sidewalk before facing Eve and Reid with arms crossed over her chest. "They shouldn't have called you. I'm an adult. I can make my own decisions."

"I know that," Reid said. "I don't want to tell you what to do. I really don't."

Tara snorted. "You've been telling me what to do my whole life. Why stop now?"

"Damn it, Tara." Reid rubbed the back of his neck. "Can't we just talk? Like two adults?"

Not wanting to intrude on their personal conversation, Eve took a tiny step away. She shifted to the side, her focus on the people trudging along with grins and laughter because their lives weren't filled with alcoholic fathers or dangerous stalkers. She wished she could be one of them. No troubles, no worries, just a sunny day of fun with friends and family.

A subtle bump against her shoulder moved her another step away from Reid. She braced herself against the impact.

A hand gripped her bicep, steadying her. A clean-shaven man wearing a crisp white button-down shirt and dark jeans stared at her from under the bill of a baseball hat. Shadows hid his eyes, but nervous energy poured off him in waves. He moved so he stood between her and Reid. "I'm so sorry. I didn't mean to knock into you. I'm just… I'm a little frantic. My daughter wandered away. My wife is on the other side of the street looking for her. She's so small, only three years old. She's probably scared and lonely. Have you seen her?"

"Do you have a picture of her? Have you called the police?"

"My wife spoke to a deputy, who's helping. But I can't sit still and just wait. I have to find her. There are so many people here." He fished his phone from the front pocket of his jeans. "This is her."

Eve glanced at the screen, and terror squeezed her lungs until it stole every breath from her body.

"She's a real pretty little girl," the man said, his voice becoming hard and cold. "I'd hate to see anything bad happen to her. Don't you agree?"

A picture of Suzy dominated the screen. Her nose was tilted up and her smile wide as she stared up at a police horse wearing a cowboy hat.

Eve's gaze flew up and connected with the man's. The hard glint shining through his green eyes sent a wave of nausea crashing against her abdomen.

He lifted his finger to his lips. "Quiet. Don't do or say anything you'll regret and the girl won't get hurt. If you want to keep her safe, come with me now and don't make a scene."

Chapter 24

Reid clenched his jaw to keep from losing his cool. Tara's annoyance wasn't surprising, but he'd hoped she'd be open to a calm and rational conversation. If that was his goal, he couldn't misstep and raise his voice.

Not like that would help anyway.

Tara pursed her lips, to match his pissed-off expression. "So you're going to talk to me like I'm an adult now, huh? Not a baby sister you have to always look out for? Is that why you had your friend keep an eye on me and call you when I'm about to do something you won't like?"

"I never told Madden to keep an eye on you. He called because he knew how important it was." He threw his hands in the air. "He called because he knew you wouldn't. And you should have, Tara. You can't just run away and leave me wondering where you are."

"Like you did?"

Her words hit him harder than the IED that took out his tank overseas.

They'd had this argument so many times, and this time, he really needed Tara to hear him. He gripped both her shoulders and ducked his chin so she couldn't look away. "I did run, and I left you behind, and I'm sorry. But I couldn't take you with me and I needed to get out to save myself. I was afraid if I stayed, I'd become Dad."

Tara's facial expression softened. "You could never."

He lifted a shoulder. "I might. Every time he called, it made me want to drink. Every time he needed me to bail him out or he guilted me into giving him money or walked away from rehab, I wanted to drink. If I didn't put distance between me and him, it would have created the same demons in me that he has fought all these years. It would have killed me. And now what kills me is thinking the same thing might happen to you."

Tears hovered above her lashes. "I won't ever be like Dad, but I can't walk away and not help him. I can't give up hope."

"You might not end up like him, but my fear is you'll end up like Mom."

She squeezed her eyes closed for a beat and the tears rolled down her cheeks.

"I don't want you to lose hope," he said, pressing on. "Not in Dad and not in anyone. You have a big heart. It's one of your best qualities. But you've given up so much. Lost so much. When will Dad be forced to look out for himself? Clean up his own messes?"

"He's all alone. He doesn't have anyone looking out for him." Tara wiped her eyes and sniffed.

Reid struggled to hold back his frustration. "He's our *father*. He's supposed to look out for us, not the other way around."

"I know that, but… I don't know. That's just never the way it's been. He's always needed me more than I needed him."

"But that doesn't make it right or mean it's the way

things always have to be." He gave her shoulders a little squeeze. "Eve and I talked about this last night. She helped me to see the flaws in the way I've viewed things all these years. Seeing that doesn't mean I'm cured of my bad thoughts or self-destructive behavior. But realizing I need to make a change is the first step, right, Eve?"

He glanced over his shoulder and frowned. "Eve?"

She wasn't there.

A boulder of apprehension sat in his gut as he bounced onto his tiptoes to peer above the growing crowd. "Eve!"

A few curious glances from passersby were the only response.

Tara gripped his arm. "She was just right there."

"I know," he snapped and grabbed his phone. He dialed her number and pressed the phone to his ear. "Come on. Pick up. Pick up."

Her voicemail message came on, and his apprehension turned to cold, blinding panic.

"We'll find her," Tara said. "She couldn't have gone far."

He stared into the reassuring eyes of his sister as fear pressed against his windpipe, blocking the path of his breaths to escape. He struggled to take in air, to let it out. Struggled to see beyond the suffocating reality that Eve wouldn't just walk away. She wouldn't wander off or do anything to make him worry.

"Reid, look at me." Tara kept her voice calm and steady. She flattened her palms on either side of his face. "Eve may or may not be in trouble. Either way, we have to find her right away, okay?"

Unable to speak, he nodded his agreement.

"You know what to do now. So do it."

He finally let out a shuddering breath. Tara was right. This was his job, and he wouldn't stand here and fall apart when Eve's life could be at stake. With his phone still in his hand, he called Madden. While he waited for an answer, he said, "You head south. Call out Eve's name and keep your eyes open for anything unusual. If you see anyone who looks familiar, ask if they've seen Eve."

Tara took off, her pace quick.

When Madden answered, he headed north.

"Hey, man. How'd it go with Tara?"

"No time for that," he said as he waded through the crowd. He scanned each face, praying one of them would be Eve. "Eve's gone."

"What? How did that happen?"

"I don't know, man. She was right there when I was talking with Tara. Now she's missing." He pounded forward. His heart threatened to beat through his chest with each step. "Tara and I split up to find her. I need your help."

"You got it. I'll get Dax and Ben to search and have Lily make some calls. Maybe someone got ahold of her and needed something. Don't worry. We'll find her."

Disconnecting, Reid dialed Eve one more time. When she didn't answer, unshed tears stung his eyes. This couldn't be happening. He'd taken his focus off her for one second. How could someone take her from practically right under his nose?

As he pounded the pavement, pulse racing and gaze scanning every face he passed, the cold, hard truth formed a hard ball in the pit of his stomach.

Tyson Brown had gotten his hands on Eve, and it was all his fault.

* * *

The hard grip on Eve's arm bit through her long-sleeved shirt. Instinct told her to yell, to scream, to yank away from the man leading her through the maze of people.

But if he had Suzy, she had to do whatever he told her. Had to stay strong and calm, prepare herself to fight tooth and nail to keep the little girl safe.

The farther away from Main Street they walked, the thinner the crowd became until they left the chaos and laughter behind. She kept her mouth shut as her mind raced. Once she had Suzy in her arms, she'd scratch Tyson Brown's eyes out if she had to in order to escape.

Tyson steered her down a back alley that bled out to a side street where his truck was parked. "Get in and don't try anything stupid."

Her heart pounded as she reached for the handle. Her arms ached to wrap around Suzy. To hold her close and let her know everything would be okay. Opening the door, she hopped inside while Tyson hurried around the front and climbed into the driver's seat.

She searched behind her in the tiny space between the bench seat and the window. Desperation lodged in her throat. "Where's Suzy?"

Snickering, Tyson hooked an arm on the seat, his fingers skimming the top of her shoulder, and shot out of the alley. He sped forward, putting distance between them and the town faster than she could wrap her mind around what was happening. "Did you really think I had her? That she was just patiently sitting and waiting for us in my truck?"

"I don't understand," she said, voice shaking. "What did you do to her?"

"I didn't do anything with her. She's probably still back at the parade. I just took her picture because I needed to get you away from that macho baboon that's always panting after you."

Anger clashed with relief, leaving her dizzy. "So she's safe?"

He shrugged. "How should I know?"

Blowing out a ragged breath, she rubbed her temple, trying to regain her senses. He didn't have Suzy. He'd used the girl to break down her guard and keep her quiet while he got her away from safety.

And now she was screwed.

She struggled to regain her composure. Keeping her wits was paramount in making it out of this alive. She stared out the window, keeping mental track of each turn as he navigated out of town.

"So what now?" she asked. "What do you want from me?"

He spared her a quick look and maneuvered his hand from behind her shoulders to slide down to rest on her thigh. "All I wanted from the start was to thank you for your kindness. I mean, you bought my meal. That means something. I understand my enthusiasm scared you, and if that jackass wouldn't have interrupted, I could have made you see how great we could be together."

Digesting his words, her stomach dipped. He wasn't just dangerous and violent, he was delusional. She debated the best way to handle him. As much as she wanted to smash her fists against him and scream, she feared it wouldn't get her anywhere.

"And what about you breaking into my home? Was that supposed to make me feel better?"

His jaw dropped, as if befuddled by the question. "Of course. You love flowers. I left you my best work, then I picked as many as I could find. If *he* wouldn't have taken you away, we could have had a perfect evening." He tightened his grip on her thigh, the cold edge creeping back into his voice.

Her body stiffened. She didn't want to upset him any more but was afraid whatever she said would only push him closer to the dangerous edge where his mind teetered. She needed to take a different tack. Get him talking about what he planned so she could figure a way out. "Is that what you want for today? To make up for losing out on the perfect night?"

He shot her a wide grin before returning his focus to the country road. "Exactly."

"And where are we going?" She watched the scenery fly by, noticing the road sign she'd spied not long ago when she'd been sitting in Reid's truck on the way to the fairgrounds.

Maybe that's where he was taking her. Back to a place he was familiar with, where he'd been while stalking Dana. She and Reid had assumed he'd stayed close to the rodeo circuit, slept somewhere he'd been before. It made sense he'd been close to the fairgrounds all along.

She made mental note of all the places she'd gone when visiting the rodeo with her parents. If she could get away from him, there were a dozen places she could hide— places she could find help.

"Someplace special. Someplace where we can be completely alone."

The turn to the fairgrounds passed by her window and crushed her plan before she'd fully gotten it off the ground.

She had to shake off her disappointment and figure out another idea. If she was going to escape, she needed to buy some time. Distract him and maybe make him believe she bought into his twisted delusion. "I appreciate the effort you've put in, but I'm not sure how comfortable I am taking things to such an intimate level when I don't know much about you."

He snorted. "With those posters plastered all over town, I bet you know plenty." He patted her leg then snaked his hand to rest at the back of her neck. "You're so tense. Don't you worry. I'll make sure and wipe all that stress away when we get where we're going."

She suppressed a shudder. She didn't need to give him any more reasons to be annoyed. She forced a laugh that came out clipped and brittle. "I've been so busy, I haven't seen any posters. Why don't you tell me what brought you to Cloud Valley?"

His fingers gently dipped into her stiff muscles at her neck. "Apparently, fate."

She frowned. "What do you mean?"

He blew out a long breath and shook his head. "My wife left me, and I thought it was the end of the world. But I followed fate to this pretty little town, leading me right to your doorstep. Now I can show you what the others didn't want to see. I can love you the way they wouldn't let me love them."

Dread pushed her past her limit. She couldn't sit alone in this truck and listen to a murderer spouting nonsense about love. His nearness made her skin itch, and she stared at the door handle, contemplating her options.

He hadn't used a weapon on her—hell, he hadn't even shown her one. If she could wait until the truck slowed, maybe she could hurl herself out of the vehicle and run. Without a weapon of her own, it might be her best chance of escape.

"So will you?" he asked, bringing her back to the moment.

She swallowed hard. "Will I what?"

"Let me love you?"

Forcing a tight smile, she nodded. "Sure."

"Good, because we're almost there."

He turned onto a familiar road, and she straightened in her seat. He was taking her to her favorite park. She knew these woods better than anyone. All she had to do was get away from him and get a big enough head start to find all her favorite hiding spots—places she used to hole up in as a child while playing with her father.

The empty parking lot loomed ahead, but Tyson drove past, opting to bump along a narrow trail that wove through the trees. He removed his hand from her neck, circling both fists around the steering wheel. The truck slowed as he navigated around upturned roots and over bumpy terrain.

Now was her chance. Steeling her nerves, she slowly inched her fingers toward the handle. Her pulse thundered like crazy in her ears, and she'd swear he could hear the frantic pounding of her heart. Keeping her eyes fixed straight ahead, she closed her hand around the cool metal.

"You're going to love what I have planned. I promise

you. This will be a day you'll never forget. As long as you live. I promise—"

Before he could finish, she threw open the door and launched herself out of the truck. She slammed against the ground, skidding over loose stone and dirt, the impact knocking the air from her lungs.

The truck screeched to a stop.

Without wasting another second, she staggered to her feet and ran.

Chapter 25

With Eve nowhere in sight, Reid sprinted the two blocks to her house. He had no other idea where Tyson could have taken her. The man had broken into her home a couple of times. Maybe he'd taken her back there to finish what he'd started.

Houses and trees passed by in a blur. Panic stretched his nerves tight and threatened to break through his skin. He kept alert for any signs of Eve or Tyson Brown's truck.

The ringing in his pocket slowed his stride as he plucked out his phone and prayed to see Eve's name.

Madden.

"Did you find her?" he asked as he answered.

"Not yet. Where are you?"

Eve's house came into view, along with his truck in her driveway. No other vehicle was parked beside his, and disappointment slapped him harder than the wind barreling across his cheek. "Almost to Eve's place. I thought maybe he brought her there. I don't see his truck, but that doesn't mean anything."

"No one's seen her. I spoke with the sheriff's department. They're figuring things out, but I don't want to waste time. I'll meet you at Eve's and tell Dax and Ben to do the same. Can you get inside?"

He jogged down the driveway and tried the handle. "It's locked."

"I'll have Lily call Becca. She might know where a spare key is. Hold tight. I'm on my way."

Normally, knowing Madden was close by to help solve a problem eased some of Reid's anxiety, but not this time. His friend's presence wouldn't do anything to help Eve.

Fisting his hand, he pounded on the front door. "Eve! Are you in there?"

Nothing.

He yanked at the door again, but it refused to budge. He could run to the back door or try the windows, but he'd made sure the place was locked up tight. Besides, the sinking feeling in his gut told him she wasn't inside anyway.

With his phone still in hand, he dialed Eve again. This time the line went straight to voicemail. Shit.

Needing to do something, he peered into the windows for any sign of movement.

Any sign of Eve.

When he arrived at the broken bedroom window, he squared his shoulders and prepared to shimmy his way through the tight space. The window was already busted, and if there was any chance she was inside, he had to get in and fast.

"Reid!"

The sound of Madden's voice stalled his momentum, and he redirected himself to the front of the house.

Madden hunched over a flowerpot and straightened with a key in his hand. "Becca told Lily where the key was. She's a mess. She wants to help, so Lily stayed back to speak with her and Tara to see if they could think of anything useful. I thought it'd be best if Becca didn't come here, just in case we found something."

Reid leaped up the front steps. "Fine. Just get inside the damn house."

Madden unlocked and pushed open the door.

Reid worked his jaw back and forth, waiting for Madden to step inside before flying in behind him. The overpowering scent of dead flowers lingered, greeting him like an unwelcome guest. "Eve!"

He ran through the house, searching every room, even though he knew before he'd entered he wouldn't find her. Defeat knocked him off balance in her bedroom. He sank onto the side of her mattress and hung his head in his hands, the rose petals that had been left behind dried and sprinkled behind him.

Madden's low, long whistle lifted his head. "I didn't realize this place hadn't been cleaned yet. This is extremely disturbing." He flicked his wrist toward the bed.

Reid squeezed his eyes shut, unable to look at the offerings Tyson had left for Eve. "We didn't have time. I forgot it was all here. I should have called someone to take care of everything while we were gone. Before she could come home." Emotion stole his words and cracked his voice.

A heavy hand gripped his shoulders. "Look at me, man."

Reluctantly, Reid opened his eyes.

"You can't give up. We'll find her. She has to be somewhere. All we have to do is figure out where."

He huffed out a snort. "Yeah. No problem." Jumping to his feet, he paced the length of the room and shoved a hand through his hair. Irritation and worry crushed his lungs, making it hard to breathe. "I'll just step outside and call out her name. I'm sure she'll answer. I mean, she's *somewhere*, right?"

Rolling his eyes, he stopped in front of the picture hanging on her wall. The explosion of colorful flowers with the mountains in the distance stared back at him. He'd swear he could actually see the movement of the petals, the wind flowing over the canvas.

His breath caught in his throat. "Wait a second."

He ran down the hall to the living room, where wild-flowers had been vomited around the space. The colors had dulled, the life draining from the blooms that had once held so much vibrancy. He knelt on the floor and studied the shapes of the petals then moved to the couch, studying another type, then another.

"What is it?" Madden asked. "What's going on?"

He ran back to the bedroom, back to the picture.

"Dude, are you going to tell me what's going on in your head?"

"Here—" He pointed at the painting. "The day after Tyson attacked Eve, she took Suzy here with Lily. It's her favorite spot in the entire world. He had to know. I mean, that morning she had one of those damn wooden carvings dropped in the driveway and another in her car. He'd fol-lowed her home. Chances are high he followed her there, too. Hell, even the flowers picked and left here match the ones in the pictures."

"Okay," Madden said, drawing out the word. "You're right. We know he followed her, stalked her, kept tabs on the best time to try and grab her. But what does that have to do with where she is now?"

Reid ran the tip of his finger over the raised paint. "He brought the flowers to her in an attempt to give her something she loved. That didn't work. Maybe now he's taking her to the flowers. Taking her to spot that means the world to her."

Tightening his jaw, Madden tipped his chin. "It's the best lead we've got. We'll head there while Dax and Ben keep searching the area. Let's go."

Reid made a mad dash for the door and prayed his instincts were right and would lead him straight to Eve.

Pain ricocheted up Eve's body as she ran through the dense patch of trees. Her palms stung and her knees ached. But she couldn't dwell on the discomfort, or the tiny pebbles embedded in her skin. She had to focus on putting one foot in front of the other and creating as much distance between her and Tyson as possible.

Muttered curses sounded behind her, mixing with Tyson's heavy footsteps. "You'll never outrun me," he screamed, causing a flock of birds to scatter into the sky.

She swallowed her fear as adrenaline pumped through her system with each step. The urge to check and see how far Tyson was behind her was hard to ignore, but she kept her focus forward. Her mind as sharp as the branches reaching out to snag on her clothes and slap her cheeks. Tears threatened to fill her vision, but she blinked them back. She didn't have time to fall apart.

Her lungs burned as she picked up her pace. The muscles in her thighs screamed. She shoved her way through overgrown brush and past towering pine trees, thankful the abundant leaves provided some coverage.

"You can't hide from me," Tyson taunted, his voice far too close for comfort.

As she ran, she snagged her phone from her pocket.

If she could call Reid, let him know where she was, she could hide long enough for help to come. She swiped at the screen, but it remained black. The muted sunlight streaming through the trees showcased the cracks splintering the phone.

Crap.

She must have broken the phone when she'd jumped from the truck.

The tears she held back started to fall, and she shoved her phone back in her pocket. Her hair stuck to the moisture on her cheeks. She wiped the strands away from her eyes and her foot struck an upturned root, sending her flying to the rough ground.

She winced, the impact knocking her breath from her body. The scratches on her palms and knees throbbed. A part of her wanted to curl into a ball and give in to the fear and tears. But she couldn't give up. She had to keep moving. Eventually she'd run into someone. She had to. She couldn't believe she was about to meet her end in a place that had always meant so much to her.

Crawling to her hands and knees, she leaned on a moss-covered tree and hauled herself onto her feet. She filled her lungs with air, the effort enhancing every ache pulsing against her skin. She struggled to calm her pounding heart and regain her ever-slipping mindset.

She could keep running, hoping to stumble upon someone, but most of the locals were at the parade. She had to think straight and figure out the best path to get out of this situation. Closing her eyes, she visualized the layout of the park. Tyson had driven past the parking lot. If she could turn toward the opening of the trail, she could follow the road back toward town.

Plan made, she steeled her nerves and peeked around the tree. She kept as still as possible, tuning her ears into every snapping twig or rustling leaf. No footsteps sent her heart to her throat, no curses or threats reached her ears.

Staying low, she shot out from behind the tree. The road shouldn't be too far. If she could keep moving, keep pushing herself, she'd make it.

A hard yank on her hair sent her reeling backward. Her feet flew out from under her, and her bottom slammed against the ground, pain vibrating up her spine. Long fingers snaked through her strands, tightening at the top of her head.

Warm breath skimmed her face. "I told you not to do anything stupid. You said you'd let me love you. You lied, just like the rest of them."

She stared up into Tyson's cold green eyes, and terror punched her in the gut. She pedaled her feet in an attempt to scamper away, but he pulled harder on her hair. "Please. Let me go. You don't have to do this."

He bared his teeth before slamming her head against the ground.

Agony exploded at the back of her head. A sob sat trapped in her throat. She opened her mouth to scream, and a heavy hand clamped down on her face, muting any sound.

Lowering to the ground, he placed one knee on either side of her. "Stop it! Stop being so difficult. I tried to do something special. To show you how much I cared. And how do you repay me? By jumping out of the damn truck and running away. How do you think that makes me feel?"

Spit flew from his mouth and landed on her chin. She

winced and thrashed her body from side to side, trying to buck him off.

"You don't listen. You never listen." He moved his hands to circle her neck. Each word made him tighten his grip, making it harder and harder to breathe.

Tears fell from the corners of her eyes, and dark spots dotted her vision. She clawed at his hands. She needed air, needed to get him off of her. "You're hurting me. Stop. Please." The words were barely above a whisper, almost impossible to squeak out of her mouth as he continued to press on her windpipe.

This wasn't how she wanted to die. Trapped under a monster, alone in the forest with only a brief taste of what her life could have been. Memories of Reid ticked by one by one. As scared as she'd been the last couple of days, she'd also never been so happy. Never experienced so much joy and love.

Oh God. She loved Reid. She'd been in love with his smile and charm and wit for months. But now she knew it was more than that. She was in love with a man who brought all her dreams to life, and now she'd never get to experience those dreams with him. Never build that life.

She'd never even get a chance to tell him.

"You're just like the rest of them," Tyson screamed, his hands pressing harder against her windpipe. "You were supposed to be different."

Energy leaked from her body. She couldn't move, couldn't breathe, couldn't fight. Not wanting Tyson's face to be the last thing she ever saw, she closed her eyes and pulled forth an image of Reid. His shaggy hair and kind brown eyes. The grin that melted her insides and the booming laugh that always made her smile.

I'm so sorry we couldn't do life together.

The grip around her neck loosened, allowing her to pull in a large gasp of air. She swallowed, the motion like needles along her raw throat. She opened her eyes, and the slimy smile on Tyson's face made her wish he'd finished what he'd started.

He rested his palms along the delicate dip of her collarbone. "I won't make the same mistake I made before. No need to end things here, with neither of us getting the satisfaction we really want. Nah, I'll take you to that special spot and show you exactly the kind of man I am. The man you've been waiting for your whole damn life."

Chapter 26

Reid burst out the front door, and the crisp air hit his face and spurred him on. He sprinted down the porch steps and dug his keys out of his pocket. Thank God his truck was parked out front. He didn't have to waste time finding a ride.

"Hold on a second," Madden said, following him outside.

"Not gonna happen. Time's not on our side. I'm not slowing down for anyone." He continued to his truck until a hard grip on his shoulder stopped him. He whirled around, anger mixed with impatience and fear gnawing at his gut as every worst-case scenario played on repeat in his brain. "What the hell is your problem?"

Madden held out his hand and wiggled his fingers in a give-me motion. "Hand over the keys."

"No way. My truck. I drive. Now get your hands off me and get your ass inside so we can go."

"You're not in the right headspace to be behind the wheel. You're upset and you're scared. I totally get it. But if we get into a car accident, you won't be any good to Eve." Madden made the hand gesture again. "So give me the keys."

Reid considered Madden's words for just a second and

then tossed him the keys and stomped to the passenger side of his vehicle. There was no reason why he couldn't drive his own damn truck, but he wasn't about to spend precious seconds arguing.

Once buckled, he rubbed his hands up and down the thighs of his jeans. Nervous energy whipped around inside him. He darted his gaze between the side window and the front, hoping to catch a glimpse of Eve.

Madden backed out of the driveway then shot down the road. "The park Eve met Lily at with Suzy isn't that far away. We should be there in about ten minutes or so. If you're right, they don't have much of a head start. We'll get her back."

He didn't respond, couldn't get the words out of his mouth. He'd never known fear like this. Never experienced the gut punch of emotion holding him in gridlock.

His phone rang, and hope sprang forward. Maybe it was Eve and this was all a big misunderstanding. Tara's name and photo on his screen sent those hopes crashing right back down. He didn't want to answer, didn't want to focus on anything other than the all-consuming need to find Eve and hold her in his arms. To kiss the hell out of her and tell her what an idiot he'd been for waiting so long to tell her how he felt.

For waiting so long to tell her that he loved her.

The realization sent another bolt of pain through his heart.

"You gonna answer that?" Madden asked, tilting his chin toward the phone. "Could be important."

Knowing he was right, Reid answered the call. "Did you find something?"

"No, you?"

He sighed and stared out the window as the patches of land grew wider and fewer houses dotted the landscape. "We're heading to the park she loves. Hoping he took her there. It's the only place I can think of." His voice caught, cutting off any more words.

"You'll find her, Reid. I know you will."

He huffed out a humorless laugh. "How do you know that? I can't keep anyone safe. I can't help you. I turned my back for one second and Eve was taken. I lost control."

"You stop that right now," Tara barked. "You're amazing. I haven't always really heard you, haven't let your advice seep in. But you've never given up on me, just like you'll never give up on Eve. You can't control everything, no matter how hard you try. Things will always happen to you, not because of you. And now you'll fight like hell to find her. Just like you've always fought like hell for me."

Her faith in him made unshed tears burn his eyes. "A lot of good that's done."

"It's done more good than you realize," she said. "This is the last thing you need to be thinking about right now, but I canceled my flight. You need me here, and I want to help look for Eve. Lily, Becca and I are doing our part and I'll reach out if we come up with anything. You do the same."

He should be happy, tell her how relieved he was, but not even her good news could break through the paralyzing terror keeping all his thoughts on Eve. "Okay" was all he could manage to say.

"I love you." She clicked off, and Reid crushed his phone in his hand.

"Everything all right?" Madden asked.

He blew out a long breath. "Yeah. Tara's staying in town to help find Eve."

"That's good. All help is good help."

He grunted his agreement and went back to staring out the window. They were close, the entrance to the park only a couple miles away. "Once we get there, I don't have the first idea where to look."

"I understand this is personal, but we treat it like any other case," Madden said. "We follow the clues. Search for signs that could lead to where he might have taken her."

His heart thundered like a herd of stallions, and he rubbed the heel of his hand over his chest. Madden was right. He had to calm down, get his head on straight, and attack the problem with logic and not emotion.

They approached the turn to the parking lot, and Reid held his breath.

Madden drove into the empty lot and stopped in the closest spot, letting the vehicle idle.

"They're not here." The statement sliced through him like a knife. "No way he could have carried her here from the parade, and there's no truck around."

"Shit," Madden said, slamming his fist against the steering wheel.

Turmoil built in Reid's stomach until he thought he'd be sick. Needing fresh air, he hopped out of the truck and connected his hands behind his head. He drew in large gulps of air, trying to keep himself from going crazy. He kicked a large rock, which skittered across the cement to land on a wide dirt path. Tire tracks caught his attention.

He gestured for Madden to join him and ran to the trail.

"What is it?" Madden asked.

Reid crouched low, studied the marks. "They look

fresh." He peered down the lane, and an old, rusty truck stared back. Jumping to his feet, he sprinted toward the vehicle, Madden right behind him.

"Eve!" he called, reaching the open passenger door. "It's empty."

Madden grabbed his phone. "The license plate matches Tyson's truck. They have to be close. I'll call it in, but we need to keep looking."

Reid sprinted down the dirt path, trusting Madden would stay close. "Eve! Where are you?"

He kept on alert as he moved, his gaze continually shifting as he listened for any sign Eve was nearby. The trail narrowed and spilled into a dense patch of woods until it disappeared. He moved through the weeds and past the brush, thorns gripping his clothes and scratching his face.

An outline of dark green nestled against the light green moss surrounding the trees. He picked up his pace, his heart in his throat. His feet pounded over twigs and leaves, and he secured his weapon in his hands as he moved toward whatever was hidden in the brush.

Madden's footsteps crunched behind him, steadying his nerves. They'd been to war together, been to hell and back. If there was anyone he could trust, it was his best friend.

Slowing, he approached the structure with caution. "Looks like a tent," he said over his shoulder.

"Might be where Tyson's been sleeping," Madden whispered. "Be careful."

Reid moved methodically to the front of the tent. His pulse raced in his ears, the frantic sound like white noise against the call of birds overhead. No shadows moved against the nylon material from the inside. But she could be in there. He just hoped she was alive.

Finding the zipper, he slowly opened the door and shoved the fabric aside.

The sickening scent of flowers greeted him, the petals strewn across an air mattress. Candid photos of Eve were taped to the walls, and a bottle of champagne sat in a bucket of ice.

He stumbled backward, his hand covering his mouth to keep the bile sliding up his throat from leaking out.

Madden looked past him and cursed under his breath. "What the hell?"

Fury shook Reid's head back and forth, and he fisted his hand at his side, resisting the urge to tear down the tent. "He's a sick bastard, that's what."

"This had to be the plan," Madden said. "So where are they?"

"She got out of the truck," Reid said. "That's why the door was open, the truck stopped in the middle of nowhere. The champagne isn't open in there. They haven't made it here yet. But she's out there somewhere. We just have to make sure we find her before Tyson does."

Eve's scalp screamed as Tyson maneuvered her through the forest. He kept one hand threaded through her hair and the other clamped on her bicep. Her body was weak, the loss of so much oxygen wreaking havoc with her system.

Her mind buzzed and her limbs were heavy. She struggled to keep her focus on not tripping over her feet as she willed her brain to come up with a plan. Running blindly into the woods hadn't worked. And now that he had his slimy hands on her, he wouldn't let her go until he got what he wanted.

A chill skidded down her spine. She'd rather die than let him touch her. But she had to be smart. Make him think she was not only willing to participate in whatever sick nightmare waited for her but was excited.

She slowed their frantic pace and rested her hand on the one gripping her arm. "I'm sorry I ran. I was just scared. Please, can we slow down? You're hurting me. I know that's not what you want. You want to love me, remember?"

He hesitated, his pace matching hers, but he loosened his grip a fraction. "How can I believe you?"

Twisting, she ignored the ripping pain in her head and faced him. "I was scared. You wouldn't tell me where we were going. Now I know. You're trying to make things special for me. I should appreciate that."

"Damn right you should." He spat out the words as if disgusted by her. "All I want is to show you how much I care."

Her stomach revolted, but she couldn't let her true emotions show on her face. She forced a smile. "I see that now. I'm sorry."

His sneer twisted into something softer, something that scared her even more, but she kept her smile firmly in place.

"Because I'm a good guy, and I love you, I'll give you one more chance." He lifted a finger as if to emphasize the point then linked his hand with hers.

His sweaty palm engaged her gag reflex, but she swallowed hard to hide her reaction.

With her fingers still entwined with his, he brought

his face inches from hers. "Don't mess this up again, do you understand? I'm running out of patience."

She nodded.

He released her hair and tightened his hold on her hand, tugging her forward. "You're going to love what's waiting for us. And we can stay as long as we want. Then we can move on, leave all this nonsense behind us. Find the perfect place to start fresh."

She let him ramble while her mind went into overdrive. He might prattle on about a future and starting over, but she knew what he was capable of. Her throat throbbed at the memory of his hands squeezing the life from her. Memories assaulted her of being trapped against her bar and his hard body pressed against her.

Then there was Dana. She hadn't survived to share the horrors she'd experienced at Tyson's hands.

Eve couldn't go anywhere with this man. He was unpredictable and dangerous. The moment he got what he wanted, or she said the wrong thing, she was dead.

"We're almost there," he continued. "Right up ahead. I'm so excited to show you."

The outline of a tent appeared. Dread slowed her steps. Doing what he said might be key to her survival, but she wasn't sure she could go through with it. Wasn't sure her body would listen to logic when all she wanted to do was kick and scream and fight.

She had to fight.

A renewed urgency flowed through her bloodstream. He still hadn't used a weapon on her. If she could find something to defend herself, she stood a chance at survival. As they closed in on the tent, she scanned the forest floor until she spied a long branch near her feet. Perfect for swinging at an asshole's head.

She just needed to figure out how to get it.

Plan made, she pretended to stumble over her feet, yanking her hand from his to brace herself on the ground. "Goodness. I'm such a klutz." As she balanced herself on the balls of her feet, she lunged forward and grabbed the stick. The rough wood in her hands was heavy, and she gripped it with both hands.

Tyson's eyes went hard, and he dived toward her.

She swung the branch as hard as she could. The thick wood bounced off his face and he staggered backward. "Son of a bitch!"

Dropping the branch, she ran, but a hard shove between her shoulder blades catapulted her into the air before she slammed against the ground. She skidded across the fallen leaves and dirt. No. She couldn't be back in this spot. Helpless on the forest floor. He'd kill her this time.

"I told you not to mess it up again." He grabbed her ankles then flipped her so she landed on her butt. He hovered over her, his face red and voice shaking. "I told you I'd give you one more chance."

She stared up at him, panic swelling like a giant bubble, swallowing her insides. She was all out of ideas.

All out of hope.

The crunch of footsteps pricked her ears.

Tyson yanked on her arm and pulled her to her feet then pinned her to his chest. He hooked one arm across her throat, the other around her waist. He spun in a circle. "Who's out there?"

Eve trembled in his grasp, the smell of cigarettes and sweat making her nauseous.

Reid emerged from the cover of trees, a gun aimed in front of him. "Let her go."

Hope swept in and popped the bubble of panic and brought tears to the corners of her eyes. Reid had found her. Now she could jab this bastard with an elbow and Reid could take him down. Get her the hell out of here.

A subtle click of a pocketknife echoed in her ears, then a hard, sharp point pressed against her throat.

She hissed out a breath. Her body was rigid, and she kept her gaze locked on Reid.

Reid stopped. "Don't do anything stupid."

"I'm not the one being stupid, she is," Tyson said, digging the tip of the knife into her skin. "If she would have done what she was told, if you would have left her alone, everything would be fine."

"Please," she said, her voice nothing more than a whimper. "Please don't do this."

Tyson took a step backward and dragged her along with him. "I'm not doing anything except taking us back to the truck. Your boyfriend's going to stay put unless he wants me to kill you right here in front of him."

Reid's jaw tightened. His gun stayed in place. "You'll never escape. Never get away with any of this. Just let her go and don't make things worse for yourself."

Tyson laughed. "Do you think I'm an idiot? No way. She's my ticket out of here. I'll never let her go."

The statement rang in her ears, and she knew he meant every word. She'd rather die right here than be a pawn in his twisted game. Better to act, to make the sacrifice so Reid could finish the guy off and he couldn't hurt another woman again.

Steeling her nerve, she sucked in a deep breath and

braced herself for the slice of the knife against her throat as she balled her fist. She shifted her head as far from the lethal point of the knife as she could then jammed her elbow against Tyson's stomach. She stomped on his foot with all her strength then threw her head back, connecting with the soft cartilage of his nose.

The strong grip around her neck loosened and she dropped.

The blast of a gunshot echoed through the trees, and Tyson collapsed to the ground.

Reid rushed forward, kicking Tyson's knife away and flipping him to his back then slapping a pair of handcuffs onto his wrists.

Madden rushed forward from the cover of trees, shoving his gun in a holster at his side. "Got his leg. Wish I could have put that bullet in a place he wouldn't wake up."

"Get off me," Tyson spat with more venom than a poisonous snake. "I'll make you pay. All of you."

Reid hauled Tyson to his feet and pushed him toward Madden.

Tremors overtook Eve's body, and she covered her mouth to muffle her sobs.

Reid flew to her side and engulfed her in his arms, turning her away from the blood trail Tyson left behind as he was marched away through the woods.

"How? How'd you find me?" Shock made her words choppy, her thoughts a cluttered mess. She blinked back tears and stared up into Reid's brown eyes, unsure if he was real. If she was really safe and Tyson apprehended. None of it made sense.

"I went to the one place you loved the most." He

pressed his lips to her temple. "I was so damn scared. But you're safe now, baby."

She buried her face in Reid's neck. Sobs shook her shoulders and relief washed over her, so swift and sweet. She curled against the hard security of Reid's body.

"You saved me," she said. "You saved my life. You saved me from whatever horrors waited for me in that tent."

He smoothed a hand over her head. "You don't have to think about that. I've got you, and I swear I'll never let you go."

Her body relaxed and she closed her eyes. He was right. She didn't have to think about Tyson Brown and his intentions ever again. She was safe in Reid's arms, and she never wanted to leave.

Chapter 27

Reid refused to leave Eve's side while the medic looked her over in the back of the ambulance. He'd carried her to the parking lot, memorizing the way she felt in his arms. And now he couldn't wait to pull her close again and never let her go.

Chaos had taken over the once-empty lot. Cruisers with flashing blue and red lights filled spaces. Deputies marched between the crime scene and their vehicles, hanging yellow tape to preserve the scene and collecting evidence.

Madden stood with Deputy Hill, probably replaying the events that had led them to this moment.

Dirt smeared Eve's face and holes in her clothes broadcast her struggle, but it was the ugly purple marks around her neck that made Reid want to put a fist through a wall. Tyson Brown might not have gotten exactly what he'd planned, but he'd put his hands on Eve, had almost killed her.

And it was all Reid's fault.

"Can you lift your head a little," the medic asked. She gently touched a sensitive spot along Eve's collarbone with her fingers.

Eve winced and tightened her hold on his hand.

"You're going to be sore for a couple of days, but no serious injuries. You have a slight concussion and wound on your head. I've cleaned your cuts and scrapes, and I don't see a reason to take you to the hospital. Lots of rest the next few days, and I recommend finding someone to talk with about what you just went through. Trauma takes time to heal. Be good to yourself."

"Thank you," Eve said.

"So she's free to go?" Reid asked.

"Whenever she's ready." The middle-aged woman hopped out of the back of the ambulance and walked across the busy parking lot to speak with Deputy Silver.

Reid shifted on the hard gurney inside the ambulance. He wanted to whisk Eve away from this place, give her all the time she needed to put this whole nightmare behind her. He stared down at her dirty face, and guilt stung his heart like a pack of angry bees. "If I'd lost you, I would have never forgiven myself. I'm so sorry I let this happen."

"You didn't let anything happen," Eve said, her voice hoarse and quiet. "This isn't your fault."

He shook his head, unwilling to let her words penetrate the thick cover of blame wrapped around him. "I shouldn't have taken you to the parade. I should have kept my eyes on you the entire time. If I would have done my job right, he wouldn't have taken you away from me."

She flattened her palm on his jawline. "Not today. But he would have kept trying."

"I'm so sorry." Regret like he'd never known waged a war inside him.

"Do you remember what you told me the first night Tyson attacked me? You told me I wasn't allowed to apologize for things that weren't my fault. He did this, not you. You have nothing to apologize for. You saved me."

Reid squeezed his eyes shut for a beat and let her absolution rain over him. Blowing out a long, steadying breath, he looked at her. "No, honey. You saved me."

She quirked up a brow, but he didn't expound. Now wasn't the time to focus on anything other than getting her someplace warm and comfortable. "You ready to go home?"

Dropping her hand to her lap, she stared up at him with wide eyes. "I'm ready to leave, but I'm not ready to go back to my house. Not after everything…" Her voice trailed off and tears fell down her face.

He folded her against him, careful not to hurt her. "Honey, we can go anywhere you want. My apartment, the safe house—hell, how about I take you to the beach or a cabin in the mountains? Get away for a few days and recover. Just know that no matter where we go, you'll be safe. I'll keep you safe."

A smile curved up the corner of her mouth. "We?"

Tucking his thumb and index finger under her chin, he stared into her eyes. He'd hidden his feelings for too long, too afraid that his emotions would lead to disaster. And look where that had led him. With the woman he loved in danger and him a wreck, knowing he'd held back.

"Yes, we. If that's what you want. I want to stand by your side as we battle back to your new normal. As we navigate our future. As we process all our baggage and grow and learn together. Because as uncertain as things are right now, the one thing I know is that I love you, Eve."

A soft gasp puffed through her perfect lips. "I love you, too, Reid. I thought I'd never get a chance to tell you."

His heart swelled and he kissed her softly. "So where should we go? Hawaii?" He wiggled his eyebrows and was rewarded with a short laugh.

"Anywhere with you is paradise, but for now, can I stay at your place? At least for a night or two?"

"You can stay as long as you want, as long as you don't mind an extra houseguest."

"Tara?"

Grinning, he nodded.

"Perfect. Can we leave now?" she asked, resting her head on his shoulder. "I'm so tired. I want to go home."

"Absolutely." He climbed out of the ambulance then helped her down before sweeping her off her feet and into his arms. *Home.* Such a simple word with so much meaning, and now he understood deep within in his soul that wherever Eve was, that was home.

And he hoped she'd stay there with him forever.

Eve curled next to Reid on the sofa at his apartment and sipped the warm tea he'd made her after breakfast. The lemony liquid soothed her throat, even if swallowing hurt like hell.

She hadn't slept well. Nightmares had plagued her, pulling her into a kaleidoscope of fear with Tyson Brown as the leading man. Each time she woke, drenched in sweat and afraid of where she'd find herself, Reid was there. Holding her close and soothing her with sweet kisses and gentle words.

"Morning!" Tara called, sneaking her way into the kitchen for a cup of coffee. Once she'd doctored her drink, she joined them in the living room, sitting in the chair across from the sofa. "How you feeling?"

Eve shrugged, words to explain her emotions hard to find. She slipped her hand into Reid's and grinned up at him, choosing to focus on the positive. "I'm good, with things only looking up from here."

"You've got that right." He kissed her forehead then snuggled her close. "What about you, Tara?"

She tipped her head from side to side as she sipped her coffee. "Okay. Dad called again last night."

Reid tensed.

Eve set her mug on the end table then rested her free hand on top of the one already joined with Reid's. "What did he say? Is he upset you stayed in Cloud Valley?"

Tara blew out a long breath. "He wasn't happy, but I think it shook some sense into him. Maybe it's wishful thinking, but he seemed to understand his actions were driving everyone away. At least that's what he said before telling me he was headed back to rehab."

"Let's see how long he lasts this time." Reid snorted then glanced down at Eve. Something skittered across his face, a peacefulness that resembled acceptance. "But I hope he stays. It's about time he figures out how to slay his own demons. Just like the rest of us."

His answer buoyed her spirits. His feelings about his father were complicated and filled with sadness. He might never forgive the man who'd raised him, but letting go of his anger and resentment was a necessary part of healing.

Something she'd have to do in time where her feelings toward Tyson Brown were concerned.

But that's what time and therapy were for. This morning she was grateful to be in a safe home with the man she loved beside her.

A loud knock at the door tensed her muscles and her

heartbeat went into overdrive. "Are we expecting company?"

"No." Frowning, Reid stood and crossed to the door. He glanced through the peephole and tossed a smile over his shoulder. "Although I think you'll be happy about these unexpected guests."

He opened the door, and Suzy flew into the room with Becca behind her.

Suzy's blond hair was tied back in pigtails, and she carried a small bouquet of wildflowers. She hopped onto the couch, stopping abruptly before launching herself at Eve. "I brought flowers."

Eve's breath caught as she stared at the sweet offering. The scent permeated her senses, making her dizzy and threating to suck her back in time. Back to a place filled with fear and dread.

Suzy gently rose to her knees and leaned forward to press a slobbery kiss to Eve's cheek. "I lub you."

Joy and love washed through her, erasing the ugliness clinging to her brain. Tyson Brown might have tried to steal the things in her life that brought her so much joy, but he'd failed. She didn't have to avoid places and things because a monster had weaponized them against her. She just had to remember it was the meaning behind the gesture—the gift—that was important. "I love you, too, honey bunny. Give me a hug."

"Mama said be careful." Suzy's lip pouted out. "You got hurt."

Eve pulled Suzy onto her lap and held her close. She breathed in the smell of baby shampoo and sugar. Having the little girl she loved so close was worth every ache and pain. "I did, but I'm okay. And no matter what, your hugs and kisses always make me feel better."

"And flowers?" Suzy asked, wide eyes latching onto hers.

Eve smiled. "Yes. And flowers."

"We won't stay long." Becca rounded the side of the couch. She hooked an arm around Eve's shoulders. "We just wanted to say hello and see for ourselves that you're all right. Suzy insisted on bringing you some magic."

Eve booped the girl on the tip of her nose. "She knows exactly how to make my day better. You all do."

Becca sucked in a shuddering breath, tears brimming over her lashes. "We're so glad you're safe and sound. But we have pastries waiting for us."

"I don't want to leave," Suzy said, clinging to Eve.

"Remember what I said. Quick visit today so Eve can rest." Becca's voice was sweet as sin, but Eve could detect the underlying message, warning Suzy to listen.

Tara jumped to her feet. "Can I go with you, Suzy? I'm so hungry and I'd love something chocolate! Do you like chocolate?"

"Yeah!" Suzy hopped off the couch and ran to grab Tara's hand. "It's so yummy."

Becca gave her another gentle squeeze and glanced at Reid. "Take good care of her."

"Always."

As she watched her makeshift family walk out the door, Reid reclaimed his spot next to her. He pointed at the flowers. "Do you want me to throw these away?"

"No. They were given with love by a person who means the world to me. They're beautiful."

"Just like you." He slid his arm around her and pulled her close. "Have I told you yet today that I love you?"

He had, but she couldn't wait to hear it again. "No, I don't think so."

"My apologies. I love you, Eve Tilly. And I'll tell you every single day."

"I love you, too." Melting against him, she listened to the soothing sound of his heart beating against her ear. Relished the protectiveness of his arms. And enjoyed the tingles of happiness he brought to life inside her.

Despite the hardships, life was good. And she couldn't wait to do that life with Reid.

Epilogue

Eve hopped out of Reid's truck. Warmth from the afternoon sun promised the coming of spring. The winter had been long, but the only thing about it that had been hard was testifying against Tyson. Something she'd do a hundred times over to get justice for both Dana and herself. She'd spent every day since appreciative of the love and happiness Reid had brought into her life, and every night in his bed.

Meeting her at the hood of his vehicle, Reid reached out a hand.

She took it and glanced around her, curiosity rippling her brow. "What are we doing here?" The snow had melted around the safe house that held a special place in her memories. They hadn't returned since the night they'd spent here months before.

"I have something to show you." He stepped in front of her, blocking her from the cabin. "I want you to close your eyes."

"Excuse me?"

"Just for a few seconds. Trust me."

"You're lucky you're cute," she teased but closed her eyes then covered them with her free hand for good measure.

Reid tugged her forward. "Watch your step. Nice and slow."

Her foot crunched over dirt instead of gravel, telling her they'd ventured off the driveway. She moved carefully, appreciating the care Reid took as he guided her to the surprise destination.

They hadn't gone far when Reid rooted his hands on her hips and stopped her. "Okay. You can open your eyes."

She let her hand fall away from her face and stared at the green tips bursting through dark brown mulch.

He hooked an arm around her waist and stood beside her, flicking his wrist at the sprouts. "I stopped by the other day and noticed the flowers we planted were starting to grow. I couldn't help but stand here and look at them, realizing how much had changed since the day we put them in the ground. When we planted those bulbs, we hadn't given in to our feelings for each other yet, hadn't really opened up and discovered how much we love each other."

She sniffed back happy tears. "I can't remember a time when I didn't love you."

"I feel the same, and these little bulbs are a constant reminder that we planted something together that was loved and nourished and will continue to grow into something so damn beautiful. So damn special."

She leaned against him and let her head fall to his shoulder. "I wish I could see them every day."

Pivoting, he faced her and took her hands in his. "What if I said you could?"

"What do you mean?"

"Well, I've loved having you stay at my place, but it's

a little crowded with the three of us, and Tara's not ready to commit to getting her own place yet."

Her stomach dipped. They hadn't exactly discussed her moving in with him. It had just kind of happened. Maybe she'd been wrong and had taken advantage of his kindness. She struggled to keep her smile in place. "I'm sorry. I don't want you to feel like I'm taking up your space."

He grimaced then rubbed the back of his neck. "No, that's not what I mean. I bought this place off Madden."

Her heart sputtered on a gasp. "You did what? How? I thought this was for your business?"

He shrugged and reclaimed both of her hands. "We didn't realize how much time it'd take to get it ready. We decided it'd be better to find something turnkey. Besides, this house holds some of my favorite memories. Memories that I want to cherish and relive every day with you."

"*With* me? You want me to stay here with you?"

"No, I want you to move in here with me. I want this to be our home, our safe place, our little cabin in the woods with a lawn I can maintain while you find the right paint color for the living room."

Her grin grew and she threw herself into his arms.

"Is that a yes?" he asked. Laughing, he lifted her off her feet and spun her in a circle.

"I love every single thing about that idea, and I love you. Thank you for being what I needed—for giving me everything I didn't even know I wanted."

He set her back on the ground and lowered his forehead to hers. "Right back at ya, babe. Now, are you ready to get to work on this place?"

"Trust me, I can't wait to see those skills of yours put

to good use." She looped her arms around his neck and sealed the deal with the sweetest kiss.

Her life had been turned upside down, and she'd landed exactly where she was meant to be—with Reid, their new home and a future filled with limitless possibilities.

* * * * *

Get up to 4 Free Books!

**We'll send you 2 free books from each series you try
PLUS a free Mystery Gift.**

FREE
Value Over
$25

Both the **Harlequin Intrigue**® and **Harlequin**® **Romantic Suspense** series
feature compelling novels filled with heart-racing action-packed romance
that will keep you on the edge of your seat.

YES! Please send me 2 FREE novels from the Harlequin Intrigue or Harlequin Romantic Suspense series and my FREE gift (gift is worth about $10 retail). After receiving them, if I don't wish to receive any more books, I can return the shipping statement marked "cancel." If I don't cancel, I will receive 6 brand-new Harlequin Intrigue Larger-Print books every month and be billed just $7.19 each in the U.S. or $7.99 each in Canada, or 4 brand-new Harlequin Romantic Suspense books every month and be billed just $6.39 each in the U.S. or $7.19 each in Canada, a savings of 20% off the cover price. It's quite a bargain! Shipping and handling is just 50¢ per book in the U.S. and $1.25 per book in Canada.* I understand that accepting the 2 free books and gift places me under no obligation to buy anything. I can always return a shipment and cancel at any time by calling the number below. The free books and gift are mine to keep no matter what I decide.

Choose one: ☐ **Harlequin**   ☐ **Harlequin**   ☐ **Or Try Both!**
             Intrigue   **Romantic**   (199/399 & 240/340 BPA G36Z)
             Larger-Print   **Suspense**
             (199/399 BPA G36Y)   (240/340 BPA G36Y)

Name (please print)

Address   Apt. #

City   State/Province   Zip/Postal Code

Email: Please check this box ☐ if you would like to receive newsletters and promotional emails from Harlequin Enterprises ULC and its affiliates. You can unsubscribe anytime.

Mail to the **Harlequin Reader Service:**
IN U.S.A.: P.O. Box 1341, Buffalo, NY 14240-8531
IN CANADA: P.O. Box 603, Fort Erie, Ontario L2A 5X3

Want to explore our other series or interested in ebooks? Visit www.ReaderService.com or call 1-800-873-8635.

HIHRS25